the
Undateable

Also by Sarah Title

Kentucky Home

Kentucky Christmas

Home Sweet Home

Snowed In

Two Family Home

Practice Makes Perfect

And read more Sarah Title in

Delicious

The Most Wonderful Time

the
Undateable

SARAH TITLE

ZEBRA BOOKS
KENSINGTON PUBLISHING CORP.
http://www.kensingtonbooks.com

ZEBRA BOOKS are published by

Kensington Publishing Corp.
119 West 40th Street
New York, NY 10018

All Kensington titles, imprints, and distributed lines are available at special quantity discounts for bulk purchases for sales promotion, premiums, fund-raising, educational, or institutional use.

Special book excerpts or customized printings can also be created to fit specific needs. For details, write or phone the office of the Kensington Sales Manager: Attn.: Sales Department. Kensington Publishing Corp., 119 West 40th Street, New York, NY 10018. Phone: 1-800-221-2647.

Zebra and the Z logo Reg. U.S. Pat. & TM Off.

First Printing: March 2017
ISBN-13: 978-1-4201-4183-2
ISBN-10: 1-4201-4183-X

eISBN-13: 978-1-4201-4184-9
eISBN-10: 1-4201-4184-8

10 9 8 7 6 5 4 3 2 1

Printed in the United States of America

For Brock,
who keeps me sane on Sunday mornings.
You're electric, darling, and I love you for it.

ACKNOWLEDGMENTS

The plight of the misunderstood librarian is a real one, and I want to thank Jeff Waller for his help with the realities of academic librarianship in a small-ish college library. I'm glad I was able to give Bernie some coworkers.

Also, thanks to Trixie Stix and the Chemical Valley Roller Girls for introducing me to the world of roller derby back before I was even thinking about writing romance novels. I'm glad I finally got to use some of the knowledge I picked up.

That said, any errors I made vis-à-vis college libraries or roller derby are totally my own, the former because I am a bad listener, the latter because I was drunk on adrenaline. And beer.

I always have to thank Alicia Condon for being gentle with me as I fight with plots and politics. Ladies, if you can find an editor who lets you talk about the gender dichotomy in your romance novels, go with that editor.

Louise Fury, agent extraordinaire, thank you for believing that big things would happen.

For my mom, who pushes my books on all of her unsuspecting friends, and my dad, who reads them all even though we don't talk about it. We don't have to talk about it, btw. Mom told me your secret.

Thank you to Aunt Barb for being the OG Bernie, who lives her principles and made me the fresh-mouthed independent woman I am today.

And thank you thank you to all the readers who have reached out or reviewed my books. I still can't believe people I don't know IRL read my books, and it does wonders for my delicate (fresh-mouthed, independent) ego.

Kisses!

Chapter One

Dear Maria,

I'm about to graduate from college and I think my boyfriend is going to propose. My parents really like him, but they say we're too young to get married. I really want to start a family, and I love him so much! We've been through everything together. We lost our virginities to each other. We've been talking about what we'll do after graduation, but he's never brought up marriage.

If he asks, should I say yes?

Distressed About Saying Yes in Alamo Square

Dear Distressed,

You are so young. I can barely remember what it was like to be that young, except that marriage was the last thing on my mind. Marriage is a lifelong commitment, and who knows what will happen when you get out in the real world? You might discover that the path you set yourself on is not the path you were meant to be on.

*Your boyfriend might find the same thing. Hell,
you might want to have sex with other people!*

*Think about that. He is the only person you'll
have sex with for the rest of your life. Unless you
have an open marriage, which is definitely
something you should bring up before he asks.*

*Imagine your perfect life together. Imagine
what your house will look like, how many kids
you'll have, what your career will be. Nice, right?
Now imagine that none of that happens. You have
a dead-end job that you took just to pay the bills.
You can barely afford the kids you have, or maybe
you find out you can't have kids. You live in the
Bay Area, so guess what, you can't afford a house.
Life sucks. Is your boyfriend still the person you
want to be with?*

*I can't tell you what to do, Distressed, but if I
could, I would tell you: when he asks, say, "Hell, no."*

Kisses,
Maria

It WAS SEVENTEEN PAST ONE and Bernie was hangry.

She thought longingly of her midmorning banana,
abandoned and lonely on her kitchen counter, and of her
leftover lentil soup, waiting patiently in the insulated bag
under her desk. All of her food was so far away. And
even if it was right in front of her, she wouldn't eat at the
information desk. It would set a bad example. She had
enough trouble keeping her student workers off their cell
phones while they were on the desk; she didn't need
them eating, too.

She looked at the clock again. Eighteen after one.
Carly was a wonderful employee in many ways; she was

friendly and she seemed unflappable in the face of panicked procrastinators. She had ended up in the library as her work-study assignment, but after four years, she was now considering library school. Bernie was glad. She'd be a great librarian.

A late librarian, but a great one.

As if Bernie's rising hunger-induced annoyance had conjured her up, Carly came sprinting through the lobby, slowing down to a power walk once she crossed the threshold of the library. She mouthed a wincing apology to Bernie, who just shrugged. She could write her up, but Carly was a senior. She'd be graduating in a few months, and anyway, Bernie was about to eat lunch so she didn't really care.

"I'm so sorry." Carly was breathless when she finally reached the desk. She dropped her heavy shoulder bag on the floor next to the reference computer. "Evan was . . ." She blushed, then stopped. Bernie was grateful. She'd learned way too much about Carly's personal life, and the oversharing had only multiplied since Carly had started dating Evan. Evan was a musical theater major—not gay—and they were supposed to be saving themselves for marriage. Bernie ignored the alarm bells and minded her own business, or as much as Carly would let her mind her own business. For example, a few weeks into the new semester, Carly was floating around and more tardy than usual, and when Bernie asked her what was up, she got a long, metaphor-filled description of Carly's deflowering by the not-gay (and apparently not-waiting-for-marriage) Evan.

It was sweet, Bernie reminded herself. Young love and all that. She had been young and foolish and in love

before. Carly would grow out of it, just as surely as
Bernie had.

That was depressing, she thought.

Which was surely just the hunger talking.

"There's nothing carrying over," Bernie explained, her
mind half on her lunch. In addition to soup, there was also
a cupcake. She had forgotten all about the cupcake. Her
stomach growled. "It's art history time again," she said,
referring to the annual Intro to Art History term paper
rush they got this time in the semester. "I pulled a few
of the books this morning"—she pointed to a small cart of
giant art books near the desk—"so if you could check the
links on the Web site, make sure they're all still good . . ."

Bernie was distracted by a big crowd of students enter-
ing the library. Her heart sank even as her public service
smile lit up. She couldn't leave Carly to handle this many
students by herself. Carly was unflappable, but Bernie
wasn't a sadist.

"Hi, can I help—"

Bernie started to greet them, thinking they'd all come
over from a class together and maybe they wanted a tour.
Bernie didn't have any tours on her calendar, but that
never stopped a professor from sending a group over.
But then they all stopped just shy of the desk and turned
their backs to her. Were they protesting? Who would
protest the library? Then she heard music coming from
the back of the Student Blob, and she was just about to
launch into her autopilot Please-Use-Headphones, when
the Blob started to shake.

Oh my God, she thought. They're dancing.

She looked at Carly, as if The Young Person might
have some explanation for the Undulating Student Blob
(was this a thing the kids were doing, Bernie wondered
while reminding herself that she was only thirty-one, still

a kid, maybe). Carly, however, looked like she was on the amused end of the bemused spectrum. Kids, Bernie thought. Then: I am very, very hungry.

Then the lyrics started, and Bernie recognized the pop song—something about love forever and crap like that. But her Old Person Brain remembered that it was sung by a woman, and this was not a woman singing. The Dancing Blob parted and there, like a singing Moses, was Evan. He was holding a small microphone plugged into his cell phone, karaoke-ing over the original song. As he sang and the music crescendoed, the dancers moved in a joyful, if not totally coordinated, circle around the information desk. Bernie watched them swish and swirl around, wondering where they were going to go next. She started to say something to Carly, but Carly was not watching the dancers. She was watching Evan, who had swirled up to her and *onto* the desk. He was dancing on the information desk. That was not allowed. Bernie should stop him.

Then a couple of the burlier dancers were behind the desk—another thing Bernie should stop—and they lifted Carly, who squealed, but took Evan's hand as he led her in a few complicated but clearly familiar moves on the desk.

Two people dancing on the information desk. Bernie should definitely not just stand there with her mouth open.

Then the dancing stopped, and so did Evan's singing, although the music continued in the background. Bernie remembered this part. This was the part where the singer talked to the singee about how much she loved him and there were some metaphors about sunshine and butterflies. But Evan wasn't metaphorizing. He was getting down on one knee. Then he was reaching into his pocket. Then, accompanied by the sound of dozens of undergraduate cell phones taking pictures, he pulled open a small square box.

"Carly Monica Hilbert, you have made me the happiest man in the world. Will you make me even happier by becoming my wife?"

No, no, no, thought Bernie. This isn't right. They are way too young. They just started drinking legally—they couldn't possibly be ready to get married!

But Carly wasn't listening to Bernie's silent objections. She wasn't looking to her mentor for advice or approval. She was just looking at Evan, her eyes shining, and she nodded.

There was a surge from the crowd as Evan stood and twirled Carly in his arms, then shakily put the ring on her finger.

Bernie was never going to get to eat lunch.

Colin woke up on a couch that was not his own.

He knew this because his legs were hanging off the end, and his legs did not hang off the end of the giant lounging sofa he had in his living room. Also, he was sticking to the fake leather. Not only would he never own a fake leather couch—and this one was really fake—he also knew that he didn't own a fake leather couch. He didn't own a real leather couch. Steph would never allow such an affront to the animal community as a leather couch in their house. Never mind that she had a pretty extensive collection of leather shoes, which he regularly pointed out, as was his prerogative as an older brother. However, since he was not on his own couch, the chances of his little sister being here were pretty slim.

He sat up, unsticking his legs from the couch while

wondering why his legs were so sticky when he was pretty sure he had been wearing pants last night. He lifted the edge of the *Transformers* comforter covering his legs and confirmed that, yes, he was in his boxers. Also, his head hurt. Also, where the hell was he?

He looked around the room with squinting, hungover eyes. There were posters for martial arts movies in cheap frames on the wall, an artful tower of beer cans in the corner, and a bed with three heads sharing the lone pillow.

Where. The. Hell. Was. He?

As if sensing Colin's very confused perusal, one of the heads lifted and offered Colin a weak, groovy smile. "Hey, man," the head said, and Colin nodded hello.

"Have you seen my pants?" Colin whispered. This was a phrase he'd hoped never to say again after a particularly wild semester abroad in college. And yet, here he was. Wherever he was.

The head lifted an arm and pointed to the easy chair in the corner, on which another guy was sleeping, his mouth open and drooling onto Colin's jeans.

Great.

"I got 'em," the head said, and Colin went to stop him—surely he could retrieve his own pants—but the head was already climbing up and over his bedmates, who barely stirred, and deftly extricating Colin's jeans with barely a jostle of Drooly's head.

"Thanks," Colin said, and stepped off of the couch and into his pants. "Uh—" he started. He wasn't sure how to address this situation. He'd had drunken one-night stands before, and he'd woken up with a woman whose name he'd forgotten more times than he should probably admit. But this was new. A platonic drunken crash with strangers.

At least, he assumed it was platonic. He couldn't really remember. . . .

The head, which was attached to a tall, skinny body, tilted toward the door out of the living room or bedroom or whatever it was, and Colin followed him into a small but bright kitchen. He wished he had sunglasses. But at least he had pants.

Tall Head started making coffee, and Colin thought he might kiss him, which reminded him that he had no idea what had happened last night.

"Drake," Tall Head said, holding out his hand.

"Colin," said Colin.

"I know," laughed Drake. "You told us last night. A lot. Colin Rodriguez, Party Reporter." Oh, God. That was Colin's line from his first job as a nightlife reporter at an East Bay alt-weekly. He thought he'd left that particular bro persona behind after his immediate post-college life.

"Geez," he said, recognizing Drunken Asshole Colin Who Thought He Was Being Funny. "Sorry."

Drake shrugged. "Happens. We tried to put you in a cab home, but you couldn't remember your address. Figured it was better if you just slept it off here."

"I really appreciate it, man."

Drake waved him off, then poured him a cup of coffee. Colin thought he might love Drake.

"I think we're out of milk," Drake told him.

"S'cool. Black is good," Colin said, and he meant it. If he could have injected the coffee into his veins, he would have.

It was good.

"So . . . you live here?"

Drake laughed at him again. Colin blushed. This was the most awkward morning-after conversation he'd ever had, and he'd had plenty. And this time, he hadn't even gotten anything for his trouble.

Well, he was pretty sure he hadn't gotten anything. He hadn't gotten anything memorable, at least.

"Yeah," Drake said. "Me and my boy who was on the chair. The two girls were . . . .visiting."

Oh my God, Colin thought. I slept through an orgy.

"Listen," Drake told him around a mouthful of toast. Where had he come up with toast? "I gotta get ready for work. You're welcome to hang out. . . ."

"No! No, that's okay. I'll, uh. I'll just go. Thanks for the coffee." Before anything else dumb could happen, Colin walked out of the apartment, down the hall, and into the bright San Francisco day.

At least he hoped it was San Francisco.

Chapter Two

Dear Maria,

My boyfriend won't grow up. All he wants to do is hang out with his bros all night, either at a crappy bar or playing video games online. When I mention it might be nice for him to take me to a restaurant that doesn't have paper napkins, he says sure, but he won't do it. Sometimes I feel like I'm dating a child! How can I get him to change?

Feeling Like Peter Pan's Wendy in Hayes Valley

Dear Wendy,

It sounds like your boyfriend has different priorities from yours. You want to hang out with him; he doesn't. You want him to spend a lot of money on you; he doesn't. You can sit around and pretend that, someday, he'll grow out of it—but maybe that's just his personality. The job of a girlfriend is not to take a shitty guy and make him great. I think the best thing you can do for your love life is to find a new man.

Kisses,
Maria

"YOU'RE NOT DEAD!" Colin heard as he tried to sneak unnoticed through the unlocked front door.

Colin scowled at his little sister as she sat at the kitchen table in front of her laptop. Working again, even though it was the weekend. "You knew I wasn't dead. You gave me directions home, remember?"

Steph shook her head in disapproval. "You grew up in this city. Your lack of understanding of the public transit system is appalling."

"You could have sent an Uber."

"I'm not the one who lost his wallet in a bar last night. Someone brought it over, by the way. All your cards are in there. I took the cash."

Colin muttered a curse and took the wallet from Steph's outstretched hand. Sisters.

"She was cute. Seemed disappointed you weren't home."

"Shut up," he told his sister, then went over to the cof-feemaker. He drained the pot into the nearest mug and plopped down on the chair next to hers.

Steph held up her mug for a refill. Colin pretended not to notice. She muttered something unflattering, then got up to make another pot.

"What are you working on this weekend?" he asked, turning her laptop toward him.

"Hey!" she said. "What if I was looking at something personal?"

"This doesn't look personal."

"It could have been! What if it was a picture of boobs or something!"

Colin shrugged.

"What if it was a picture of MY boobs?"

"Fine," he conceded. "Although why would you be looking at a picture of your own boobs on your computer?"

"Why would you be getting blackout drunk with strangers?," she said.

"It was for a story."

"A story on how it's a man's privilege to lose consciousness and end the night with only a lost wallet?"

"Yup," Colin said, decidedly not taking her bait. It was too early for a discussion about the patriarchy. And by discussion, he meant a lecture from his little sister on how the world was designed in his favor, which would inevitably lead to a lecture on how he wasn't doing the women of the world any favors by writing for a fashion start-up that perpetuated an impossible standard of beauty and tied those standards to rampant consumerism. He was well aware that Steph's beauty would not be commodified; he had been told many times before. But he had to make a living.

Even if writing for Glaze was not how he really wanted to make his living. But he liked writing, and he was good at the kind of writing Glaze readers demanded of him (a slightly pandering version of "brutally honest guy's perspective"). He didn't totally hate it, usually. And sometimes it meant he was able to get into a new club or find out the top-secret location of a pop-up restaurant . . . or spend the night in a post-college dive bar and get blackout drunk with strangers.

He might not have Steph's drive to better the world and fulfill her career ambitions, but, dammit, he was good at his job.

Mostly.

He ignored the little voice in his head—the one that sounded unfortunately like his little sister—that told him it sure looked like he was losing his touch.

Preferring exercising his rights as a nosy older brother to painful self-reflection, Colin scrolled idly through the message board for Steph's softball team, not really reading anything, just waiting for his coffee to kick in. Then he got to one of the girls' responses—a meme of a woman with a sour face and the caption "Disapproving Librarian Disapproves." He snorted. The woman looked disapproving, all right. He should know. He'd gotten that look from women before.

"What's so funny?" Steph said, retaking her chair and her laptop. The look she gave him as she shoved him out of the way was not entirely dissimilar to the Disapproving Librarian's. "Holy—" she started as she flopped down into the seat.

"Funny, right?"

Steph didn't say anything, just started typing madly.

"Steph?" He must not have read the messages closely enough. He thought it was just an argument about someone not cleaning the helmets right. He had no idea those helmets even got cleaned.

"This is terrible!" she said without taking her eyes from the screen.

"What is it?" Someone must have really broached some softball etiquette that Colin didn't understand. In the interest of journalism (and nosiness), he reached for her laptop again, only to have his hand slapped away.

"Ow!" he said, mostly for attention, because Steph was ignoring his questions and he was the older brother, dammit.

"This can't be right." She squinted and leaned into the screen. She sat back. "It really is her."

That was it. Colin had had enough of his authority not being respected (also, he was dying of curiosity). He stood up and put his sister into a headlock. "What are you talking about?" he asked, as he rubbed his knuckles into her scalp.

"Quit it!" she shouted, and then, because Colin's ego was bigger than his brain, he momentarily forgot that, although he was older and bigger, his sister did that crazy workout that involved flipping tires, and soon he was facedown on the table, her forearm holding him in place.

At least the laptop was in his line of vision.

"Uncle?" she asked. He was tempted to kick her legs out from underneath her, but he didn't think his pride could take two beatings from his little sister in one day.

"Uncle," he muttered. "What are you so upset about?" He rubbed the back of his head when she let him up. It did not elicit an ounce of sympathy.

"I know her." She pointed to the Disapproving Librarian.

"Yikes."

"Shut up. She's really nice."

"She looks nice."

"That is not her normal face! Someone is obviously playing a joke."

"How do you know her?"

"She works at Richmond. Remember when I told you about that really cute librarian?"

"This is the cute librarian?"

"This is not how she normally looks! She's very nice, and fun, and . . . stop laughing!"

"I can't help it! This meme is speaking to me. God, I'd hate to be the one to let her down."

"You're a jerk. Anyway, don't you have some story to write about how you're way too old to drink like you're twenty-one?"

Colin wanted to tell her to shut up, and that he could drink any twenty-one-year-old under the table. But his head was throbbing from a combination of hangover and headlock, and so he was grateful when she slammed her laptop shut and stormed out of the kitchen, shooting him a look that was decidedly more murderous than disappointed.

Women.

He went for a mouthful of sweet, sweet coffee, but his mug was empty.

Chapter Three

Dear Maria,

Is it possible to die of embarrassment?
I'll Be Hiding Out Until You Answer in Nob Hill

Dear Hiding,

I hate to sound like an old fart, but whatever it is, this, too, shall pass. The good, the bad—it all becomes memories, and memories fade like dust in the wind, to borrow a phrase from your grandparents' favorite song. You know, time heals all wounds and all that crap.

But what should you do to get through the part before it gets better? Take comfort in the fact that you are merely a speck on a grain of sand in the great dune of the universe, and you're probably more aware of the embarrassment than anyone else is. If that's not the case, you better just own it. You did something dumb, you were made a fool of, but every supermodel that trips over her heels on the runway gets back up to sashay again.

Chin up, Hiding. You'll get over it.

Kisses,
Maria

BERNIE LOVED HER JOB. Really, she did. Her students were mostly wonderful, the occasional flash mob notwithstanding. The college had a decent budget for resources and access to larger universities in the Bay Area. The staff was small but dedicated, she worked on research projects, and the campus had a really good cafeteria, thanks to the hospitality program. Sure, there were some things she didn't love—professors who didn't take her seriously as an academic equal, the weird hours during finals week, her pathetic salary—but on most days, the good far outweighed the bad.

Mondays were still a total drag.

Especially since she'd spent the weekend off the grid. One of her best friends, Marcie, led female empowerment workshops around Mount Tam, and she'd finally talked Bernie into going. It wasn't easy to convince her—Bernie loved Marcie, but she imagined the workshops were all women in crushed velvet drinking homemade tea, and examining themselves with hand mirrors. But Bernie needed a break and someone had dropped out at the last minute and she liked tea, so she went.

In some ways—the crushed velvet and the tea and the hand mirrors—it had been exactly what she'd expected. But there was decidedly more naked bonfire-dancing and funny baked goods than she was quite prepared for.

Nonetheless, she returned to the city refreshed and empowered. Then her other bff, Dave, insisted that she meet him at work so he could hear all about it. He had a new job at a new bar, and it was sure to be dead on a

Sunday night, he said. And it was, until it wasn't, and then Dave insisted that she stick around so she could watch him flirt, and take notes as needed since she was notoriously terrible at flirting. She wasn't interested in facing her return to normal life, so she did.

She wasn't sure if Dave's flirting methods would exactly work for her, but it beat doing laundry and making lunches.

This break from routine made her way happier than it probably should have.

Marcie said it was because she spent so much time adulting that her idea of rebellion was having a nonsensible dinner.

Which wasn't fair. She rebelled all the time.

Okay, she didn't rebel at all, she thought as she unlocked her office door. But she did enjoy the occasional popcorn for dinner.

Did she know how to party or what?

She reached over the pile of reference books she was supposed to have spent the weekend reviewing (rebel!) (or maybe just procrastinator) and turned on her computer. Her phone was lit up, which meant she had a voice mail, which was a little strange. People hardly ever used voice mail at Richmond anymore. It was all e-mail, which, frankly, she preferred. She pulled open her desk drawer to find the scrap of paper she'd written her voice mail password on. It was a whole mess of numbers, and Bernie didn't have a head for remembering numbers. And since IT had made her change it from 1234, she couldn't keep the darned PIN straight.

"Ha!" she said as she stumbled on the old Post-it: 4321. Very clever, she told herself. That'll show those IT guys.

Rolling her eyes at herself, she went through the 6 million

prompts that finally got her to her messages. Seventeen new messages, the nice robot lady told her.

Seventeen messages! She didn't think she'd had seventeen messages altogether in the two years she'd been at Richmond.

As she listened, she realized why. There were fifteen hang-ups, one sobbing message from Carly saying she was "so so sorry," which was alarming, and one vulgar message promising impossible things with the caller's tongue that would "wipe that look off her face," and which she assumed was a wrong number. An alarming wrong number, but how else to explain it? She'd never gotten dirty messages before. Hearing this one made her grateful for that.

The wrong number, plus the fifteen hang-ups, was concerning. She must have forgotten something. How else to explain why so many people were calling her? She didn't think she'd ever gotten fifteen phone calls in one day, even during finals week. She didn't think there were fifteen people at the library who wanted to talk to her.

Maybe that was it—finals week was coming up. She needed to get her stuff organized, make sure all of her LibGuides were up to date, get petty cash for late-night pizza for the procrastinators.

As she started to make a physical list, her computer finally came to life. She logged in, tapped her fingers as each icon popped to life, and then opened her e-mail. She tried not to think about the irony in the fact that the public computers in the library were state-of-the-art and replaced every year or so, but the staff computers were older'n dirt, as her friend Helen would say. They only got upgraded when whatever software they were running was so old that it was no longer supported by the manufacturer. And then they got complaints from professors that the new software was broken (a.k.a. they didn't know how to use it). So Bernie supposed she understood IT's hesitation. But still. When it was faster to work at public computers (which were always available since most of the students had their own laptops), it all felt a little silly.

Blergh. Mondays.

Also silly was the flood of e-mails in her inbox. She'd developed a pretty good rapport with a lot of students over the past few years, so she was used to coming back from a few days away with lots of requests for appointments and panicked questions about citing blogs according to *The Chicago Manual of Style*. Plus lots of meeting requests from colleagues. The new library director loved a meeting, and both librarians and academics loved a committee, and Bernie was always in the middle of both.

This, however, was ridiculous.

Three hundred e-mails.

In two days.

Her palms started to sweat.

She'd definitely forgotten something.

Part of her wanted to just turn the computer off and go back home. Retreat back to the woods with her hand mirror. Remember two days ago? she asked herself. Remember when there was nothing to forget so you couldn't go into a panic about forgetting it?

But there was another part of her that was curious. She didn't realize how important she was if one forgotten something warranted three hundred e-mails. She felt a little like George Bailey, and her inbox was her Clarence. Or maybe something terrible had happened in the library over the weekend. Security incidents tended to set off an explosion of reply-alls. Too bad she'd lost her cell phone charger somewhere between home and Mount Tam. She'd bet she had a butt-ton of messages there, too.

Well, only one way to find out what was going on, she told herself. She started at the top, with the newest messages. From Liz, her direct supervisor, asking what this was all about. Bernie had no idea what "this" was. She left it open and moved on. Carly had sent her fourteen apologies, without making it clear what she was apologizing for. Was it the flash mob? It was annoying, sure, but Carly hadn't been involved in planning it—that much was clear based on the look on the poor girl's face when Evan started dancing. Bernie'd seen Carly in plays before. She couldn't fake that kind of enthusiasm. Was she apologizing for getting engaged when she was so young? Maybe she'd come to her senses over the weekend. Although why she would apologize to Bernie for that was not entirely clear.

Bernie shot off a quick reply—there's nothing to apologize for, see you during your next shift—and moved on.

She eventually slogged into an e-mail from an old friend from library school. Liam had sent her a short message and a link to a tumblr page.

"You're famous!" the message said. "Hilarious!"

Bernie thought back to what she'd done recently that was noteworthy. Occasionally the local media would do a story on something at Richmond—a display she'd put up, some new technology they'd spent a lot of money on. She'd been a talking head in several stories about e-books and textbooks. She didn't love watching herself in the media—her voice always sounded strange and she wanted to tell herself to smile more—but curiosity got the better of her and she clicked the link.

And it was her face.

Up real close.

Scowling.

Above her face in big white block letters, were the

words *Disapproving Librarian* Underneath her slight
scowl-induced double chin was the word *Disapproves*.

Disapproving Librarian Disapproves.

With her face.

Holy crap.

She was a meme.

Colin pushed his way through the glass doors of the
Glaze.com office. They'd moved in during their last round
of funding after hiring an interior designer, so the whole
place was very shiny and open. The result of this very
modern and very expensive makeover was that it was a
terrible place to work. Every sound echoed off the cav-
ernous warehouse ceilings, and fashion people were not
a quiet people. Nobody had assigned workstations, so
colleagues were constantly fighting over scissors and
pens and someone using someone else's personal coffee
mug for kombucha.

Colin avoided the office as much as possible. For one
thing, all of the bright white surfaces and perfume smells
gave him a headache. Jeanaeane Ng, the beauty editor
who seemed to add an extra vowel to her first name every
six months or so, was forever spraying samples around. He
supposed it was fair—she did traffic in beauty products—
but the fact that there was no barrier between her odors
and the rest of the office made it . . . smelly. Never mind
the fact that, as an online-only magazine, there was no
way to actually get samples of the scent to the consumer.
Logic did not deter Jeanaeane.

And then there was whatever corner Makeda, the fashion
editor, had commandeered as her samples closet. The interior designers didn't believe in closed doors, or doors
at all, or spaces that could theoretically hold a door. Instead,

they had installed built-in closet rails at various random intervals around the office walls. It would make designer samples like a showpiece, they said. And it was kind of cool, when they were full, except that the layout had Makeda running back and forth across the office whenever she was working on a spread or planning a shoot or trying to fit models.

Makeda's compromise was an unlimited number of rolling wardrobe racks with special removable shelves for shoes. Because there was no actual storage, the empty racks lived in the stairwells behind the fire doors, which was definitely a safety hazard, but it was aesthetically pleasing.

Colin always felt there was something cosmically appropriate about that.

He really hated coming to the office. Not because he was always tripping over stilettos in an effort to find an unclaimed work space—although that was not great either. There was just too much chaos. He couldn't write around the noise of the people shrieking about whether or not the bolero jacket was coming back for spring or which rose-scented towelette absorbed the most oil from your T-zone. Especially now that he knew what bolero jackets and T-zones were. He was a writer, dammit. He was a man. He didn't care about that stuff.

Except, as Steph pointed out, he was a writer for a women's fashion and lifestyle Web site. So he should care about that stuff. He didn't have to care about that stuff to write about nightlife, he argued. He was there to offer a male perspective. You're right, Steph said. You should not care at all about the things women care about when you're offering your perspective on those things.

It wasn't that he didn't care about fashion and makeup.

He just didn't get it. He appreciated it when women put in the effort, and he'd spent enough time around fastidious women to recognize the art and the work involved. He could understand the appeal of an eye enhanced by the application of mascara. But telling the difference between thick and super-thick and mega-thick mascara?

That was where Maria came in.

Maria was his beloved, crotchety, no-nonsense, advice-wielding alter ego.

Maria was way more successful than Colin was, than he would probably ever be. Not financially—definitely not financially. But her blog had a cult following online and name recognition that sites like Glaze would kill for.

Too bad he couldn't tell anyone.

Besides, Take a Letter, Maria was just a hobby. It had started as a lark, and that was all it would ever be. He liked the mental and emotional stretching it took to channel Maria, but he wasn't interested in becoming a real-life advice guru. He wasn't really interested in anything except having a good time. The only reason he even had his job at Glaze was that his parents insisted. Which sounded pathetic, to be pushing thirty and still following the orders of your parents. But when they sold their law practice and retired down South, they agreed that he and Steph could continue to live in the house, rent-free, on the condition that they both remained gainfully employed. Steph had dutifully graduated with a degree in horticulture—ha, horticulture!—and landed a job with the city as the Assistant Green Spaces Coordinator. Colin had abandoned his sporadic attempts at novel writing (it just wasn't in him) and bartending (he preferred to be in front of the bar) and joined a just-starting-up online beauty magazine as their Resident Guy.

He didn't remember exactly how he'd gotten into that headspace the first time. He supposed he was cranky. His parents were breathing down his neck, Steph was wearing him out with her success, and he'd just broken up with a girl who told him that he was just stringing her along. Which he wasn't; he just didn't always immediately reply to her 16,000 daily text messages. So he did what any self-respecting millennial did.

He started a blog.

He wasn't into navel-gazing—or at least he wasn't into *obvious* navel-gazing, so he thought long and hard about a framing device, one that would let him air out his issues without him just writing paragraph after boring paragraph about how his life was so hard. He knew his life wasn't hard. He was very grateful for that. But sometimes . . .

Then he heard a little voice. Well, not a little voice, a loud, brassy, used-to-smoke-a-pack-a-day voice. The voice slapped him upside the head and told him to pull himself together, he was being ridiculous. Which he knew. He knew he was being ridiculous, but sometimes, he thought, it helps to have someone remind you of that.

And maybe the voice could help other people. With great power and all that. So he started.

Dear Maria,

> *Why won't my man write me back?*

> > *Desperate on Divisadero*

Dear Desperate,

> *Because you write too many texts. Send one, and if he doesn't respond, it wasn't meant to be. Send another, and he was never yours to begin with.*

> > *Kisses,*
> > *Maria*

THE NEXT DAY, someone e-mailed his blog, asking Maria a question.

So, he figured . . . why not?

For his day job, he got paid pretty well, considering how little work he did. He had some friends who were actual reporters, and he couldn't imagine having to stay up all night during election season, or tracking down interviewees who did not want to be interviewed. All Colin had to do was meet with Makeda and Jeanaeane, find out what was hot, and talk about what guys thought of it. The most extensive research he ever had to do was to find out which of the new restaurants that sprouted up in San Francisco like mushrooms was the best place for a date. He'd just finished his series on Date Deciphering, which included such meaningful insights as what it meant if your date takes you to a food truck (he's a hipster with no game) or a rom-com (he's hoping to get laid; that's the only reason men ever, ever go to rom-coms).

But that series reached its natural conclusion by addressing the issue of to kiss or not to kiss. ("If he doesn't try to kiss you on the first date, there's not going to be a second. No man has ever considered whether or not he should kiss on the first date. If he wants a kiss, he'll go for it. If not, it's not because of manners.")

He also had his weekly assignment of piggybacking on one of the other features, from his "guy's perspective." Once he accompanied Makeda to Fashion Week. His guy's perspective was that it was nuts and he didn't get it. Another time he went on a tour bus through Napa Valley. Most of the time, though, his features had more of an editorial feel. Usually he got to do this from the comfort of his own home, or a coffee shop, or the bar on the corner. But not today. Today was—

"Okay, everyone, time for pants!"

Dali, assistant to Clea, Glaze.com's editor-in-chief, was a gender-fluid New Age musician with blue and pink hair and an obsession with office supplies. She also reveled in the weekly editorial meeting—Colin suspected it was because she got to take color-coded notes—which she dubbed "pants" because all of the staff writers had to come in from their cushy, comfortable non-office work spaces and dress in a manner presentable to the public.

One day, Colin swore, he was going to come in in his boxers. Except he didn't want to give Clea a reason to fire him. She probably had enough of those already. If it wasn't for his winning charm, or, more likely, the fact that he was the only straight man on staff and the only writer who more or less respected a deadline, he expected he'd be out the door.

This was the one thing that made his cushy job a little less cushy—the fact that it could disappear at any moment. All he needed was for some other dude to come in with great ideas and an actual work ethic.

The staff made its way to the large, white conference table in the center of the room. Whatever makeup samples Jeaneaeane had been toying with were long gone, and it was just chairs, table, and a plate of bagels no one but Colin would touch.

Clea was in her usual spot, perched on the corner of the table, sipping green tea from a glass mug, waiting for them all to arrive. Back in their old office, she'd taken that spot because it gave her the perfect vantage point to unleash her death glare on anyone who dared walk in the door late. Now they didn't have doors, and they didn't have wall space to waste on a wall clock. Anyway, the new conference table was so slick and high that all of her time-management energy seemed to now be devoted to not falling on her butt every time she moved.

Sitting at her right hand, of course, was Pia Wallington, former intern and current pain in Colin's ass. Pia was five feet tall when she wore her signature platform heels, had a short, Mia Farrow-style pixie cut dyed silver, and wore so much jewelry, Colin was sometimes worried she would topple over. She was also a twenty-year-old college dropout who'd had a fashion blog in high school, which qualified her for the job of junior staff writer. This meant she wrote a lot of product descriptions and small stories and spent a lot of time wondering aloud why Colin was the one who got to go to Fashion Week.

If she was a fellow straight guy, Colin would be worried.

But under the circumstances, he had nothing to worry about.

"Okay, folks, what do we have this week?" Clea asked from her perch.

"Blue lipstick," said Jeanaeane. "It's hot."

"Great. Fashion?"

"Clothes that go with blue lipstick?" Makeda hedged.

Clea sighed. "Anything that is not blue?"

"Well," said Pia. "I want to talk about the Internet."

"Sounds like a great scoop for an online magazine," Colin muttered. Makeda laughed. Jeanaeane pursed her blue lips at him.

"I'm starting the pitch nice and slow so people who weren't born digital can keep up," said Pia.

Nothing at all to be worried about.

She stood, her giant platforms clomping on the polished concrete floor. "I was doing some research over the weekend," she began. Colin snorted. Pia's idea of weekend research was celebrity-spotting at trendy restaurants and pitching features on whatever pet projects they had sold her on.

Totally different from what Colin did.

Colin just went out to try new bars and ended up sleeping through someone else's threesome.

He didn't deal with celebrities.

Pia swiped a few screens on her tablet, and the office projector buzzed to life. "Clea, you're always talking about how we are positioned to become the boutique for every part of a woman's life."

Clea's eyebrows were raised so high in expectation that they disappeared under her Wintour-esque bangs. Colin shot a quick look to Makeda, who looked as astonished as he felt. "Lifestyle boutique" was Clea's mantra. It was her dream to grow the site from fashion and beauty to include travel and work and relationships. That was what Colin did, more or less. Relationships. Well, dating. He did that because Clea was nudging him in that direction, because that was where she wanted Glaze to grow.

He hadn't thought that Pia was paying attention.

Still. Nothing to worry about. Probably.

Pia nodded at Dali, who hit a button on the office remote, dimming the lights. Everybody scooted their laptops and coffees back a little as a presentation projected onto the center of the table. Pia pushed the bagels toward Colin.

The Beauty Business is War, Clea had told them the first time she showed them the cutting-edge projection unit. This is our War Room. Someone had pointed out that, no matter which way the presentation was oriented, someone would be reading it upside down. That person did not work at Glaze.com anymore.

"*Webster's Dictionary* defines a meme as—"

"We know what a meme is," Colin interrupted.

Pia just shrugged, her statement necklaces clanking. "Just making sure." She reached over and took the remote from Dali. The image on the table flickered between cats and babies and horses with their lips flopping around. "Usually these are cute animals being hilarious." A husky gave them a bright smile from the center of the table. Grumpy Cat cut them down to size. "But sometimes, memes are people." She brought up some classics—Overly Attached Girlfriend, Ehrmahgerd Girl. "What is that like, to be a meme?" Pia clicked again.

It was the face of the Disapproving Librarian.

Colin flinched. It was funny, sure, but he couldn't help but feel bad for this girl. Maybe it was some of Steph's sympathy rubbing off on him. Whatever it was, this was not a flattering picture. Being projected large on a glossy white table did not improve it.

It was too bad, really. She probably wasn't bad looking. Her hair was pretty tragic, and the face she was making was definitely unflattering. But he'd bet she wasn't completely hopeless when she smiled.

"This meme is pretty new, so you guys might not have seen it yet," Pia said, picking up on the surprised laughter around the table.

"Poor girl," said Makeda.

"Poor girl's eyebrows," said Jeanaeane.

"I've heard rumors that she lives here," Pia said, her eyes lighting up with mischievous glee. "I'm going to track her down—"

More power to ya, Colin thought as the librarian disapproved of them all. I wouldn't want to meet that glare in a dark alley.

"God, has she totally gone into hiding?" Jeanaeane asked.

"I would—"

"That's the story!" Pia interrupted. "What's it like to be a meme? To have your face involuntarily the butt of a joke?"

"I read that on Buzzfeed a few months ago," Clea said.

"Cyberbullying!"

"One unflattering picture is not cyberbullying."

"It is unflattering," Makeda agreed.

"I'd love to get at those cheekbones," Jeanaeane said.

"The pout would go down a little easier with some lipstick," Clea agreed.

"I'd be pissed if I had to wear a shirt like that," said Makeda.

"Colin?"

Colin looked up at Clea, not sure what she wanted him to contribute. The librarian didn't look great; he agreed with that. He had no idea how to make her better. "Maybe if she smiled?"

"Ugh, nothing worse than a man telling me to smile," Makeda grumbled.

"But you can sit here and talk about how tragic her face is?"

"She can still scowl," Jeanaeane said. "But she could work a little harder on giving us her best scowl. With lipstick. And eyebrow shaping."

"What's wrong with her eyebrows?"

Jeanaeane just rolled her eyes at him.

"That's it!" Clea shouted.

"What's it?" Colin asked.

"Making Over a Meme."

Pia beamed with pride. "Exactly!"

"She doesn't look like the kind of woman who'd be interested in a makeover," Colin said. He didn't know why he said it, or why he thought it. She just looked like . . . like maybe she thought about other stuff.

And yet . . . there was something about that face. He was curious about that face.

"The woman clearly needs help," Jeanaeane said. "At the very least, she needs to learn what her best angles are."

"It's gonna take more than angles," Pia said. "This is probably something that's more suited for a senior writer."

Colin's ears perked up. Was Pia . . . giving him her story?

"I can see this being a series of articles, one on each aspect of her disastrous face. Jeanaeane, we can do a whole spread on eyebrows."

Jeanaeane's eyes lit up.

What was the deal with her eyebrows?

"I can see the potential," Clea said, squinting at the Disapproving Librarian. "I like the idea of a series. Colin, what do you think?"

"Well, this isn't really Colin's wheelhouse, is it?" Pia asked, her face completely artless. If Colin wasn't mistaken, she was batting her eyes at Clea.

Now would probably be the time to start feeling threatened, he told himself.

"I mean, maybe this would be easier if I was just made a senior writer."

And there it was.

Colin braced himself for the speech, that they had only budgeted one senior writer for features, maybe that could be expanded in the future, but for now it was one senior and one junior, although there were opportunities for freelancing.

That was the speech that saved his ass every time Pia brought up the great idea that she should also be a senior writer, despite her lack of experience and the lack of a budget.

"I know there's only room in the budget for one senior

writer," Pia said, and alarm bells went off in Colin's head. "I'm not suggesting you change that."

"Then what are you suggesting?" Clea's expression indicated a mix of annoyance and curiosity. Colin was most worried about the curiosity.

"Nothing, really. Just that, well, there's only room for one senior writer, and I'm the one with all the good ideas."

"I know the librarian!"

All eyes turned to Colin, who was only barely aware that he had spoken. He just felt the panic of losing his cushy job and the hot breath of Pia's ambition breathing down his neck, and he blurted out the ace he didn't realize he was holding. Probably because it wasn't much of an ace, what with it not really being true and all.

"Do you?" Clea asked, very, very interested.

"Sure. Pia's right. She's local."

Pia looked momentarily panicked, but she recovered quickly. She was quick, the little sneak. "Great. You can put me in touch."

"Um, no." He could also just hand her his job, which he was not interested in doing.

"My idea, my story," Pia said, and it sounded like she was starting to whine.

"My contact," Colin said. God, was he really trying to steal Pia's story? This was a new low for him.

Dear Maria,

I knew I didn't have much professional integrity, but today I learned the depths of my desperation. What should I do?

                            Soulless in SoMa

Dear Soulless,

 A man's gotta eat.

Kisses,
Maria

"*I* HAVE AN IDEA," Clea said. She didn't exactly rub her hands together in maniacal glee, but it was close. "I want a proposal from each of you by end of day tomorrow," Clea said.

"But it was my—"

"Colin, share the unfortunate woman's contact information with Pia. The two of you reach out to her, I don't care how. Then I want a proposal from each of you for a month-long series on this, starting with the makeover."

"But what if—"

"The advertisers will love this. Makeda, can you get clothes in her size?"

Makeda gave Clea a side-eye that meant yes.

"But this was my—"

"Before and After. Jeanaeane, call Jack. Tell him it's an emergency. Book him for later in the week. Wednesday at the latest."

Jeanaeane whipped out her phone, presumably to text their on-call hair guy, Jack.

"But Clea!"

"Geek to Chic," Clea said, tapping her finger against her chin. "No. Dowdy to Drop-Dead Gorgeous. Maybe." She turned to Colin and Pia, her War Room face dead serious. "I don't have to tell you that we need the hits on this. I won't play second fiddle to *Cosmo* anymore. I'm not paying rent in the most expensive city in the country to be laughed at by Nina Garcia. I want nothing less than world domination," she added, and Colin would have laughed but he didn't think she was joking.

"Pia, I'm sick of your whining, and Colin, I'm sick of you not pulling your weight. As of next month, there is no more junior staff writer and senior staff writer. There is only a staff writer. Get it?"

Pia scrunched her nose in confusion. "But—"

"She means one of us is getting fired."

"Oh."

Clea patted Colin on the cheek. "You're smart, good. Now get me that story." She took the remote from Pia's limp hand and tossed it to Dali, who caught it while still managing to furiously continue taking notes on Clea's ultimatum. In red pen.

"It's not that bad."

Bernie lifted her head off the café table long enough to give her friend Marcie a look that she hoped would kill. Or at least significantly maim. Or, at the very least, get Marcie to shut up about the stupid meme that was now Bernie's life. This was not what she'd wanted when she'd called her best friends together for an emergency lunch. "You look thin," Dave suggested, and Bernie was going to punch him in the arm, but Marcie beat her to it. "What, she does!" he said, rubbing his poor, stupid arm. "It's not entirely unflattering."

"The most important thing is that it will pass," Marcie said. "That's what Take a Letter, Maria said. You read the column I sent you, right?"

"I'm never going on the Internet again."

"The gist of it was that you'll be old news in no time."

"Helpful," Bernie told the table.

"The humiliation will pass, too," Dave assured her. Bernie took a little more comfort in that. Dave had tended bar at almost every hip restaurant in San Francisco. He'd seen his share of flash-in-the-pan celebrities rise and fall.

Not that she was a celebrity. God, she hoped she wasn't a celebrity.

The Internet was supposed to be really big. It was supposed to have diverse pockets of communities that developed their own codes and languages that took years to become part of the everyday lexicon. Years! Not days.

The Internet was a big, dumb lie.

Maybe not too much of a lie. Her parents hadn't called yet, which meant they hadn't seen her new online persona. Would her parents even know what a meme was? Would they even recognize her?

Yes, her mother would. In the meme, Bernie was making the face that had driven her mother to redo many a family picture. "Can't you just smile?" her mother would say.

Bernie should have listened to her mother.

"It's not the worst picture you've ever taken," Marcie added, helpfully. "Remember that time when you met Junot Díaz?"

Junot Díaz had come to San Francisco on a book tour, and since Bernie had a huge literary crush on him, she'd dragged Marcie along to the reading. They waited in line for a signed book, then Marcie insisted on a picture. In her heart, Bernie was completely fangirling and trying her best to shut up about Oscar Wao for long enough for Marcie to take the photo.

She did not succeed.

In that picture, Bernie looked like a maniac. A smiling maniac who appreciated great writing, but a maniac all the same.

That picture, however, was not on the Internet.

Certainly, this meme had traveled. Aside from Liam, she'd heard from several of her other library school friends. Maybe it was because they were connected, digitally speaking, for professional reasons, and maybe it was because the meme was both generally appealing (unfortunately) and industry-specific, but she'd gotten four different "how are you" e-mails.

She was also the subject of more think pieces than she cared to admit to reading, mostly on professional blogs that covered issues of librarianship. They were a diverse lot of bloggers covering a wide range of topics in the field, but they all agreed on one thing: Bernie's meme reinforced tired stereotypes, and Bernie's meme was bad for business.

It wasn't her fault. She hadn't taken the picture. She didn't put that stupid caption on it. She didn't make terrible faces when her too-young students took a plunge they were ill prepared for.

Well, yes. She did make the face. It was not a great face, but what kind of face was she supposed to make? Carly and Evan were babies. Carly had just moved out of the dorms last year. They'd never dated other people or seen anything of the world, and now they'd be tied together forever. If Bernie had married her college boyfriend, she'd be a pastor's wife in Ohio. Her college boyfriend wasn't even religious when they were together, which was exactly the point. Carly and Evan were still finding themselves, so how could they possibly know that this was the person they wanted to spend the rest of their lives with?

And why why why was every emotion she felt so apparent on her face?

The whole thing gave her heartburn.

It was never going to pass.

Chapter Four

Dear Maria,

    My friends think I'm too good for my boyfriend. I make more money than he does, but I still feel like we are partners in everything. They think I'm settling, but it took me so long to find him, I don't think I should give him up. What should I do?

        Floundering in the Outer Sunset

Dear Floundering,

    There may be other fish in the sea, but do you really want to put that worm on the hook again?

          Kisses,
          Maria

BERNIE HEARD HER PHONE BUZZ from the bottom of her purse, where she'd buried it once she found her spare charger and discovered that, while she was dancing naked around a bonfire, everyone she knew in the Bay Area was sending her some form of message asking if she'd seen the meme and wasn't it hilarious. Her friend, Helen, a fellow librarian halfway across the country in Kentucky, had sent her a link to a popular librarian blog that was asking Important Questions about the image of librarians, and whether or not Bernie had set them back decades. Bernie wanted to add to the comments that it wasn't her fault she couldn't control her facial expressions. Then she read what some of her anonymous colleagues had written and decided it was better if she just let them duke it out among themselves.

Never read the comments, she reminded herself.

The first person to find her Tuesday morning was Liz, the head of reference, who asked if she knew anything about the meme and whether it was too soon to laugh. Then Carly stopped by and told her that it was kind of cool that she was so famous, although her attempt at cheering Bernie up was somewhat marred by her apologetic tears. Then she got a call from the director's secretary, saying he wanted to see her in his office.

You're not going to die, she reminded herself as she walked down the carpeted hallway to the director's office. You just might get a little bit fired.

"Miss Bernard, right on time," Director Dean said, standing as she entered his office. Maxwell Dean, Director of Libraries, was relatively new to the job and had the unfortunate habit of referring to the library as the "Googleplex." But he was her boss's boss, and he respected her ability to wield usage statistics, even though his complete reliance on numbers undervalued a lot of the good work the library did. He was obsessed with the idea of being hip and connected, and liked to include at least one hashtag in each departmental e-mail, even though it made him look kind of stupid, since hashtags didn't track in their e-mail program.

He also had an unfortunate habit of deferring to her

student workers when he wanted a decision made. Not that students shouldn't have a voice in their library, but she was the one with the MLS. And she was the one who supervised the students, when they weren't dancing on the reference desk. Although she supposed she was, technically, supervising the students then, too.

Which had to be what this was about.

Oh, God, what if he had seen the meme?

Dean was always getting on them about busting stereotypes and making the library a dynamic learning environment. She was all on board with that. She was pretty sure a dynamic learning environment did not mean inadvertently being part of an Internet trend that reinforced negative stereotypes.

"And how is your semester going so far?"

She blinked at Dean across his desk. Was he making small talk?

"Great," she replied. Until she became Internet Famous.

If he was going to make an issue of this, there was no way she was going to be able to follow the ignore-it-and-it-will-go-away path for dealing with her infamy.

"Getting down to the wire for some of the kids, huh?" he small-talked.

"Yup," she said, acknowledging the impending end of the semester and the chaos that usually ensued.

She blinked at Dean some more. He blinked back.

Productive meeting.

"Sorry, what did you call this meeting for?" Bernie didn't want to be rude, but she also wanted to know why she had been called to the principal's office.

"Miss Bernard—Melissa—you've been supervising the undergraduates here at the library for, what? About a year now?"

"At the end of this semester it will be two years," she corrected.

"Yes. You've done a wonderful job, so Liz tells me. And the student workers do seem well-trained and well-prepared for their work. And they speak highly of you."

She blushed. Compliments always made her blush. Even though it wasn't a compliment; it was true. When she was promoted, she'd worked hard to whip a bunch of disorganized, dispassionate students into the well-oiled, if sometimes tardy, machine that made the library function. And every semester, she started all over again.

"I understand that last week there was an . . . incident at the library."

Crap. She knew she should have written it up. But what was she supposed to put in the incident report? Two kids danced on a desk and got engaged, and then they all left. But not before taking a totally unflattering picture of me and plastering it all over the Internet.

"It was quick, and I didn't see any danger of it happening again, so I didn't see the need to—"

"Yes, I understand it was over *in a flash*."

She looked up at the strange tone of his voice. Was Maxwell Dean, Director of Libraries, giggling?

"I'm sorry, I should have put a stop to it right away. It just caught me by surprise—"

"No, no, Miss Bernard, you misunderstand. I'm thrilled! A flash mob—is that what the kids call it?—right here in our library! I'm only sorry there wasn't a video."

There probably was. And she wished the video had gone viral; then maybe her stupid face would be left alone.

"Just the other day, my daughter-in-law sent me this." He typed the pass code on his phone and turned it toward her.

It was her face.

Looking disapproving.

Sigh.

"I couldn't believe it! I was just tickled!"

Now he definitely was giggling. Had she fallen down a rabbit hole?

"Do you know what this means for the library?"

Nothing, she thought. At best, it means nothing. At worst, it means everyone will think a bunch of sour-faced old ladies work at the library. Which a lot of people thought anyway, so it really isn't that bad.

"Melissa, I see a real opportunity here." He steepled his fingers in front of his chin. "Our own meme, right here in our very own library!"

"Sorry?"

"This is quite a coup."

"Well, I can't really take any credit for it." Although she supposed she had spent thirty-one years perfecting her look of disdain. The inability to control her facial expression just came naturally.

"I had Marketing work some of these up." He pulled a foam-core poster out from under his desk.

It had her face on it.

It said DISAPPROVING LIBRARIAN . . . WANTS YOU TO CITE YOUR SOURCES.

Then he pulled out another one that said DISAPPROVING LIBRARIAN . . . DOES NOT USE WIKIPEDIA.

Then he pulled out a few more, all with pithy, useful library tips, all with her frowning face staring back at her.

"And there are matching bookmarks!"

She had definitely fallen down a rabbit hole.

With matching bookmarks.

Chapter Five

Dear Maria,

   My boyfriend won't wear the expensive tailored shirts I bought for him, even after I threw his crappy old band shirts away. What should I do?

   Distressed in Balboa Park

Dear Distressed,

   If you want to play dress up, get a Ken doll. If you want to be with a real man, buy your boyfriend some new band shirts.

   Kisses,
   Maria

THE LIBRARY WAS OFFICIALLY CHAOS.

Bernie usually thrived during finals week. It was a great chance to show off what the library had to offer, especially since she essentially had a captive audience.

The building bustled with nervous energy, and desperate students came to Bernie with problems that she could solve. You need three sources for your paper on medieval morality plays? No problem. You need to access translated newspapers from Uzbekistan? Here you go. You need to see how shoe size affects performance in track and field events? Let me introduce you to this database. She loved it, almost as much as she loved the week after finals when everyone was gone and she could put her feet up—literally—and catch up on all the stuff she'd missed during the madness.

This year, the madness was starting early.

If one more student came to the desk and told Bernie to make a disapproving face, she was going to confiscate their phone and run up overdue fines on their library account.

Worse, when she got dressed that morning, she changed her outfit half a dozen times, because in each one, she looked way too much like a spinsterish, Disapproving Librarian. Why did everything she owned involve a cardigan?

Dammit, she was a librarian. Of course she was going to dress like one. No, that wasn't the worst part. The worst part was when students asked her to make her Disapproving Librarian face and she tried to ignore them but they took the picture anyway and went away happy. Was the Disapproving Librarian face actually just Her Face?

God, did she look like that all the time?

Bernie was not a vain person, but this whole experience was really testing the limits of her less-is-more approach to her appearance.

Unfortunately, they were short-staffed and she couldn't call in replacements because she needed to save those student worker hours for next week, when finals actually started. Liz had been on the reference desk for most of yesterday, but she had other stuff to do, too. As much as Bernie wanted to hide in her office all day again today, she couldn't do that to Liz.

This whole experience was also testing the limits of her welcoming smile.

She thought about the e-mail she'd written last night, the one where she really let her pity party go hog wild, admitting that being the subject of a meme made her feel pathetic and angry. In the cold light of the morning (and the harsh fluorescent lights of the Richmond College Library), she was glad she hadn't sent it. She didn't need to be asking for advice from anonymous bloggers, no matter how sassy or wise they were. Maria might have all the answers for other people, but what could she possibly say to make Bernie feel any better?

Besides, Bernie still had a job to do, so when the pixielike girl in giant platform sandals approached the desk, Bernie smiled at her.

"Hi, can I help you?" she asked, because she was a Friendly Librarian, not a Disapproving One. Even if those shoes were making her very worried for the poor girl's ankles.

The girl studied her face for a moment, and Bernie braced herself for the inevitable cell phone picture.

"I like your sweater," the girl said, sounding almost as surprised as Bernie felt. "Is it vintage?"

Bernie wasn't sure if it was vintage. It was old, she knew that. And secondhand. "It was three dollars," she said, as if that explained it.

"Cool," the girl said, and jotted something down in the purple notebook she carried. Bernie noticed that the notebook was the same color as the big flowers on the girl's dress. She wondered if that was on purpose.

"Do you get a lot of your clothes secondhand?"

"Um . . . yes?" Bernie hated shopping. Most of her clothes were the first thing she picked up in a store that fit her, or castoffs from the more conservative end of Marcie's wardrobe. So, technically, yes. Secondhand. Thirdhand. It didn't really matter, as long as it was convenient hand.

The strange little pixie took more notes.

"Have you always dressed like this?" she asked.

"Dressed like what? Like crap?" Bernie asked with a laugh. She knew how she looked. Meme or not, she knew.

She tended to make unfortunate wardrobe choices. She really did look like what the rest of the world assumed a librarian looked like—messy hair, fussy sweater, big glasses. It was not a cute look. That was what made the meme especially embarrassing. When she'd left the house that morning, she'd thought she looked good.

"Um, maybe? Or maybe like a librarian?"

"Well, I am a librarian, so no matter what I wear, technically I am dressed like a librarian."

The pixie thought about that for a second, then wrote it down.

"Have you ever thought about dressing . . . differently?"

No, Bernie wanted to say, but that wasn't true. Just this morning she had been wishing for some clothes that were a little less nouveau-spinster. She wasn't even dressed not-hip enough to be considered a hipster.

But what did that have to do with this student?

"I'm sorry, did you have a research question?"

"Yes!" the girl said, brightly. "Well, no. I'm a writer for Glaze.com."

The girl didn't look old enough to be a writer. Or maybe

Bernie was getting old. She sometimes thought the juniors didn't look old enough to be freshmen.

Then something the girl said stuck out. "Glaze.com? The fashion site?"

"You know it?"

"You don't have to look so surprised."

The pixie blinked at her.

"Everyone knows Glaze. Clea Summers went here."

"She did?"

"Yup. She worked in this library, too. Well, not this library. The old library. Way before my time. The one before we got computers."

The pixie blinked again. She probably didn't understand a time before computers.

"So, ah, if there's nothing else . . ." Bernie suggested, nodding as subtly as possible to the line of students forming.

"Do you want a makeover?"

"What?"

"You're the meme, right? The Disapproving Librarian? I saw it and I thought, there's a woman who could use a makeover."

And just when Bernie thought her day couldn't get any worse.

It was shabbier than he'd thought it would be.

That was Colin's first thought as he entered the Richmond College Library.

It wasn't a very kind thought, but it was true—the furniture was worn-out looking, and though it looked like pretty good quality, it had not stood the test of years of student abuse. He also noticed there were lots of computers. Where were all the books? Did libraries even have books anymore?

It had been a while since Colin had been to a library. He immediately felt guilty about that. He didn't know why, except that the feeling was familiar. Every time he went into a library, it was like the building was saying, Hey, haven't seen you in a while. You should come here more often. It's good for you.

He shook his head. He didn't like doing things that were good for him.

"Mr. Rodriguez?"

He shook off his guilt—since he had nothing to feel guilty about—and looked at the woman in front of him.

She was younger than she looked in her meme, and, if he was frank, hotter. The meme gave her a vaguely double chin. In real life, her brown hair had a hint of red, and her face looked, well, if not exactly relaxed, at least a lot less like she was taking a dump. Far from being the pudgy book-pusher he was expecting (he felt a mental slap from Steph, which he deserved), there was something strong about her posture, something appealing about her whole bearing. Nothing at all like the Mean Lady Pia had described, the one he was prepared to discharge his Prince Charming arsenal upon in order to defeat the tiny dragon and protect his job.

So not what he was expecting.

Maybe this wasn't her. Maybe this was her more pleasant twin.

"Hello?" And now she looked annoyed.

Yup, definitely her.

"Hi," he said, shaking off his rudeness and sticking out his hand. "Call me Colin. My dad's Mr. Rodriguez."

She had a firm handshake. He thought she rolled her eyes at him.

"I'm Melissa."

"I know. I recognize you from—" And now she definitely did roll her eyes at him.

"So what can I do for you?" She didn't seem vicious or defensive at all, not the way Pia had reported. He hoped it meant she was up for anything.

Like going along with a cockamamie scheme in order to help him keep his job.

"Is there somewhere we can talk?" He looked around the library. Busy. He needed to stop being surprised at how different the library was from his preconceived notions of it. If he wasn't careful, soon he'd be learning a lesson from this experience.

"Sure, let's go to my office."

Librarians had offices? Colin was smart enough, at least, to keep that observation to himself.

They stopped by the reference desk where Melissa checked in with the student working there; then they walked through a glass door to the windowed office that Colin should have noticed when he'd walked in.

"So," he said, settling into the chair across the desk from her. It was not ergonomically sound. He toughed it out. "My sister, Stephanie, gave me your contact information. . . ."

"Sure, I remember Steph."

"You do?" Steph had just graduated. Not that his sister wasn't memorable. But Melissa wasn't even one of her professors, just the librarian.

The librarian who smiled as she remembered a former student.

And what do you know, she was pretty.

This might be easier than he'd thought. Once he got her to agree, of course.

"She was my first ever student on my first ever desk shift. I remember those reference questions fondly. How is she doing?"

"Great. She's working for the city."

"Oh, I think I read about that. The new Green Spaces Coordinator?"

"Assistant Green Spaces Coordinator."

"Still. Quite a coup for a recent graduate."

"Hmm."

"Supportive older brother."

"Sorry, yes. I'm very proud."

"So. What can I help you with, Steph's supportive older brother?"

How was she doing that? How was she making him feel flustered, throwing him off balance? He was the charming one, dammit.

"I understand that you met with my colleague, Pia."

Her face fell. Ah. So there was the Disapproving Librarian.

"She's a little green," Colin said, trying to distance himself from whatever blunders Pia had made. "She's very good with hashtags."

Then she turned the Disapproval on him. "What do you mean, 'green'?"

"I mean, she's young—"

"Do you have a problem with young people?"

"No, I—"

"Or is it just a problem with young women?"

What? "No—"

"What is it? Is she trying to take your job? Is she better at it than you are?"

"Hey, now."

"I'm just wondering what she's done to make you feel so threatened."

"Are you kidding me? That kid couldn't write her way out of a paper bag unless she bought the bag factory." What was he talking about? Whatever it was, he didn't seem to be able to stop. "I'll have you know that if I dislike Pia, it is not because she's young, or a woman. She earned my dislike strictly on her own merits."

"You're turning red."

"Shut up."

And . . . he'd just told the woman he was supposed to be charming into a makeover to shut up.

You still got it, Rodriguez.

But to his surprise, the librarian smiled.

She really did have a great smile.

"Mr. Rodriguez—Colin—let me put you out of your misery. I don't need a makeover."

He took a deep breath. So, this would be a challenge. He loved a challenge. Hell, he secretly wrote a woman's advice column in the voice of an old woman.

"I agree," he said. "No woman *needs* a makeover."

He thought he saw her eyes soften.

"I have no problem with the way you look."

"So glad you approve."

"Let me guess. You hate shopping. . . ."

"Do I look like I hate shopping?"

Ack.

She sighed. "Fine, yes, I hate shopping."

"So, great. This is a chance to get some free clothes. Clothes you don't have to shop for."

"You're gonna let me keep the clothes?"

He wasn't actually sure if that was how it worked. "Of course."

"Here's the thing," she said, and leaned forward. Colin did his American best not to look down her blouse. "I would love to never go shopping again, but what you're offering is not free clothes. In order to get these clothes, I would have to give up my dignity."

"It's a chance to re-form your image."

"That meme is not *my* image. It's an image of librarians. If I let you do a story about making *me* over, then it is about my image."

"Yes, but it's making it over in a good way."

"No, it's not. It's making it over in a more socially acceptable way, in a way that reinforces the idea that women can be smart and capable and accomplished, but if they look sad and undateable, all of those accomplishments don't mean shit."

"Who said you look undateable?"

"Really? Would you go out with this?" She held up a bookmark. The bookmark looked back at Colin with disapproval.

"Heck, yes," he lied. What guy doesn't love getting his head bitten off every time he opens his mouth? "Wait, is that what this is about?"

"What?" she asked, clearly irritated.

"You hate this meme because it makes you look undateable?"

"No, I hate this meme because it reduces my existence to a shrewish stereotype."

"But you still think you're undateable."

"I don't think that. I know it."

"How?"

"What do you mean, how? I know because I don't go on dates."

"Do you look at guys like that?" he asked, pointing to

the small stack of bookmarks on her desk. Good grief, she had a whole stack of them?

"I don't know!"

She was getting upset. He should back off. But he was also getting an idea. He should pitch it to Clea first. Or he could seize the moment and finally put Pia in her place.

Chapter Six

BERNIE WATCHED COLIN RODRIGUEZ and his handsome hands fiddle with his phone while he continued to talk to her. He was hot. There was no sense denying that. She had a thing for broad-shouldered guys with striking green eyes and dark, wavy hair that was just a bit too long. So, she was a straight woman with eyesight. This did not mean she was going to jump at Mr. Handsome's every whim.

Especially when he made it clear that his whim was to follow her around and watch her pathetic dating life.

Not that her dating life was pathetic. In order for it to be pathetic, it would have to exist. But Bernie liked her life. She just didn't like dating. She liked hanging out with her friends and reading books and the occasional one-night stand with a guy from pub trivia night. All of her needs were being met. Well, she wanted a dog, but that was a dream that would have to wait until she left San Francisco, which she hoped was never. She had a hard enough time finding an apartment she could afford that was not either shared with six other people or the size of a shoebox. She couldn't afford to be picky about pet policies. Besides, she borrowed her neighbor's dog frequently enough that little Starr was half Bernie's. Her neighbors might not think that, but they didn't have to know.

Dog needs aside, she was fine. She was great. She was currently being humiliated on the Internet, but that would pass. And it would definitely not pass any faster if she drew extra attention to herself.

And yet, here she sat, in her hard-earned office, across from the man who was trying to ruin her life. But Colin Rodriguez was handsome, and she liked watching him talk. Not just because he was handsome—those lips were pretty tempting, or they would have been tempting if they weren't describing her absolute worst nightmare of laying all of her romantic problems bare to the public. He was also fascinating to watch. He couldn't seem to sit still. He would focus on her eyes, then on his phone, then back to her, then to something on the wall, then the phone. It was like he really just wanted to be looking at his phone, but someone had told him not to do that and he would get a guilty reminder every time he did. Which was interesting, because he did not strike her as the type of person who was easily bossed around. He seemed like a guy who was really used to getting his way.

Which was part of what gave her a great, sick pleasure in what she was about to tell him.

"No."

Bernie was pretty sure the idea had just come to him while they were talking. When they'd started the conversation, it was clear that Colin wanted the same thing that rude little woman with the fake silver hair wanted: to replace Bernie's offensively unfashionable wardrobe with something more acceptable to society's notions of what a woman should look like.

But now he was talking about helicopter rides to vineyards and flying to L.A. for movie premieres and great relationships with advertisers who were really interested in her story. Now he was talking about dating.

Thirty dates in thirty days, he told her, siccing that intense gaze on her. She squirmed, but she did not cave.

Bernie was not most people.

He raised an eyebrow at her, which she thought he did because it made him look charming. "Don't you want to hear the rest of the idea?"

"Let me try finishing it for you," she said, leaning her elbows on her desk. "I am currently the subject of a humiliating, but not life-ending, meme. You want me to capitalize on that humiliation to quote-unquote combat stereotypes, which really means to just force me out of my comfortable, spinster life so I can be paraded around in front of the state of California and the world and find true love and the patriarchal definition of what is Good For Me."

He lowered his eyebrow. "That's not exactly how I would have said it. . . ."

"I should apologize for being rude, but I'm not sorry. You're taking a relatively innocent, definitely temporary, embarrassment and turning it into some kind of desperate cry for help."

"Hey, now."

"I'm not like that, Mr. Rodriguez. I'm not one of those women who hit thirty and panicked because I wasn't married. I'm happy. And I know my life doesn't look like what everyone thinks is supposed to be a happy one, but it is for me. I like my life, and I wouldn't change a thing." Which was a lie.

She would totally get her own dog.

But still hang out with her neighbor's dog.

As she talked—and she did try to stop herself, but she was on a roll and she couldn't seem to prevent the words from spewing forth—she noticed Colin getting red. It started at his neck, just a mild flush. Then it spread in uneven patches along his face. It was not particularly attractive. She realized she was making him mad.

She took way too much perverse pleasure in the realization.

So she kept going.

"Frankly, the whole thing is insulting and I think you and your whole industry need to take a step back and look at the harm you're doing to society."

"Are you done?" he asked through clenched teeth.

She sat back, assessed the verbal spewage. "Yes."

"Good." He stood up and walked toward the door. She tried not to look at his butt. But she was a feminist, not a robot. He had a great butt.

He turned back toward her and she quickly looked down at her keyboard. Totally not looking at your butt, Mr. Patriarchy.

"You know," he said, and she braced herself for the I-was-just-trying-to-help speech that usually followed her expressing any kind of opinion that indicated a man had somehow behaved incorrectly. "This could have been fun."

That was not what she was expecting. "But I'm incapable of having fun, right? I'm just a man-hating feminist who can't take a joke? It's totally my fault that it's not funny, right?"

He shook his head. "You've got some really crazy ideas, you know that? Dating is fun. It's not a plot of the patriarchy. Fun. You could have learned a thing or two."

"Oh, and you're gonna teach me?"

"Argh!" Colin growled and stomped out of the library.

Ha, real mature.

"I showed him," she said to her empty office.

That was why she didn't feel victorious, she thought. Because there was nobody to gloat with.

Not that she minded being alone.

She liked it.

She liked it, dammit.

"Dang, was that a student?"

Bernie didn't have to lift her head from her desk to know that Liz was talking about Colin Rodriguez, the very handsome writer who had just left her office after shattering her self-esteem into even tinier pieces than the Internet had. A makeover for the undateable librarian. Great.

But Liz was her boss, so she lifted her head to see Liz leaning out of the door, presumably to catch a last glimpse of the handsome writer who thought Bernie was the Great Sexless Wonder of the Internet.

Still, Liz's leaning was convenient, because it gave Bernie a chance to wipe her eyes, because in addition to being unable to control her face, she had also apparently lost the ability to control her tears. She shouldn't be crying in front of her boss. Everyone knew you cried in the bathroom at work.

"Oh, hey, I was kidding." Liz kicked the door closed and put a coffee mug in front of Bernie. It was full and hot and it made Bernie cry again that her boss was being so nice to her even though she was the worst thing to happen to librarianship since Google.

"He's not a student," Bernie said shakily.

"Oh. Well. Um, that's good, right? Because he's hot, I mean."

"He's a reporter."

"Really? What did he want?"

Bernie held up a Disapproving bookmark.

"Ech. I tried to talk Dean out of them, but they were already being printed when he showed me. Do you want me to accidentally lose the box he just sent over?"

"There's a whole box of them?"

Liz hesitated. "There are several."

Bernie put her head back on her desk. If she couldn't go to the bathroom to cry, she could at least pretend she was hiding.

"Sweetie, I'm so sorry. We won't use them. I didn't plan on using them. They're . . . they're not great."

"It's fine," Bernie mumbled as she tried to get her shoulders to stop shaking.

"It's not fine, but I'll take care of it. But what does this bookmark have to do with the reporter?"

Nothing. Everything. Just her life spinning totally out of her control. Well, at least now her life matched her facial expressions.

"I guess that means you're not going to ask him out."

Bernie snorted at Liz's suggestion, in spite of herself. "Even if I wanted to . . ." She let the rest remain unspoken: that Colin Rodriguez was hot, and hot guys didn't go out with women who spent less than fifteen minutes getting ready for work. Besides, he wrote for a fashion site. He was probably gay.

Of course, gay men didn't generally sneak looks at her cleavage.

"Even if you wanted to what?" Liz asked, and Bernie felt a comforting hand on her crooked arm.

"Never mind. He's a jerk."

"What did he say?"

Bernie lifted her head and wiped her eyes. She couldn't

help but smile at Liz's protective tone. "Slow down, Mama Grizzly. He just wants to do a story on me."

"On the meme?"

"Sort of."

"What do you mean, sort of?"

Bernie took a deep breath. "I mean he wants to do a story where I get a makeover. And then he suggested that he would set up a bunch of dates for me to prove that even the Disapproving Librarian is not undateable."

Liz's eyebrows shot up into her hairline, then she burst out laughing.

"What? You think I can't do a makeover?"

"No, no. I'm just imagining how you must have eaten that poor man alive when he suggested it. You're very protective of your aesthetic."

"I don't have an aesthetic."

"I know, and you're very protective of that."

Bernie waved Liz's teasing away. "Anyway, I'm not getting a makeover, and I'm not going on dates. He just wants to capitalize on this stupid meme, and I think we've probably done enough of that."

Liz winced. "I can't believe those bookmarks."

"Well, if it gets Dean off our backs for finals week . . ." It was just her pride. Nobody died from losing their pride, right?

"Did you know he wants to start a policy review?" Liz asked, swooshing right past Bernie's broken pride and into professional indignation. "Every single one of our policies."

"Well . . ."

"I know, I know, you kids and your rethinking libraries. But he wants us to do it this week."

"This week?"

"Or next. Whichever is more convenient."

Bernie dropped her head to the pile of papers on her desk. At least she'd be too busy to worry about a little thing like public humiliation.

"I suggested he come work at the reference desk for a few shifts to help us manage the time," Liz said.

"And he said yes, sure, that would be wonderful?"

"I believe it was more along the lines of, 'Let's make this project a priority, blueprint it, and let me know your timeline.'"

"Blueprint is not a verb."

"Right? But who cares? We'll fight about policy over the summer. Are you going to do it?"

"Sure, I guess. I've been wanting to look at our loan periods—"

"No, the article."

"What? No! I can't think of anything more humiliating."

Liz arched her elbow toward the bookmarks.

"I'm hoping this will just go away soon. You know what will not make it go away? An article that follows me on a month of humiliating, unsuccessful dates."

"An article?"

And there was Maxwell Dean, hovering in her doorway. Great. Now everyone was here. If she tried, she could probably get her parents on a conference call from Ohio.

"Oh, I'm glad you've got some more," he said, reaching out for the stack of bookmarks on the corner of her desk. "The ones outside are all gone."

They weren't really gone, per se. They just hadn't been put out yet. Bernie watched in fascination as Liz's gaze narrowed on Dean's outstretched hand. She thought for sure it would go up in flames. Maybe it would take the bookmarks with it.

"So, tell me about this article," Dean said, making himself comfortable in the other uncomfortable chair in front of Bernie's desk with an unburned handful of bookmarks.

Oh, it's not an article, it's a series of articles that focuses on all of my physical shortcomings, then another series on the shortcomings of my personality that make me completely repellent to men, Bernie thought. "It has nothing to do with the library," Bernie said, with a little more heat than she meant to. Dean was an idiot, but he was her boss. Well, her boss's boss. But she supposed the boss of her boss was still her boss. Either way, she could not, in the interest of keeping her job, tell him that he was an idiot.

"Oh. Can we make it about the library?" he asked.

"No," Liz and Bernie said together. At least Liz had her back, even if Dean wanted to pimp her out to the city. The idea was ridiculous. The idea that anything good could come of this disaster was even more ridiculous.

So ridiculous.

So why did she get a twinge in her gut whenever she thought about rejecting Colin outright?

It was probably just a twinge of righteous victory. Because there was no way that rejecting his stupid dating idea was anything less than absolutely the right thing to do.

"Well, any exposure is good exposure, right?" Dean said. "Just think, Melissa, you could be our first celebrity librarian."

Bernie's eyes went so wide, she thought they'd pop out of her head. Celebrity librarian? That was so not what she signed up for. That was not what anyone who went into librarianship signed up for. Was a celebrity librarian even a thing?

"The article really has nothing to do with the library," Liz insisted.

"What is it? Maybe we can brainstorm a way to bring it back to our core message."

Good God. Now her boss's boss was trying to use her sex life as a way to sell library services. She blinked, hard. No way was she going to cry in front of him. The problem was, when she got frustrated or angry, she cried. The Hulk turned green; Bernie cried. It was humiliating, and she'd had just about enough of that this week. This whole thing was spiraling out of control. It was just a stupid meme.

"You okay, Melissa?" he asked.

Bernie pursed her lips and nodded. She would *not* cry in front of her director. She would do it in the bathroom, like a normal person.

"Bernie and I were just talking about how she hasn't taken a vacation in, what, a year or so?"

Liz seemed to be shooting Bernie an encouraging look. Trouble was, Bernie had no idea what Liz wanted her to say. "I've never taken a vacation," she said. Which was mostly true. She hadn't used any of her leave time since she'd started at Richmond. She just took short weekend trips to the woods when she needed a break. Then, when she came back, her face was plastered all over the Internet.

She blinked again, hard. She would *not* cry. Once per day was her professional limit.

"Really? Never?" Dean looked surprised. "That's not healthy."

"No, it's not," Liz agreed. "That's why I'm encouraging her to take the rest of the week off."

"The rest of the week?" she squeaked. Next week was

finals week. It would be nuts in the library, and there was
a lot to do to prep for that. There was no way she'd leave
Liz alone to deal with it, no matter how many dumb self-
ies she had to take with students.

She felt something wet on her cheek. She hoped the
ceiling was leaking. But it was probably a tear.

"That's too bad. I was hoping to . . ." Dean waved the
bookmarks around vaguely. "But I guess if this was already scheduled."

"Already scheduled and booked," Liz said. "We were
just talking about whether or not she could afford that and
the three weeks after that."

"Three weeks!"

"It's just that, if she doesn't take it, it won't roll over
into next year."

One of the libraries farther down the coast had just
gone through the process of unionization. It hadn't come
up at Richmond yet, but the situation had made Dean
very sensitive about employee benefits.

Which must have been the reason why he told Bernie,
"Bernie, I insist you use your leave time."

"But—"

"The only time I want to see your face for the next . . .
for the next month—a whole month!—is on one of these
clever bookmarks. So I'm going to restock the desk while
you two, uh . . ."

Dean whizzed out of their office so fast, it was funny.
Bernie would have laughed if she could have stopped
crying.

"Liz! I can't leave you to this mess all by yourself.
There's no way. Finals!"

"Bernie, you're a sweet girl, but the world does not fall
apart when you're gone. Go. You need a break. Anyone

would under the circumstances. And by the time you get back, everyone will have forgotten about that silly meme."

"But—"

"And if the library does fall apart, think how fun it will be to take on a new construction project!"

"Liz—"

"Bernie. You need this."

Bernie sighed. She did need a break, a real one. She thought fondly of the stack of books by her nightstand. Maybe she could even go somewhere. Surely she had enough money to do an airbnb at a beach somewhere. She could go to the beach, read books for a few weeks, and come back to a world where nobody remembered that stupid Disapproving Librarian.

"And think about doing that article. It would do you good to get out," Liz said, and she was through the door before she could see the look on Bernie's face.

Chapter Seven

COLIN WAS NOT USED TO REJECTION. He had been lectured on privilege by Steph many (many!) times before, but awareness of his privilege did not make its absence any easier to take.

He used to be able to just turn on the charm and get whatever he wanted. Mostly from women, but he wasn't unable to charm his fellow fellows as well.

In just one week, he'd been rejected by the same woman twice.

What was that word for doing the same thing over and over and expecting a different result each time?

And now Pia would be right. Pia, who'd probably learned to tie her shoes just last week. Pia, who ate chocolate cereal for lunch every day. Pia, who had a different matching notebook for every outfit she wore. Pia was right.

The worst part—worse than Pia being right—was that he'd been excited about the story. He was intrigued by Bernie, even when she was biting his head off. Every little thing in life that he'd ever taken for granted about women was contradicted in Bernie. He had been looking forward to finding out what made her tick. Plus, it was nice to see everyone at Glaze so excited about a project. The clothes, the makeup. And everyone was on board to see what kind of fireworks would happen when Bernie was polished up and unleashed upon the city.

Except now that wasn't going to happen.

Oh, and he'd probably lose his job.

At least Pia hadn't had any success with the librarian, either. Although given what he now knew about Bernie, he wouldn't be surprised if she did the story with Pia just to spite him.

Yeah, Colin, because the woman who wanted to avoid publicity would suddenly change her mind in favor of his rival just to spite him.

He wondered if, when he was jobless and homeless, his inner voice would continue to sound so annoyingly like Steph.

At least he still had his anonymous advice blog in which he pretended to be someone he was not in order to tell people what to do.

Dear Maria,

> *What the hell have I been doing with my life?*
>> *The Man in Your Inner Monologue*

Dear The Man,

> *I have no friggin' idea.*

>> *Kisses,*
>> *Maria*

"Want another?"

Colin looked up at the bartender. He'd been chewing his cud so long, he hadn't noticed that he'd finished his beer.

At least his unconscious mind would get what it wanted.

Which was a drink.

He ordered another beer and turned to survey the crowd.

Mostly men, especially this early in the day. Steph still couldn't believe that his neighborhood bar of choice was a gay bar, but what did she know? He could walk home from here—which he frequently did—and the place was just a hole-in-the-wall pub, the last place in San Francisco that wasn't a gastropub or a fusion cuisine or a brewery that served small batches brewed in the bathtub. Not that he had a problem with those kinds of places. He loved those kinds of places. But those places were work.

This place didn't have shared work spaces and interns who were after his job and a boss who would gladly give away that job if he couldn't convince a librarian to put on some damn lipstick. Besides, he was around women all day. It was nice to go to a place where he didn't accidentally learn about different absorbencies of tampons.

What the hell was he doing with his life? Fighting with a child for bylines. Going out and partying with strangers. Hiding from women in a gay bar.

The one thing he really liked to do was Maria. It made no sense. He didn't feel like he particularly related to older women, or that an older woman lived inside of him. It was just . . . fun. He could pass on advice from a guy's perspective without, well, being a guy. When he was writing as Maria, he felt like he could really be unfiltered. He wasn't beholden to advertisers or his reputation as Colin Rodriguez, Studly Reporter Guy.

And if he didn't deliver on this story, there would be no more Studly Reporter Guy. There would just be Maria. And Maria was a side project; there was no way Maria could be more than that. The whole point of Maria was that she was a side project. He'd be out of a job in one of the most competitive markets in the country, and his parents would probably kick him out of the house and tell him that if he wanted free rent, he would have to move down to San Diego to live with them, and then he'd be stuck babysitting his brother's kids and helping the old people in his parents' development hook up their computers.

He shuddered. He needed this story. Even though talking to Bernie again made elderly tech support seem like a tempting option.

No, he needed this story.

First, he needed another beer.

Chapter Eight

Dear Maria,

   *I pride myself on having very strong
principles, but an opportunity has presented itself
and I am tempted to take advantage of it, even
though it goes against everything I stand for.
What should I do?*

     Thinking of Selling Out in the Richmond

Dear Sellout,

   *Let me get one thing out of the way and say
that if the thing you are tempted to do is not legal,
then I might suggest you get your rocks off in
some other way.*

   *There. That's out of the way. Now, most people
might think this is a question of the head versus
the heart: your principles lie in your head, but
your desires lie in your heart. This ignores the fact
that principles come from somewhere, right? And
if these principles are things you truly believe in
(assuming you're not being brainwashed by some
cultlike society, in which case, see my answer from*

*the first paragraph), then they come just as much
from your heart as your desires do.*

So . . . which do you do?

*Is it possible this is not an either-or situation?
You seem to look at the world like it's black and
white, but honey, it's all different shades of gray.
It's not shady (ha!) to live in those gray areas.
That's where all the interesting stuff happens.*

*Unless we're talking about something illegal, in
which case, I would like to remind the authorities
that these questions are anonymous and therefore
I should not be considered an accessory.*

> *Kisses,*
> *Maria*

IT WOULD DO HER GOOD TO GET OUT, Liz said. She needed
to get laid, Marcie said. What's the worst that can
happen? a tiny little voice in the back of her head asked.
Can it really get worse than it is now? What would
Maria say?

"What is my threshold for public humiliation?" she
asked Starr, her next-door neighbors' toy poodle who
Bernie sometimes liked to pretend she coparented. She'd
stopped by Maddie and Al's after work, as she often did.
She liked to check up on them because they were elderly,
and, conveniently, Maddie was a fabulous and generous
baker and they let her borrow the dog for long walks. It
was good for the dog, they said.

They had no idea the dog was also part therapist.

"Clearly my threshold for public humiliation is high
since I am talking to a dog," she said to Starr as the dog
sniffed a particularly offensive blade of grass. Inside the
restaurant they were walking past, kids were smacking
the glass and making faces at Starr. The parents were

making a face at Bernie, which meant they'd seen her talking to herself. She was half tempted to go in and explain that she wasn't talking to herself, she was talking to the dog. Then she heard what that sounded like and gave Starr a gentle tug so they could move on.

"And now Maria says it's a good idea," Bernie told Starr, who looked up at her briefly, then continued on her happy trot down the street. They got to the little neighborhood park that was always empty this time of day, and she let Starr water the lawn a little before she sat down on the nearest bench.

Starr investigated the grass under the bench to make sure it was an acceptable place to sit, then she hopped up on Bernie's lap, circled three times, and lay down with a sigh.

"It's wrong to get advice from some anonymous old lady on the Internet, right?" Bernie asked. "But then, is it really that much more wrong than asking the cutest, sweetest dog in the world and yes, yes, I'm talking about you and your face," she said, adding a vigorous rub behind the ears for emphasis.

Bernie pulled out her phone and looked at Take a Letter, Maria again. Her letter was still on top of the page. "That's where all the interesting stuff happens," Bernie read. "Interesting stuff happens here, too." For example, she was sitting on a bench and talking to a dog who was not her own. That was interesting.

Interesting was one word for it, certainly.

"Everyone thinks this dating thing is such a good idea. Is my life really that pathetic that my friends think *this* is the best thing for me? There's nothing wrong with my life, you know," she told Starr, who turned her head for more scratches. "I'm totally happy." She wiped her eyes.

It was so windy, that was all. There was no way she was crying again. "I'm not crying, Starr. I'm totally happy."

Starr stretched out and licked her cheek.

"What am I supposed to do, change my personality? I can't help it if men don't like me!"

Starr climbed onto Bernie's chest. Her little ten-pound body was a comforting weight, keeping Bernie tethered to reality.

Even though reality sucked.

Reality was going on a first date with a guy and having to laugh at his terrible jokes or be impressed with his powers of acquisition. She wasn't good at that. She didn't like to laugh at things that weren't funny. That was why she didn't get second dates.

Or worse, the first date with a guy who she thought was nice and funny and who never called again.

But then there were the gray areas. "I don't need a man," she reminded Starr. "But . . . maybe it would be nice to have one. Sometimes. Right? Is that terrible?" She said that last bit on a whisper. Starr licked her cheek again.

She grabbed her phone before she lost her nerve.

Chapter Nine

COLIN FUMBLED FOR HIS PHONE. It was not where he had left it, on the coffee table next to his beer. Also, someone had emptied his beer.

He really needed to stop drowning his professional sorrows in alcohol.

But alcohol was so good.

"Steph!" He called out to his sister. She would know where his phone was. "Steph!"

She was ignoring him.

No, she was on a date.

"Dammit, Steph, I need you!" he shouted in a way that he would not have shouted if she had been home. It was cathartic. And it made his phone stop ringing.

Satisfied, he got up to get another beer, since someone had emptied his. But there was no beer in the fridge. Someone had emptied all of them. Also, the fridge was ringing.

"Huh," he said, picking up his now-cold phone. "Who put that in there?"

He should find some food.

He should also answer the phone.

"Hello?"

"Colin?"

He didn't recognize the voice, but it was a woman. Good. He liked women.

"Hey," he said, happy to talk to a woman.

"Hello?"

"Hey," he repeated.

"Are you okay?" the woman asked.

"Mmm-hmm," he purred.

"Are you having a stroke?"

He didn't know what to say to that, so he didn't say anything. He just leaned his hip against the kitchen counter and tried to place the woman's voice. She sounded familiar. He knew that he should remember her.

There was a sigh, and then "This is Bernie."

Bernie was not a woman.

Oh, wait. Yes. Bernie was Melissa, the librarian who hated men.

Or maybe just him.

She definitely hated fun, and he was fun.

"Hi," he said warily. Why was she calling him? She hated him.

"I've been thinking about your offer—"

What did he offer her? Oh, yes. To write an exposé on the Life of a Meme. And to set her up on dates. A ridiculous idea. What was he thinking, that this woman who hated men (or just him) (or just fun) would want to go on dates with other men that he picked out for her? He had terrible ideas.

"I'll do it."

Colin nearly dropped the phone, but managed a surprisingly dexterous bobble that prevented the destruction of both his phone and his job. "What?" he shouted, because he'd almost dropped his phone and because he wanted to make sure.

"But I want to set a few ground rules."

Rules. Of course. The librarian wanted to set rules. How fun.

"First dates only, and all in public places."

"Okay." That was easy enough. San Francisco had lots of public places.

"I get to call off the dates at any point in the night."

"After you've given the guy a chance."

She sighed. "I'm not putting myself in danger to give a guy a chance."

"I'm not going to set you up with ax murderers." At least, not on purpose.

Well, maybe on purpose. He'd see how this experiment went.

"So if I'm getting a bad vibe from a guy, I need to sit there until he's ready to leave? How is that fun for me?"

You hate fun, he thought.

"There won't be danger," he said. "You'll be in public. I'll be there with you."

"Wait, what?"

"I'm the reporter. I have to be there to report on what happens." Because if I don't report on it, I will be out of a job, not that you care, mean old librarian lady.

She sighed. "Fine," she said, finally.

"What else?"

"No crazy dates, like bungee jumping."

"Okay." He wondered what his budget was going to be.

"But not all boring stuff. I don't want to just go out for coffee with every straight man in the city."

"And I won't feed you after midnight."

"What?"

"Never mind."

"And I reserve the right to stop the story whenever I'm done."

That, he wasn't sure about. If she quit, the story would be over. And so would his cushy job. Although this conversation was making him rethink exactly how cushy it actually was. "Only if I have the right to try to convince you otherwise." He could be very persuasive when he wanted to be. Despite all the evidence that Bernie was completely immune to his charms.

"Fine."

"Fine."

"Good."

"Great."

"So now what?"

Now he had to find some non-jerks to date the most difficult woman in San Francisco.

"I'll get back to you," he said. Then he hung up and looked for some food to soak up all the beer someone had thrown down his throat. He was doing it. He was going to find dates for the undateable librarian, and he would keep his cushy job, and life would go back to normal. He let out a little whoop, then remembered his sister wasn't home, so he let out a bigger whoop.

He could do the impossible.

He'd find dates for the undateable.

So fun.

Chapter Ten

Dear Maria,

> *My job sucks. Can I quit and join the circus?*
>
> > *Clowning Around in Potrero Hill*

Dear Clowning,

I don't know what field you're in and I don't know what your financial situation is, so I don't have enough information to tell you what to do (not that that's ever stopped me). Let me tell you this: I once had a job working with nice young people who were part of a circus collective in Oakland. They were all unique and talented performers, and it took months for me to forget the smell of their body odor.

Chin up, Clowning. Every cloud has a silver lining, and if that lining is a lame clown costume, you'll never get the stink out.

> *Kisses,*
> *Maria*

DON'T THINK, JUST DATE, she told herself as she carried Starr over the dunes to Ocean Beach. She took a deep breath of Pacific air and watched the waves roll in and out. "It's a metaphor," she told Starr, and let the dog down in the sand. "That wave is the meme, where my frowning face turns out to be the butt of a very public joke. And there it goes, back into the sea. And there goes the next wave, the wave where Glaze.com posts an online dating ad for me and nobody responds because I don't look like someone who's any kind of fun." Starr barked, and Bernie started walking, doing her best not to trip over the tangle that Starr's leash became whenever they came to the beach. The dog loved running in the sand and barking at the waves. So Bernie took her there as often as she could.

"I'm fun, dammit," she reminded Starr, who was busy investigating a seaweed pod.

Bernie didn't understand the disconnect between her and men. When she was with her friends, she could laugh. She loved a good dance party. She could talk about feelings and nonsense and make fart jokes and be spontaneous and go on adventures. It was just dating that she was no good at.

For some reason, when a date was part of the equation, she looked for subtext in every spontaneous, jokey, nonsense fun time. What did it mean that a guy took her to this type of restaurant? What did it say about him that this was the movie he picked for Netflix and chill? Everything that was said, every look that crossed every face was up for scrutiny. Every comment was turned around and around until she found something wrong with it. Every date was a new opportunity to keep her guard up, because no date was worth letting her guard down for.

What if the problem wasn't the dates?

What if the problem was her?

She took a deep breath, and let it wash out with the tide while her borrowed dog barked at it.

Chapter Eleven

DISAPPROVING LIBRARIAN IS DATING

By Colin Rodriguez, Staff Writer

Fiercely independent. Uncompromising. She's worked hard to build a life of her own. She doesn't need a man to make her happy.

But what if she does?

Melissa Bernard has worked hard to cultivate an independent, fulfilling life. She has a promising career, a cadre of creative friends, and a full social calendar.

So what does she have against love?

If you've been online recently, you know her face. She's the one giving you a look that makes you think of every time your mother said she was disappointed in you, every time your father grounded you, every time a teacher told you you weren't working up to your full potential.

Melissa Bernard is the Disapproving Librarian.

In real life, Bernie is relaxed. The lines on her face that make her meme so funny were nowhere in evidence when I sat down to talk to her the other day. That is, until we started talking about dating.

COLIN SAT BACK AND READ over the article that had just gone live. It was a bad habit of his, admiring the work he'd just posted. But his laurels were comfortable, and he liked resting there. Besides, he never really got tired of seeing his own name on an article. Take a Letter, Maria was fun to write, and he loved that Maria had such a following. It was a little frustrating, though, that he couldn't bask in any of that glow.

Bernie would have a field day with his ego if she knew what he was thinking.

If she was speaking to him.

He'd called her and e-mailed her, but she hadn't responded. At first he was just letting her know that the article had gone live, and that the story was really happening. It was going to be great, for both of them. He'd get a great story and keep his job, and she'd get the man she didn't want to admit she wanted. Win-win.

The radio silence was bothering him. Did she not like the article? Maybe he shouldn't have said that thing about the lines on her face. However, he thought her whole deal was that she wasn't vain about her looks. Besides, he was just telling the truth. When he'd first walked into her office, he didn't think she was even the Disapproving Librarian. It was only when he started explaining his project to her that the Internet-familiar face came out. The transformation was extraordinary, really. He wondered what it would take to get that look off of her face for good. It was going to take a guy with balls. Although she'd probably be offended that he had balls and that he was using them to challenge her autonomy. The thought crossed his mind that maybe she was too independent, not that he'd ever say that out loud. Not if he wanted to keep his balls.

Well, she couldn't back out now. Not now that they'd announced their intentions to the world. Not when he'd worked so hard to make her seem likable. And he'd had to work hard. Clea was obsessed with worry that the readers wouldn't relate. And, yes, it was true that Glaze.com readers didn't generally wear quite so many cardigans, but there was something about her. She wasn't like other women Colin knew, but he had the feeling that he'd be itching to tell her story, even if his job wasn't on the line.

Which it was.

Good thing there was no such thing as undateable.

He hoped.

Bernie wanted to kill him.

Lines on her face? She was not generally vain, but reading those words had her running to the mirror to see what he saw. He was right. When she wasn't paying attention, her resting bitch face totally made her wrinkly.

The worst part was, Colin's article made her care about stuff like that. She didn't care if she had lines! She was a woman! Time was happening! Of course she would get lines on her face! It wasn't like she was fighting off crow's feet and saggy jowls, and even if she was, so what? It was nature!

And then she read the comments. Apparently lines on her face were not the worst of her problems.

She should back out. She'd feel bad for Colin, but he'd

made her feel bad, so it served him right. It wouldn't do anything to rehabilitate her image, but had she really thought that putting herself up for further scrutiny from the Internet was going to make her look better? The article wasn't terrible. He'd spun the story into a real underdog case, like she was a champion who deserved something good. But she didn't know that she liked being pegged as the underdog. She wasn't. She was happy, dammit.

But hadn't she pegged herself as the underdog? Hadn't she told herself that the reason she was single was because nobody took the time to give her unvarnished appearance a second look? Didn't she lament that she never got flirted with because she didn't act like normal women, that she didn't prance and pretend? But she didn't want to prance and pretend; that was the whole point.

If Colin's quasi-journalistic treatment of her didn't kill her, all of this convoluted self-reflection would.

And if she died, she wouldn't have to go out on a date tomorrow night.

That was healthy, right?

When she'd finally decided to answer Colin's calls (and texts and e-mails), she'd agreed to meet him at the sandwich shop across from her apartment. He wanted to strike while the iron was hot, he'd said. She supposed that meant that she was the iron and the potential to tame her shrew was the hot. All she had to do was decide whether or not it was worth shaving her legs.

"Here you go, with extra sprouts," Colin said, putting a plate in front of her. She supposed she should have paid for her own lunch, and gotten it from the counter herself. But she was dating now. She needed to practice being helpless.

"What're you thinking?" he asked as he settled into the seat opposite hers.

"I'm not thinking anything. Why do you say that?"

He made a circle in the air. "Your face. You look like you're thinking."

"It's just my face!"

"It looks like the face of a woman who wants to run and hide."

"I don't!" she lied.

"So you're not going to bolt?"

"Not until I finish my sandwich, no."

"Then we'll eat and talk."

He pulled his chair around the table so he was closer to her, and pulled out his laptop.

"We had a great response to the article," he said. She snorted.

"You didn't like it?" he asked.

"I didn't say anything!"

He studied her face for a second, then he said, "Is this how it's going to be all month? You making passive aggressive noises at me while pretending everything's fine?"

"What? No—"

"God, it's like we're dating."

"I thought you said dating was fun."

"I'm starting to change my mind. Look, you agreed to do this. I understand it's outside your comfort zone and maybe you're scared or whatever—"

"I am *not* scared."

"Fine. But just . . . can you just be honest with me? If you're not fine, say you're not fine and we can talk about it."

"I thought you didn't like arguing with me."

"I'm not talking about arguing, I'm talking about a conversation."

She sighed. He was right. Dammit. She'd signed up for this, all on her own. She might as well act like she actually wanted to do it. Because she did want to do it. Sort of. No, she *did* want to do it; it just scared the crap out of her.

"I'm not going to pretend to be happy when I'm not," she told him.

"I wouldn't expect any less."

"Are you making fun of me?"

"Yes. Can we do this now?"

Bernie took a bite of her sandwich.

"The good news is," Colin said, gently extracting the laptop from Bernie, "you are not as unappealing as you'd like to think you are."

"So, basically, a bunch of dudes in their parents' basements said they'd do me?"

Colin winced. He'd clearly read the comments, too. "I apologize on behalf of my entire gender."

"I wrote an op ed for the local paper at my first job, and the responses online were all 'I've seen that hot librarian. I'd totally do her.'"

"That's alarming," Colin said.

"That's the Internet. No place for a woman."

She looked up from her homemade potato chips and artisanal pickle to find Colin looking at her, his expression unreadable. It looked like he was reading her. Like he was coming to some kind of understanding.

She cleared her throat.

"So how does this work? I just pick the ones I want to go out with?"

"No. Pia and I pick."

Her face fell a little.

"Are they all, you know . . ."

"Basement-dwelling trolls? No. We've gotten lots of serious submissions, some from the guys themselves, most from women nominating a brother or friend or coworker. Pia's going through the submissions as they come in."

"That's nice of her."

"That's her job. She's the junior writer."

He looked a little pained when he said that. Bernie wanted to make a comment about gender inequality and the wage gap, but she took pity on him. Also, she was too nervous to form a coherent argument right now. Even though she thought arguing with Colin would probably make her feel better.

She didn't know why she thought that. She had ample evidence to the contrary.

And now he was staring at her. She must have some kind of look on her face.

"Okay. So . . . I just wait? I thought we had to strike the hot iron and all that stuff."

"We do. Tonight you're going out with a friend of a friend."

"Oh, God."

"What?"

"Nothing. Just. Ack. I'm just remembering that I hate getting set up."

"It's a little late for that."

"Usually people try to hook me up with their other single friends, even though the only thing we have in common is that we're both single."

"Well . . . that might be the case here. Think of it as a practice date."

"Practice."

"Yeah. You'll look nice and make nice conversation, no big deal. It's the first of many."

"Many many."

"You've got nothing to lose."

"But my pride."

"If you screw it up, you'll have twenty-nine more chances to get it right."

"Not encouraging."

"Makeda wants to know if you have your outfit picked out yet."

"Makeda?"

"Our fashion editor."

"Oh, uh. No. Just whatever's clean."

"I'm not going to tell her that. Do you have a friend or someone who can help you pick out some date clothes?" She thought of Marcie. Marcie would probably help her. Marcie would probably make her wear a body-hugging jumpsuit, the kind that you had to take completely off when you wanted to go to the bathroom.

"This is going to be a disaster."

"You'll be fine. Pete's a nice guy."

"Pete."

"Your date."

"My date."

"Are you okay?"

"Yes. Wait, no. I'm supposed to be honest with you, right?"

"Please."

"I may vomit."

Colin laughed and clapped her lightly on the back. "Relax, Bernie. This will be fun."

Chapter Twelve

COLIN WAS SUPPOSED TO MEET HER outside the restaurant. He'd promised. He was supposed to give her moral support. She didn't even know what her date looked like. She didn't even know his name. Maybe she shouldn't have given up on Colin so quickly. But when she didn't see him, she'd gone inside to wait at the bar, where there was wine.

Wait. Pete. She remembered. Pete was her date. Good. Now where was her moral support?

Someone tapped her on the shoulder, and she turned to see . . . a guy. He was cute. Was this her date? Go, Colin.

No, wait. It was Colin.

"Nice glasses," she said, ignoring the skip her heart had done when she'd first seen him.

He waggled his eyebrows at her. "I'm in disguise."

"Why?"

"So I can blend in and observe, while remaining unobserved." He waggled his fingers in front of his glasses.

"You have written a story before, right?"

"What? You don't think I look like a beatnik?"

He looked nothing like a beatnik. He looked like a twenty-first century hipster's idea of a beatnik.

But cute.

"Very far out, man," she reassured him. "I don't think North Beach is a beatnik neighborhood anymore."

Colin just shrugged. "Your mission, should you choose to accept . . . Scratch that, you already accepted. You're not backing out now. Your date, Pete, is a software developer. He likes cooking and seeing live music, although he does not play. He's never been married, but he's had a few long-term girlfriends, and he's very nice and boring. I'm sure you'll love him."

"Pete." She could do this. She could go on a date. She had this.

As promised, the date would be in public, at a noisy and not-very-trendy Italian restaurant in North Beach. Colin would sit near enough to observe (unrecognized; hence the glasses), but not near enough that he could overhear every little word that was said. If there were words to be said. Bernie suddenly forgot all of the words that humans used for small talk. Her brain was melting into a blob of mangled incoherence. Was she having a stroke?

"Bernie? Are you okay?"

"Hmm? Yes, fine, why?" she said, a few decibels louder than she meant to. "Why wouldn't I be fine?"

"You look a little nauseous, that's all."

"Nauseated. Nauseous refers to the state of being nauseated."

"Good. Get all of your pedantic out before your date gets here." He gave her a smile that she was pretty sure was meant to reassure her. It did not.

She turned in her seat at the bar, picked up her wineglass, put it down, brushed her skirt over her knees. Why were her hands in the way of everything?

"Bernie."

She turned to face Colin and his stern voice.

"Listen to me." He whipped off his glasses and she almost laughed. But then she thought if she laughed, she might get nauseous all over his black turtleneck. "It will be fine."

"I know," she said, in a voice that was not at all convincing.

"Pete is very nice," Colin assured.

"I know," she convinced.

"You'll just make small talk, eat some pasta, and that's it. No big deal. It's just a first date."

"I know," she said, like a broken record that was stuck in the comforting groove of a daily routine that did not involve first dates.

"Don't order spaghetti," Colin advised. She nodded.

"And don't—"

"Melissa?"

Bernie turned to face her date, and away from whatever instruction Colin was about to give her that would prevent her from making a complete ass of herself. She'd already made an ass of herself. That was what all this meme stuff was about. Now she was un-assing.

Of course, having a contentious inner monologue when she clearly did not possess the will to control her facial features was probably not the way to do it.

"Pete?" she asked, brightly, and she felt Colin move off the stool behind her and disappear into the crowd.

"Was that guy bothering you?" Pete asked, and Bernie just knew she made a face in reaction to that comment, because what kind of comment was that? Like she couldn't take care of herself?

She took a deep breath. He was just being nice. That was what people did on first dates.

"Uh." She wasn't sure if she was supposed to acknowledge that Colin was there as a reporter and, if necessary, an extraction agent. They'd talked about him being there, but not about whether or not that was to be addressed. Should she address it? Would that fundamentally change the atmosphere of the date? Oh, God, what was she supposed to do with her hands?

She shook her head. Colin had been bothering her, but suddenly she wanted him back. At least she knew how to talk to Colin. All she had to do was disagree with absolutely everything he said. This guy, this Pete, she wasn't sure about.

What was she doing? She thought of the generations of women who went before her, who had managed to have first-date conversations without dying, and still go on to make scientific breakthroughs and artistic masterpieces and generally leave their irreplaceable stamps on the world.

She took a deep breath. She could do this.

"Hi, Pete. Thanks for coming."

Pete smiled. He had a good smile, this Pete. "It's an honor, being your first date. This is crazy, right?"

"Yes," she agreed, and relaxed. They were going to acknowledge the craziness. She could do this. Lay it all out on the table. It was crazy, and she could do it.

"Would it be terrible if I told you that you look a lot different from your picture?"

She laughed. "God, I hope so."

"I mean, in your picture you look kind of mean."

She laughed again, with a little less enthusiasm.

The maitre d' signaled that their table was ready, and she gathered up her wineglass and her date, and prepared to make small talk.

Chapter Thirteen

Dear Maria,

I've been out on a few dates with a guy, and he's great. He's funny and very sweet and I like the way he dresses. I think we look good together as a couple. We have a lot in common. We're sort of perfect together. The problem is, I don't really feel a spark when I see him. I don't miss him when I don't see him. But when we're together, it's great. What should I do?

> *He's Great, Right? in Cow Hollow*

Dear Great,

Where there's no spark, there can be no fire. And, yes, fire is dangerous and it can hurt, but it gets cold and foggy here on the Bay. You need fire. And you need a new boyfriend.

> *Kisses,*
> *Maria*

COLIN WATCHED BERNIE AND PETE stare at their plates and he really wished he was sitting closer so he could hear what Pete was saying to her. Bernie occasionally laughed, but mostly, she just looked like her eggplant parmesan had told her that her dress was unflattering.

God, it was unflattering. He was sure she had a figure underneath all those pleats, but it was well hidden. He knew Bernie wouldn't be the type to wear a body-hugging minidress, but she could have left the Amish couture at home. And was she wearing clogs? Nothing said "I'm not interested in carnal knowledge" more than clogs did.

He stared down at his notebook, trying to think of a way to describe the floral sack she was wearing in a way that would not make her hit him. He rubbed his eyes, or tried to. The fake glasses were, he admitted, a little silly. But he was undercover, dammit. He didn't want anyone to notice him. Not that he was recognizable—he wasn't the subject of, say, an unflattering meme—but he wanted to blend in. Be cool. Like a real reporter whose job was not in danger because of a twenty-year-old pixie who had more ambition than he did.

"Ready?"

Colin turned from his notebook to find Bernie standing next to his bar stool.

There was no sign of Pete.

"Where's Pete?" he asked, like a good reporter. He hoped Bernie hadn't eaten poor Pete alive.

"He has an early meeting at work tomorrow." She blithely swung her purse onto her shoulder.

Oh, Bernie. He shook his head at her.

"What?" she asked.

"He didn't have an early meeting."

"How do you know?"

"You got ditched."

"No, I didn't. He had an early . . . oh, I see. Hmm."

"What happened?"

"Nothing! Nothing bad, I don't think."

"What'd you guys talk about?"

She shrugged. "Work and stuff. It was pretty boring."

"Did you find out anything interesting about him?"

"No. He went to a concert last week, but it was some terrible dude rock band, so we didn't talk much about it."

"Did you share anything interesting about yourself?"

She looked up at the ceiling, thinking. "Apparently not."

Colin sighed. "Bernie. You have to at least try."

"I did! Sort of."

"You did? Then why are you dressed like you're going to a barn raising?"

"What's wrong with my dress?"

"And what the hell are those shoes?"

"They're comfortable!"

"Bernie."

"See? This is the problem. Why should I wear shoes that kill my feet and a dress that squeezes me like a sausage? Pete was wearing a T-shirt!"

"No, Pete was wearing a very nice, very expensive Oxford shirt that was ironed and tucked in."

"Well, good for him. It shouldn't matter what he wears. Just like it shouldn't matter if I show up in a sack."

"Which you did. Okay, look, don't hit me. Clothing aside, you really couldn't find anything to talk about?"

"He doesn't read."

"So? A lot of people don't read. There are other things to talk about."

"He was *proud* of the fact that he doesn't read."

Colin pulled off his glasses and ran a hand down his face. He was going to need some help with this one.

"We're not a good match." Bernie shrugged.

"How will you know when you are a good match?"

"When he's not proudly illiterate."

"But then what? Then conversation will just magically flow and he won't be insulted that you came to the date wearing a sack?"

"Hey, this is vintage, I'm pretty sure."

"Fine, a vintage sack."

"So, by your logic, if I dress with my boobies out, I'll find my intellectual soul mate."

"Boobies? Maybe."

"Of course."

"I'm just saying if you try something new, this might actually be fun."

"No, you're saying if I dress myself to please a man's gaze, he'll deign to inquire if I've got anything in my brain."

Colin thought about his job, and how he wanted to keep his job, and how Clea was worried that readers wouldn't *connect* with Bernie because she was nothing like them. Which she wasn't. Bernie wasn't like anybody. But that didn't mean people couldn't get to like her. "Look," he said. "Your way is not working."

"After *one* date."

"Just try my way, with the makeover, and if that doesn't work, I'll buy you a new pair of clogs."

"The clogs are expensive."

"I can't imagine why."

She stopped talking—finally—and Colin watched her take in the scene around the restaurant. Nothing but couples, crammed around tiny tables, sharing intimate looks over candlelight. It was a really freakin' romantic spot.

"Fine," she said, still turned toward the romance surrounding them. "We'll try it your way."

"Thank you."

"This date still totally counts."

"Okay."

"Only twenty-nine more to go."

He sighed. Only twenty-nine more.

Chapter Fourteen

DISAPPROVING LIBRARIAN
IS UNDATEABLE

By Colin Rodriguez, Staff Writer

This was the first date of many first dates for San Francisco's most eligible spinster librarian. She had an image to repair. After breaking the Internet with her look of stern unhappiness, Melissa Bernard had to prove to her profession, her city, and herself that there was no such thing as a walking stereotype.

Disapproving Librarian disapproves of stereotypes.

So does Glaze.com, despite what many—Disapproving Librarian included—think about fashion sites. Women's lifestyle is what we do, and we know that women want to look good doing it. But what about the woman who doesn't care if she looks good?

What about the woman who wears her lack of grooming like a badge of honor? What about the woman who says what's the point of dressing up when you're perpetually single? What about the woman who has branded herself undateable, and finds evidence to support that?

This woman will have many bad first dates.

My colleagues and I are here to help.

As BERNIE ENTERED the Glaze.com offices way too early the next morning, she was struck by how very new everything looked. It was the future! And the future was all glossy white work spaces and sleek laptops and pops of color in the form of racks of clothes artfully cluttering the office.

So this was what it was like to work in a place that had money.

She thought about her dull, crowded office in the library, and her small, crowded apartment. This was the other side of San Francisco, the new side, although it hadn't been new for a while. This was the future of the city, and there was less and less room for people like her, people who cared about education and art and who only cared about money as a means to create resources that made the world more equitable. She'd been a dying breed when she moved to San Francisco; now she was nearly extinct.

And she was here to get a makeover. Willingly. Because of Colin.

As if her thoughts had conjured him, Colin walked up behind her, startling her nearly out of her sensible shoes. "You're on time," he said, acting surprised. Of course she was on time. She had actually been twenty minutes early, because the bus was miraculously waiting for her on the corner, unlike the mornings when she had an early meeting and was running late and it was nothing but Google buses as far as the eye could see. Colin probably had something to do with that, too. He made the buses run on time.

"Let me introduce you to everyone," he said, holding the glass door open to her. She said hello to the receptionist, a young guy in an unprofessionally tight T-shirt, and to a few painfully fashionable young women who looked at Colin like they wanted to eat him up. She supposed she couldn't blame them; he looked good in his slim-fit pants and crisp button-down shirt. Of course, once he opened his mouth, they should have been disabused of any romantic notions. Probably their oversized scarves were cutting off oxygen to their brains. His boss, he told her, was at a business meeting. The way he said it was with a mixture of disgust and relief, which made Bernie even more curious about what Clea Summers was like. If Colin didn't like her, she was probably great.

His hand on the small of her back distracted her as he maneuvered her around the big white tables. I can walk on my own, she almost told him. But she'd promised Dave that she would be nice, and even though Marcie thought that was not necessary, Bernie agreed that if she wanted to make this experiment work, she had to do her part. Not biting off Colin's head, especially after he had already moved his hand, was a good step.

"Here's Jeanaeane. She does beauty."

Bernie could see why. She was stunning, with high cheekbones and long, sleek hair the color of dark chocolate. "Hi," Bernie said, feeling like an ogre. She didn't know why. She washed her face. She put on mascara, sometimes.

There was no law that said a woman had to spend hours on her face to make it look porcelain-perfect—like Jeanaene's.

Well, there was a law, but it was an unspoken law that everyone pretended didn't exist, acting like it was just in a woman's best interest to look as if "she took care of herself," a.k.a. was thin and perfect like Jeanaeane.

"Jenny, this is Bernie, the librarian."

Jeanaeane looked surprised and then, to Bernie's surprise, relieved. "Oh, thank God," she said. "Colin made it sound like you were a disaster."

"That's not what I said!" he sputtered.

"You have really good skin." Jeanaeane came up and ran her hand over Bernie's cheek. Bernie, who had been about to shoot Colin an offended look, froze. "Are you not even wearing any foundation?"

Bernie shook her head.

"Wow."

"Clean living?" Colin suggested.

"And good genes," Jeanaeane added. Bernie had the feeling that she didn't really have to be here for this conversation. And yet, it was her love life.

"Oh, hello," she said. "I'm standing right here."

"The hair, though." Jeanaeane pulled the clip out of Bernie's hair. It fell around her face and shoulders and she immediately wanted to pull it back up again. "The hair needs some work."

Colin stood back and put his finger up to his lips, assessing her with her hair down. "A lot of hair."

"That's why I keep it up," Bernie said, stepping away from Jeanaeane's gentle if probing hands and pulling her hair back into a messy topknot.

"Has Makeda seen her yet?"

"Not in person."

"She'll flip."

"In a good way, I hope," he said, looking mildly worried.

Jeanaeane pulled Bernie's sweater tight across her hips. "Yeah. Let's get to work, shall we?"

"Oh, are you talking to me?" Bernie asked. Her sarcasm was lost on Jeanaeane, though, and she was dragged through the office behind a curtain that looked like it had been thrown up pretty hastily. As Jeanaeane pulled it back, it came detached from the wall.

"Intern!" Jeanaeane called, and one of the waifs came out of nowhere, wielding a stapler. The room they entered was not, as Bernie had assumed, the bathroom. (She shuddered to think where the open-concept layout bathrooms really were. . . .) Or maybe it had been a bathroom at one point. Regardless of its origins, it now contained a salon chair and a sink and shelving with all kinds of brightly colored bottles and jars and things Bernie was pretty sure she had never even considered putting in her hair. It also contained a wiry man with a big belt buckle, wielding a pair of scissors.

"You must be the librarian," he said, and Bernie could have kissed his Southern accent since he was the first person to address her directly since she'd walked into the building.

"Hi," she said, shaking his hand. "Call me Bernie."

"Jack. My stars, what a head of hair you've got," he said, pulling out her clip (again!) and fluffing her frizz around her face. Jack whistled. "Lots to work with."

"Can you do something with it?" Jeanaeane asked. Jack raised his eyebrow so high, Bernie thought it would touch the converted-warehouse ceiling. Jeanaeane put her hands up in deference to Jack's superior skill and started to leave the room, pulling Colin with her.

"Wait a second," Bernie said. "Where are you going?"

"I'm going to let Jack work his magic."

"On what?"

"On your head."

"But I don't . . . but . . . but you said," she sputtered, turning to Colin. "Nobody said anything about a haircut."

"You didn't?" Jeanaeane said to him. She looked like she wanted to kill him. It almost made Bernie feel better about being in a closet-turned-hair salon against her will.

Almost.

"It's just a haircut," Colin said. At least he had the decency to look sheepish, Bernie thought. "And a little makeup."

"I don't know about this. I should be dating these people as me, not as some hyped-up version of me."

"Yes, but . . ."

"Because that would defeat the whole purpose of the experiment, right? If you want to prove that I'm not undateable as I am, how can you do that when you change how I am?"

"Well, I'm not giving you a lobotomy. A little trim isn't going to make you less argumentative."

"Yes, but I'll be argumentative with good hair. If I need a haircut to get a date, I don't want it."

"Everyone needs a little zhuzhing to catch a man," Jeanaeane added.

"I'm not trying to catch a man," Bernie said. "I'm just trying to go out on some dates."

"What do you think catching a man is?"

"I don't need a man," Bernie continued, soldiering on over poor, thin Jeanaeane's protests. "So I don't have to catch one. I can take care of myself. And if I have to make myself up like some precious doll—no offense—to get some human companionship, then what's the point?"

Bernie realized she was yelling. And breathing hard.

And everyone was staring at her. Jeanaeane looked like she might cry.

She took a deep breath, reminded herself why this was a good idea. You're just trying Colin's way, she reminded herself. It's just a haircut. Even though she totally didn't need a haircut because she'd just had it cut. . . . Actually, she couldn't remember the last time she'd had her hair cut. And the date with Pete, though not painful, was not actually good. So if all she had to do was sit in this well-lit closet and let these nice professional people take care of her . . .

She could use a haircut. And the salon chair looked luxurious. And, despite her disinclination to use multiple hair products every day, she was a little curious about what they all did.

It was just a haircut. And maybe a little makeup. It was just an experiment. That she'd already agreed to. Because it was a good idea. Because Starr had told her that she didn't want to be alone.

Ugh.

"Fine," she said, and she sat in the chair. Barely missing a beat, Jack whipped a cape over her while shooing the others out of the room.

"Call me when you're done and we'll do the eyebrows," said Jeanaeane over her shoulder.

"Eyebrows?" Bernie panicked.

"Don't you worry 'bout a thing, honey," said Jack. "This won't hurt a bit."

Chapter Fifteen

Dear Maria,

It's not fair. When I get ready to go out, I have to straighten my hair, shave my legs, and try on at least eight outfits. When my boyfriend gets ready, he just pulls on the nearest clean shirt. Then he's always complaining that I take forever. How can I convince him that perfection takes time? He just doesn't get it!

Boyfriend with Blinders in Laurel Heights

Dear Blinders,

It's not fair. You're right. But is your boyfriend doing all he can to look his best? Does he shave his face so it's smooth and doesn't leave a rug burn? Or if he has a beard, is it clipped and trimmed so it looks artfully hip? I have male friends who spend just as much time on their

*appearance as you do. I'd offer to set you up, but I
wouldn't inflict that on my worst enemy.*

Kisses,
Maria

COLIN WAS CLICKING THROUGH Pia's choices for Bernie's
next few dates when Jeanaeane's badly hung curtain
opened with a flourish, then fell to the floor.

"Oh, just leave it," Jack said, coming up behind
Jeanaeane and pushing her gently through the doorway.
She looked annoyed, but her face lit up when she saw
Colin.

"Are you ready?" she squealed, clapping her hands
with glee. Colin wasn't sure Bernie would be into a big
reveal like this, but she'd been back there for a few hours.
Maybe the blow dryer had lulled her into submission.

Ha.

Then out stepped Bernie, or a person who was wearing the same unfortunate clothes Bernie had worn into the
makeshift salon. She was smiling, but she didn't look
happy.

Still, he couldn't deny that she looked good.

Gone was the big frizzy hair tied up in a messy knot.
Now her brown hair was long and sleek and cascaded like
a river over her shoulders. It made her look totally different. But it wasn't just the hair. She didn't look like she
was wearing a lot of makeup, but the more he looked at
her, the more her brown eyes popped and her lips—had
her lips always looked that kissable? Or was that some
kind of Jeanaeane wonder product?

"Whoa," he said, picking his jaw up off the floor.

"It's not too weird?" Bernie started to tuck a piece of
hair behind her ear, but Jack slapped her hand away.

"No touching," he said. "You'll ruin the blowout."

She shook her hands and held them at her sides.

"Yeah," Colin said, taking a step closer. "You look good." Who knew the librarian was a knockout?

"I feel weird." She rubbed her lips together. "I don't usually wear lipstick."

"It looks good," Colin said, like a broken record. He couldn't help it. He was awestruck. It was Bernie, but, like, more.

"Also, I'm never plucking my eyebrows again."

His gaze traveled from her lips to her eyebrows. They looked the same to him. Then it registered what she'd said. Ouch. Plucking eyebrows.

"You have to admit, you look good," Jeanaeane said.

"I look different," Bernie said.

"Different good," Colin said.

"Are you saying I didn't look good before?"

Colin rolled his eyes. He needed to distract her. Also, he wanted to be near her. That really was some magical lipstick.

Then, while taking a moment to admire the brightness of her brown eyes, he noticed her blinking. She was blinking a lot.

"Bernie, stop," Jeanaeane hissed.

"I'm sorry, it feels weird!"

"God, you're acting like you've never worn fake lashes before."

"I haven't!"

"You look good," Colin offered, again. She did, aside from the blinking. And the scrunching her lips together.

"I feel weird," she said again.

"Do you think she's having an allergic reaction?" Colin asked Jeanaeane.

"No, she's just being a baby."

"I could be dying!"

"Nobody dies from makeup!"

"You don't know that!"

Jeanaeane threw up her hands. "Fine. No more lash extensions. Lots of girls would kill for those, you know."

"She's not lots of girls," Colin said, and Bernie smiled—for real—for the first time since her transformation.

Wow, that smile. Yeah, that looked really good.

"Remember, don't touch your hair," Jack warned her.

"Ugh, why did you say that? Now I can't stop thinking about touching my hair."

"Why can't she touch her hair?" Colin asked.

"I gave her a keratin treatment. It'll smooth her out, but no more hair clips," Jack warned Bernie.

Bernie flopped her hands toward her head, then shoved them in the pockets of her shirt.

Good grief, that ugly shirt had pockets?

"How do you feel, really?" Colin asked her. She looked good, but it wouldn't do anyone any good if she went on a date acting like she was having a seizure.

"I feel . . . heavy," she said, gesturing toward her face. "I'm not used to stuff on my face. And I have no idea how I'm going to replicate this tomorrow."

"I'll send videos," Jeanaeane said. "See? Good thing I made all those makeup tutorials," she said to Colin, as if Colin had an opinion about them. Oh, he did tease her for spending so much time in front of the mirror.

"It'll stay for tonight," Jeanaeane continued, "as long as you don't touch it."

"God, I forgot I have a date tonight," Bernie said.

"Don't touch your hair!" Jack exclaimed as Bernie's hand went to her head in what was obviously an unconscious gesture.

"What is she going to wear?" Jeanaeane asked.

* * *

Makeda Tiye was a force to be reckoned with.

Bernie almost hated to disappoint her.

But she also did not wear heels.

Or dresses that short.

Or colors that wild.

"I brought a whole bunch of everything so we can get an idea of what kind of styles look best on you," Makeda was saying as she pulled short, wild-colored garments out of the bags that had been piled on her shoulders when she burst into the office soon after Jeanaeane was done scolding Bernie about her makeup. Bernie was just starting to get into a Zen place where she could accept the changes being wrought to her head as part of a larger experiment that would bear fruit, good or bad. Then Makeda had burst into the office, declared Bernie not as bad as everyone had told her she was, but pronounced the clothes tragic. Colin was no help at all, and his silence seemed to indicate that it was better just to let Makeda do what she was going to do.

Bernie was starting to get used to the fake lashes. She could handle some new clothes. Probably.

Colin followed behind them, his arms laden with short, wild-colored garments Makeda had already pulled.

It was a train of clothes that Bernie would never wear. And, judging by the width of them, that she would never fit into. "So I'll just squeeze into them?"

"Don't you worry about it." Makeda held an animal-print minidress up to Bernie's chest, then shook her head. She tossed it into the arms of a waiting intern. Where were all of these interns coming from? Then Makeda stretched a pair of wide-leg striped pants against Bernie's waist and pursed her lips. "I'm just getting some ideas."

"From clothes that won't fit."

"Is she always this positive?" Makeda asked Colin. "I'll order the right size for you."

Colin just smiled. Makeda pulled more clothes from Colin's arms and tossed them to the interns. Then she went back and plucked a few others from the interns and gave them back to Colin. He continued to smile.

"Okay, now shoes." Makeda led the clothes train over to a corner that was laid out with rows and rows and rows of wild-colored, very high-heeled shoes.

"Um, I don't wear heels," Bernie said.

"You do now," Makeda said.

"No, I mean, I can't walk in them. I'll break my ankle."

"Mmm-hmm." Bernie was sure that Makeda heard her, but the way she was grabbing from the shoe-rows indicated that she did not care.

"Just try them," Colin muttered.

"Says the man wearing sneakers."

"Hey, these are classics."

"They're not heels."

"Heels will elongate your legs," Makeda said. "Make you feel powerful."

"Until I break my ankle and have to be carried out on a stretcher."

"Think of the stretcher as your sedan chair."

"Heels are just a way to get women to walk slower and be more dependent on men to help them cross the street," Bernie said.

"Is she serious?" Makeda asked Colin.

"Heels are the new corset," Bernie said. "Breaking women's bones so their bodies can please the male gaze."

"I can't wait until we get to foundation garments," Makeda muttered.

"No way," said Bernie. "I'm not doing Spanx."

"You need a new bra."

"I don't need a girdle."

"You're too young to have your boobs hanging down at your ankles."

"They don't hang down at my ankles!"

"Girl, if you were wearing heels, you'd trip over them. None of this is working. We gotta go shopping. Dali!" A woman with blue and pink striped hair scuttled out from behind a laptop at one of the shiny desks and handed a credit card to Makeda.

Wow. Bernie wondered if she could convince Makeda to come to her next budget meeting. For that, she might even wear heels.

"Thank you, doll. This poor girl needs some new underthings."

"You're so lucky," Dali said.

"You want to go in my place?" Bernie asked, trying very hard not to blush at how much Makeda was mentioning her underwear. Bernie was a strong, sexually empowered woman. There was no need to be embarrassed at talk of her unmentionables.

"Hush," Makeda said. "We're going shopping. Colin, call us a car."

"Um," Colin said, his arms full of clothes.

"Never mind. We've got an intern for that. Intern!"

A rail-thin man with wild blue hair and the tightest jeans Bernie'd ever seen appeared out of nowhere and took the bundle from Colin. Bernie thought the poor kid was going to collapse under the weight of all those clothes, but he surprised her by zipping along the racks, throwing things back into place. Makeda would kill him, Bernie thought. He's going to leave a mess everywhere. But as Makeda steered Bernie out of the office, she saw that the clothes were all hung neatly, color-coordinated, and the intern had disappeared.

"Wow. I need an intern," she muttered.

"You got your stuff?" Makeda asked. Bernie held up her shoddy purse, which, until a few minutes ago, she'd thought had vintage charm. Colin followed.

"Wait, you're coming with us?" Bernie asked him. Part of her didn't want to be alone with Makeda. Who knew what the woman would talk her into? But another part of her didn't really want Colin along while they were bra shopping.

"For the story," he said.

"Don't worry, I won't let him see anything he's not supposed to see," said Makeda, and Bernie believed her. If there was one thing she could take away from all of this, it was that Makeda got what she wanted.

Chapter Sixteen

COLIN HAD BEEN LINGERIE SHOPPING exactly one time in his life. He'd been a junior in college, flush with his summer job cash, dating a woman who was a few years older and basically the living embodiment of all of his sexual fantasies—tall, curvy, confident, with lots of experience and the patience to teach him pretty much anything. He was just a kid then, but he was play-acting grown-up with her. He took her shopping, like a grown-up, and she asked him his opinion and did a fashion show for him, and then they got kicked out of the store because they started having sex in the dressing room. He'd had to buy a whole pile of stuff to appease the manager—and the woman—and all he got for it was a credit card bill he couldn't afford and dumped the next week.

It hadn't quite soured him on lingerie, though.

He understood that his role in this situation was to stand back, hold the purses, and let the women shop. But he couldn't stop his brain from wandering. First, from thinking that even the most practical item sold in this store would be way too fussy for Bernie. He couldn't picture her in any of this, he told himself. It was all so lacy and frilly and girly—so not Bernie. Then he tried, and he found, to his surprise, that he could. His wandering brain told him that she would look good in purple. Deep purple, almost black. And this one, he thought, this see-through one. With the matching panties.

"Is this a sports bra?" he heard Makeda exclaim from behind the curtained dressing room.

He didn't hear Bernie's muttered response, but whatever it was, Makeda didn't seem to care. She poked her head out of the curtain and signaled to the saleslady with the measuring tape around her neck. There was a quiet conference behind the curtain, then Makeda and the saleswoman came out and dispersed into the store.

Poor Bernie, he thought. First the eyelashes, now Hurricane Makeda. He walked up closer to the dressing room curtain.

"You okay in there?"

Bernie poked her head out, but held the rest of the curtain in place, covering what he guessed was her sports bra. "I hate you."

"I know," he said. "Listen, if it's too much . . ."

"No, it's fine. I mean, what's a little abuse if I get free bras, right?"

"Right," he said, hoping she wasn't being sarcastic. He didn't really know what he would do if she wanted to bail at this point. Well, he would take her out of here, and somehow work her refusal to be made over into the story. Which probably wouldn't fly with Clea since fashion was a big part of the women's lifestyle they peddled at Glaze, and Makeda did fashion. Probably Clea'd give the story to Pia. He couldn't quite imagine Pia handling Bernie.

Not that he was handling Bernie.

"Bras are expensive," Bernie explained to him. Which

he knew, unfortunately. "And I've never had a real bra fitting. Why am I telling you this?"

"Because I'm your trusted confidant?"

"Ha ha."

"So if you've never had a bra fitting, how do you know what size to get?"

She looked at him like he'd sprouted two heads. "You just try some on until you find one that fits."

"But how do you even know where to start?"

"I don't know. How do you know what size pants to buy?"

"I just buy the size I always wear."

"Why are we talking about bra shopping? Is this going in the story?"

"No, no. It doesn't have to. Not the specifics, anyway. Although Makeda will probably want to do something on the importance of good foundation garments."

"Look at you, knowing that women's underwear serves a purpose besides just visual appeal."

"Job hazard." he shrugged. "She talks about foundation garments a lot."

"I gathered that."

"Anyway, it's kind of fun, getting to peek behind the curtain. The mysterious world of women and all that."

"What curtain?" Makeda was behind him, holding a pile of colorful, lacy, frothy things he was sure Bernie would hate.

"I thought you agreed no lace," Bernie said.

"I lied. Get out of the way," she said, hip-checking Colin.

"Good luck," he told Bernie.

"I hate you," she said back.

* * *

Colin would never find lingerie stores sexy again.

Two hours. They'd been in the store for two hours. He couldn't check his e-mail because his phone was dead, they'd been in here so long. Besides, every time he started to do something else—to check his e-mail, to suggest he go out and get them something to drink—Makeda made him wait, then, when their salesperson was occupied by other customers, go out into the wilds to find different sizes. Even with very specific instructions, he had a hard time figuring out which bra was which. They were all hot. Some were black. Some were tan. Some, he was happy to see, were purple. But beyond that, he couldn't really tell them apart, and every time he brought the wrong one back, Makeda would throw it at his head, then stomp off to get the correct item herself.

"You'd think she'd have learned the first time," Colin said to the curtain.

"I almost feel bad for you," said Bernie.

"Good."

"Almost."

"Do you know how long we've been in here?"

"Longer than I've ever been shopping for anything in my entire life," Bernie said. "I hate shopping."

"Makeda hasn't shown you the light?"

"Why do they call it retail therapy? It's stressful."

"You don't find it nice to get new things?"

"I guess. It's not really a priority for me. Especially when you have to stand naked in front of a stranger for two hours to get them."

"Can I quote you on that?"

"Shut up," she said.

"Move," Makeda said.

"Hey, Makeda, are we almost done here?" he asked her.

"Are you trying to rush genius?"

"Uh, no. I'm trying to rush underwear shopping."

"Haven't I told you about the importance of foundation garments?" She stuck her hand into the curtain. "Here, try this on. Colin's in a hurry."

"I'm not," he argued.

"Sorry, Colin's bored."

"No."

"Really?"

"Okay, yes. But we have a lot of other stuff to do, too, you know."

"How does this one even work?" Bernie said from behind the curtain.

"You see what I'm dealing with?" Makeda asked him; then she disappeared behind the curtain.

Bernie couldn't believe how much money Makeda was spending on her. It's not your money, Makeda reminded her. "And it's for the story. I'd hate to have you mess up this story for Colin."

"And for you," Bernie muttered, unkindly.

"Hey, I can do a makeover story any old time. I can probably go to your work and get half a dozen librarians who would be grateful for my expertise. But Colin's in a slump. He needs this."

Bernie looked into Makeda's thick-lashed eyes. She really meant it.

Great, another woman under Colin's spell.

"And before you get all huffy about it, I'm not one of Colin's groupies, okay? I've got a man, and he suits me just fine. I don't need to be looking elsewhere."

"Okay, sorry."

"Good. Now how are your boobs?"

Bernie looked down, as if her boobs would be anywhere else. "Fine."

"No, honey. They were fine before. Now they're fabulous."

Bernie shrugged, but secretly, she agreed. They were fabulous. She'd never think bad things about underwire again.

"Okay, fine. You can play this cool. But someday, when you're batting off compliments left and right, you'll think of me and think, Makeda was right. It's all about the foundation garments."

"I don't want to be batting off compliments left and right."

"Well, too bad. Why are you even doing this if all you want to do is sit in your sad little house and be alone forever?"

"That's cold," Bernie said, frowning. She didn't even try not to frown at Makeda.

"I think it's a fair question. Your cats don't care what your boobs look like."

"First of all, I do *not* have cats." But only because she was severely allergic. "Second, you think I haven't asked myself that question?"

"You probably have. And the answer was yes, because despite that sourpuss, I can tell you're not the sort of woman who does anything she doesn't want to do. So now it's time to try on some new clothes."

"But I don't need—"

Makeda held up a hand. "Here's the thing. You're doing an experiment, right? Because you've got this idea in your head that you're undateable. You want to know why you're undateable? Because you don't try. You say you don't want men falling at your feet, but that's exactly what you expect when you go out wearing sweatpants and a T-shirt older than me."

"Hey, it's not—"

"You don't try. And if you don't try, no man is going to say, hey, there's a woman who's interested in trying, and I'd like to try it with her."

"This shirt isn't that old."

"Let me ask you: why did you pick that shirt when you got dressed this morning?"

Bernie thought back. She'd rolled out of bed, remembered that she had agreed to meet Colin at his office uncomfortably early. She remembered eating breakfast, and getting on the bus. She didn't remember making a decision about her shirt.

"I think you either picked it out because it was the first clean thing you saw, or you wore it because you know it's frumpy and you wanted to give Colin an f-you for making you do things that make you uncomfortable."

Both of those things sounded equally plausible.

"I thought so," said Makeda. "Let's forget all this, okay? Let's just agree that we're here, we've got the company credit card, and we're going to make the most of it."

"I don't have cats."

"I know, honey." Makeda took her arm and led her out of the store. "And now, Cinderella, let's get you ready for the ball."

Chapter Seventeen

Dear Maria,

    What's the best way to grow out a mullet?

    Not As Hip As I Thought I Was in West Portal

Dear Hip,

    The lady mullet is an unfortunate trend. How did it even start? Did people look at hillbillies and think, I want that? Are they just being ironic? And who was the second person to get that cut? I can understand the first—we all make mistakes. But the second had to have seen the first and thought, Hey, that's a great idea! But why? WHY?

    Origins aside, the easiest thing to do is probably to shave your head.

                     Kisses,
                     Maria

BERNIE STOOD IN FRONT of her bathroom mirror, considering her new eyebrows and her sleek, sleek hair. She didn't look so different. Just sort of updated. Bernie 2.0. Jeanaeane had done a good job of making her look natural. It still felt weird to blink, but Jeanaeane said she wouldn't have to wear fake eyelashes again.

Fake eyelashes. What the hell was she doing?

Preparing to date. This is what normal girls do when they get ready for dates, she reminded herself. They don't have a glass of wine and read one more chapter. They put on fake eyelashes and sleeken their hair. And she had a date tonight she was supposed to be getting ready for. New bra and everything. She had some time, but she was afraid to lie down lest she flatten her hair even more. It was really flat. And smooth. And weird.

And Colin's face when she walked out of the bathroom/salon/whatever—that was what normal girls went for. She wanted to walk into a room and have the guys stop and pick their jaws up off the floor.

She started, giving herself a surprised look in the mirror.

Was that what she wanted?

Bernie had grown up knowing that her best assets were not physical. She relied on her brains to attract guys, believing her mother's assertion that smart guys liked smart girls.

So she'd focused her romantic energy on the smart guys. She'd gone out with a few who weren't that smart, too, but who didn't seem to mind that she was. But that was the problem. She was always settling for guys who let her be herself, but only at their pleasure. She could be didactic and cynical and sloppy, and they found it charming, until they didn't. Then it became inconvenient that they had a girlfriend who couldn't keep her opinions to herself. Or who didn't mind that she barely shaved her legs in the winter, until they got tired of her not shaving her legs.

Still, she looked good now. Jeanaeane was great at her job; Bernie would give her that. Of course, after tonight, she wasn't going to be able to recreate this look, ever. She hoped Jeanaeane didn't plan on coming over every day for hair and makeup. What would sweet, porcelain-faced Jeanaeane think of her decidedly non-sleek apartment stuffed with books?

She was shaken out of her post-makeover haze by her doorbell. She looked at the clock on her nightstand. Well, crap. Colin was here to pick her up for the date.

Except when she looked through the peephole in her door, no one was there. She opened it, cautiously, and still didn't see anyone, but she heard voices. Al and Maddie voices. And a distinct Starr voice, the happy one she did when someone was scratching that exact perfect spot behind her ear.

And another voice.

"So it's not a real magazine?"

"No, it's a magazine. It's just on a Web site."

A Colin voice.

"But we can't buy a copy."

"Well, you can't buy a physical copy, but you can look at the Web site."

"But it's a real magazine?"

Al was eighty-one, and he didn't do computers. Too old, he told Bernie. Never mind that Maddie was eighty-three and could Facebook like it was going out of style. Thanks to Maddie, Starr had a very popular Instagram account.

Neither of them seemed to comprehend Glaze.com's business model.

"Bernie!" Al spotted her first. "Where have you been hiding this nice young man?"

"Your hair looks different!" Maddie exclaimed. Starr barked at her from her perch in Colin's arms.

"Do you like it?" Colin asked Maddie.

"It looks different!" Maddie repeated.

Bernie wanted to arch a cynical brow at Colin, but she was afraid to dislodge an eyelash.

"You're not dressed," he said, dragging his eyes down over what she could admit was a very unflattering pair of sweatpants.

"Oh, are you two going out?" Al asked, taking Starr from Colin.

"Yes," said Colin.

"No," said Bernie.

"It's complicated," she clarified. "You're early," she said to Colin.

He just shrugged. "Nice to meet you," he said to Al and Maddie, and started up the steps to her apartment.

"Where have you been hiding him?" Al asked. Maddie reached out and touched a strand of her hair.

"He's just a friend," Bernie said. A friend who was walking into her cyclone of an apartment. Oh, God, had she left anything embarrassing out?

She raced up the stairs behind him.

The second date was not off to a great start.

Bernie looked good, he couldn't deny that. She wore a funky blouse that cinched in at her waist and slim black pants. Bernie had curves. She looked really good.

The effect was somewhat marred by the hobble she had adopted when faced with the heels Makeda had picked out. They didn't look that bad to Colin. Maybe a little pinchy in the toes, but he'd seen women with much less fortitude than Bernie walk gracefully in shoes three times as high.

"You're being a baby," he whispered as they walked up the block to the restaurant.

"You want one of these pointy shoes up your ass?"

"Can you at least try? You look good. Just quit walking like a penguin."

She muttered something under her breath he was pretty sure he wouldn't be able to run in tomorrow's story. Which was too bad. Maybe he'd let Maria borrow that line.

"Who am I dazzling with my new face tonight?" she asked.

"Paul. He's a software developer."

"Another one?"

"If software developers were a hard pass, you probably shouldn't be dating in the Bay Area. Besides, it's a nice control for the experiment, remember? How you're obsessed with the control?"

"The control is supposed to be me."

"You're the variable. If you were the control, you wouldn't need my help finding dates."

"To be clear, I don't need your help." Then her knee buckled and she grabbed his arm for support. "These shoes," she said, "are a weapon of the patriarchy."

"So you've said. Are you ready?"

"No."

"Nervous?"

"Paul? Wasn't last night a Paul?"

"Last night was a Pete. God, you just think of software developers as interchangeable pieces of meat, don't you?"

He was pretty sure he saw her smile at that.

They found Paul inside the restaurant. He did look a

lot like Pete, except Paul showed a little more enthusiasm when he saw Bernie. Colin took a seat at the bar and watched Paul lead Bernie to their table. She almost fell on the way, but Paul caught her, and they even shared a laugh.

It was the last pleasant thing to happen all night.

Paul looked like he was having an okay time. He was telling stories that involved wild gesticulations and boisterous laughter. Bernie mostly just sat there and blinked.

In record time, the check was acquired and paid, and Bernie was standing at his elbow.

"Did you even try?"

"He told me stories about illegal big game hunting in Africa while staring at my chest; then he told me he had an early meeting so why don't we cut to the chase and go back to his place."

"Yikes."

"Yeah. Plus I thought my eyelashes were going to fall off into my soup. Are you okay?"

Colin felt like he wanted to hit something. Preferably something called Paul.

That's it, he thought. No more software developers.

"Can we go home?" Bernie asked. "My feet hurt."

Chapter Eighteen

DISAPPROVING LIBRARIAN IS . . . DISAPPROVING

By Colin Rodriguez, Staff Writer

Two dates down, twenty-eight disasters to go.

After a quick office poll, it turns out that everyone has gone out with a Paul. Looks good on paper, seems nice enough, pretty good first impression. But Pauls have a problem, and that problem is with eye contact. Specifically, with eye contact when there are boobs nearby.

"PAUL COULD SUE," Clea said when she read Colin's article.

"So change his name."

"Be honest with me, Colin. Is she going to get any better?"

"Sure!" Colin said. "I mean, she can't get worse, right?"

"I still don't think people are relating to her. Our readers don't have a meltdown when they want to wear grown-up shoes."

"It wasn't a meltdown—"

"Our readers aren't paralyzed by a little eyeliner."

"It was more the fake lashes—"

"This series was a great idea, but it's not pulling in the numbers we want."

"She's only been on two dates! It's a journey!"

"A journey that's not going anywhere. It would be one thing if advertisers were interested, but your librarian throws a hissy fit whenever anything remotely girly comes within fifteen feet of her. Are you sure she's straight?"

"Why, because she's not girly?"

"Because she doesn't seem to be interested in actually attracting men. Your sister's gay, right? Can't she test her out or something?"

"That's not how it works."

"So that's a no."

"Clea, Bernie's not a lesbian."

"Then what's her problem?"

"That's what the series is all about. Finding the path from undateable to dateable. If we already knew what the problem was, we wouldn't have much of a series, would we?" He didn't exactly bat his eyelashes at Clea, but he knew he was pretty close to begging.

Clea sighed. "Colin, I know you like this girl—"

"No, I—"

Clea held up a hand. "But we are not spending thousands of dollars in clothes and beauty products and page space to watch some frumpy lesbian work out her issues with men."

"Well, she's not a lesbian."

"Maybe she'd be happier if she was."

"Again, not how that works."

"I'm not going to cut the story. Not yet."

"Thank you."

"But you're getting help."

"I had help. Jeanaeane and Makeda and . . ."

"Pia has very good relationships with places around the city. Especially those boring places that don't serve booze. Your librarian will love that."

"No . . ."

"Colin, she's already been helping you. She went through all of those dating submissions for you."

"She's the junior reporter."

"She's not your assistant. Besides, I feel like I owe her because she had to look at a lot of . . . unfortunate photography. Why do guys do that? Why do they think we want an unsolicited picture of their manhood?"

"I, uh . . ." Colin felt like the conversation was getting out of his control. Just like his story.

Not that he had ever really been in control.

"Maybe that should be your next story: a guy's perspective on why it's so superfun to stick your phone down your pants and send the results to us."

Well, at least she was talking about his next story.

"Okay, end rant. Sorry about that. But seriously, think about it. In the meantime, Pia's in charge of the dates. You wrangle the librarian."

"But I thought Pia wasn't my assistant. . . ."

"Your job is to make sure the librarian gets better at dating. Or at least more interesting. Otherwise, we kill the story. Got it? Which will be too bad, because I was looking forward to your insight into your sex's obsession with its anatomy."

He got it.

Chapter Nineteen

Dear Maria,

I've been dating a guy for a few months and we
spend a lot of time at each other's places. The sex
is great. But the problem is my leg hair. I'm
Italian, and if I don't shave every day, I turn into
Chewbacca. But shaving every day is a pain in the
ass, and it's winter and I know my bare legs won't
see the light of day for several months. But my
boyfriend loves how smooth my legs feel. How can
I ease him into my relaxed winter routine?

Hairy in Portola

Dear Hairy,

I had a friend who had hardly any leg hair, and
who never shaved because of it. She's divorced
now. Coincidence?

Of course, her husband was cheating on her

*with another man, so maybe the problem was not
a hirsute one.*

*Just remember that men are delicate creatures,
despite what they may tell you. Some men are
shocked to discover that a woman's legs actually
do grow hairy. Be gentle with him. Ease him into
your winter coat. Instead of shaving every day,
shave every two, then every three, and he may not
even notice. But if he does, take him to get his
back waxed. That'll shut him up.*

> *Kisses,*
> *Maria*

"QUIT BLINKING!"

"Quit poking my eye!"

"I'm not poking you!"

"Children!" Dave stepped in between Bernie and
Marcie, making it officially way too crowded in her tiny
bathroom, especially when Starr jumped up on her lap
and almost knocked her into the bathtub. "No fighting,"
he reminded them.

"But she's—"

"No fighting."

Bernie looked at Marcie, who looked seriously offended. She burst out laughing, and Marcie caught the
'itis, and soon they were crying and running their eyeliner
and Dave was rolling his eyes and stomping out of the
room. "C'mon, Starr. You're the only female who under-
stands me." Starr followed him, if only because he had a
reputation for being generous with the organic doggie-
friendly sweet potato snacks.

"Oh, crap," Bernie said as she wiped her eyes with a
wad of toilet paper. "This is never going to work, is it?"

"It will! I'll make a woman out of you yet, Melissa Bernard."

"This," she said, wielding a tube of mascara, "does not define my womanhood."

"Yes, but they don't make cosmetics for vaginas."

"Yes, they do!" Dave shouted from the other room.

"How does he know that?" Marcie asked.

"Your librarian friend told me!" Dave shouted.

"I saw it on Facebook," Bernie admitted.

"Yikes. Okay, now open your eyes wide."

"Eeeee . . ." Bernie squealed as Marcie, finally, applied the mascara.

"We did it! One more eye to go!"

"Why aren't we drinking right now?"

"Because you're going on a date in an hour and you called me in a panic because you don't know how to put on makeup. And I brought Dave for moral support and I'm not really sure how the dog got in here."

"She just comes over sometimes."

"What, she just, like, knocks on the door?"

"She scratches."

"And you answer?"

"I love Starr!"

"I can't believe you're single," Dave said, leaning against the doorframe with a beer in one hand and Starr in the other.

"I can't believe they just sent Bernie out without any help," Marcie said, bracing herself to mascara the other eye.

"Jeanaeane sent tutorials. I don't think she fully appreciated how nonexistent my knowledge of makeup is."

"I can't believe you've never really worn makeup. You didn't even play with it when you were a kid?"

"I wore glasses when I was a kid. Can't do mascara and glasses."

"That's not true."

"Oh. Well, then, I guess my whole life has been a lie."

"Bern." Marcie leaned in and tucked a piece of hair behind Bernie's ear.

"Wait!" Bernie said in a panic. "Don't touch my hair."

"Why? I thought you just got a blowout."

"I'm not supposed to touch it!"

"So you're going to go a whole month without touching your hair?"

"Yes . . . ?"

"What if you get lucky?" Dave asked. "Are you gonna yell at your guy like you just yelled at Marcie?"

"I'm not getting lucky."

"That's the spirit."

"I have serious doubts that any of these dates will go any better than the first two."

"That last one doesn't count. You weren't comfortable. You were too distracted by all the stuff on your face."

"What about the first date? I didn't have anything on my face."

"You were *too* comfortable then. We need to achieve the perfect balance."

"And then all the boys will fall at my feet?"

"Or you'll have a pleasant connection with someone and you'll let him get all up in your womanhood. Here, you try."

Marcie handed Bernie the tube of mascara and watched her.

Starr wiggled out of Dave's arms and yipped at Bernie's ankles.

"Uh-uh. No dog," Marcie warned. "Mascara."

"But she wants to be picked up!" Bernie said, bending down to scoop up the dog, who cuddled into her shoulder. "How am I supposed to resist this face?"

"I'm not letting you go out with only one eye made up because the dog is cute." Marcie reached over and plucked Starr out of her arms, and turned the dog to face her. "God, she is cute. Aren't you? Aren't you the cutest little weirdo baby?"

Bernie started to reach for Starr again—she was *not* a weirdo baby—but Marcie held her close.

"Uh-uh. You, mascara. I'm snuggling." She pushed Dave out of the way and the two of them—and Starr— went to the couch to admire Starr's smooshy, fluffy good girl face.

Once she was alone, Bernie leaned into the bathroom mirror. She stuck out her tongue in concentration and swiped the wand over her lashes.

She didn't die.

It looked pretty good. Like Bernie, but more.

The hair was still a problem. Was this really a thing that people did? Not wash their hair for weeks at a time to preserve its flatness?

She took one last look in the bathroom mirror. Goodbye, sleek hair. It was fun while it lasted. She reached behind the curtain and turned on her shower. Jack would kill her, but her dates would thank her in the long run. She shook herself, disgusted that she was only thinking about how men would react to her beauty decisions. This is for me, she said, and she stepped under the spray and destroyed her blowout.

Bernie looked different. Colin couldn't exactly pinpoint what it was. She didn't look as made up as she had yesterday, but she wasn't totally back to her pre-Glaze look either. She was wearing a deep purple dress that reminded him of his ideas about what lingerie she should wear and he idly wondered if she was wearing a matching bra.

That was probably inappropriate.

As she got closer—walking much more smoothly in flat boots—he realized what it was. She was smiling like she meant it. She looked happy.

"So. Who's tonight's victim?" She was practically bouncing. Huh, he thought. Maybe she shouldn't wear heels.

"Parker," he answered, ever the dutiful librarian wrangler.

"Don't tell me, he's a software developer."

"No, actually."

"Oh! Diversifying!"

"He's in software sales."

Bernie hung her head in mock despair. At least he hoped it was mock despair. She was in a remarkably good mood tonight. Maybe it was the hair.

"Hey, your hair is up."

"Oh, yeah. Don't tell Jack. He told me I wasn't supposed to wash it for two weeks."

"Two weeks!"

"It ruins the blowout. Glamor has a high price, my friend."

"So, you washed your hair and got rid of the eyelashes?"

"How can you tell?"

"You're not blinking like a maniac."

"Ah."

She looked good. She looked happy. But Colin couldn't help but remember his earlier conversation with Clea.

"Bernie, did you keep anything from that very expensive makeover we gave you?"

"Yes! The clothes! And I am wearing some makeup."

Colin stepped closer. "What's that?" he asked, pointing at her jaw.

"Crap. I'm still working on blending. Is that better?" She rubbed at her face.

"Now it's all red."

"Grr." She pulled a scarf out of her purse and wrapped it artfully around her neck. "That's right," she said. "I carry scarves now."

"Fashion."

"Fashion, baby. Bring on the men."

Chapter Twenty

COLIN STARED AT HIS COMPUTER screen and idly tapped the kitchen table. So far he'd written one sentence: "It started in Cole Valley . . ." which was already terrible. What was it his writing teacher used to tell him? It doesn't matter how crappy it is, just get that first draft down on paper. Of course, this wasn't a novel that would never get published. This was journalism.

Very Serious Journalism about the dating habits of undateable librarians in San Francisco.

He rested his head on the table next to his idle fingers. It was too heavy, his head. Too many words stuck in there. None of them were coming out.

"Blergh," he told the table.

"Rough night?"

He lifted his head enough to see Steph walk into the kitchen wearing his favorite Cal T-shirt and a pair of boxers, which he knew weren't his because he didn't wear boxers with Snoopy on them.

"No," he said, not at all pleased at the petulant tone of his voice. He was acting like a baby and he wasn't proud. "Didn't even have one drink."

"Oh, that's right! You're dating the librarian! How did Bernie do? Any better than the last two?"

"Steph, are you actually reading my articles?"

"No, I'm reading about my friend Bernie. How was it?"

"Fine. They got along, but she said there was no spark."

"Hmm," Steph said.

"What, hmm?"

"It's an improvement over the other boring dudes you set her up with. But no spark, huh? That's interesting."

"Tell that to my blank screen."

She sat down and pulled the laptop toward her. "That's interesting," she told it.

"Ha ha."

"So Bernie wasn't happy?"

He shook his head. "She seemed pretty psyched about it."

"Psyched that she had no chemistry with her date?"

Her exuberance had puzzled him, too, as they shared a cab home. "She said she had imagined it would be a total disaster. But he was nice and normal and the date was fine."

"Will she call him again?"

"Can't. First-dates-only."

"But what if there had been chemistry? What if she felt a soul connection and didn't want to let him go?"

"If she had, I would have something to write about." He glumly pulled his computer back toward him. What would Maria say about his predicament? Besides telling him to get his head out of his ass and get to work.

"You really are a baby, you know that?"

"That's no way to talk to your older brother."

"Psht. You were expecting the date to be terrible so you would have a funny story to tell."

He didn't like to admit it, but that was true. He'd seen a lot of comments from women saying they had dated a

Paul or been stood up by a Pete. He, for once, looked at the analytics on the articles and click-thrus to advertisers, and despite what Clea was saying to him, readers were connecting to Bernie. The ratio of commenters who supported her to the commenters who said they'd do her was tilting decidedly in her favor. And, before he'd left to meet Bernie, Clea had actually smiled at him.

He wasn't headed toward a Pulitzer, but things were looking up as far as his job was concerned. (He ignored the niggle of guilt in the back of his head that acknowledged that Pia had worked hard on this story, too; it wasn't her fault that he was such an amazing writer.) Still, no amount of dazzling wordplay was going to make this meh date sound suddenly interesting. There was no story there. How was he supposed to know that he'd pick the one guy in all of San Francisco who worked in software who was not completely abhorrent to his bleeding-heart librarian?

Of course, there had been no spark. So he wasn't totally . . . horrent either.

That was it. That was the angle. What to do if there is no spark.

"Thanks, sis."

"Anytime," she said, but he barely heard her as he started typing furiously.

Chapter Twenty-One

WHEN IS FINE NOT ENOUGH?

By Colin Rodriguez, Staff Writer

She looked good. She wasn't wearing heels, as she had been instructed to do, but her boots went up over her calves and her skirt was short enough that it made a difference. She even wore a cardigan, despite her insistence that all librarians do not dress alike. But this one was yellow with little elephants on it, and it fit snugly over her short dress. She looked like she was comfortable, which was a must for her, but she didn't look like she had dressed solely for comfort.

She looked like she was going on a first date.

Despite her protestations, it is prudent to put one's best foot forward on the first date. That wasn't lying, or trickery, as she'd argued; it was a way to show your plumage to its best effect and see if the guy's plumage suited yours.

This guy's plumage suited, on paper.

He was close enough to her age that it didn't really make a difference. He had a steady job that more than paid the rent. He was handsome, in a bland, inoffensive way. She said he looked like a young Paul Rudd, and the look in her eyes when she said it leads this writer to believe that that is a good thing.

When they first met, there was an immediate interest, enough to keep dinner conversation going through an evening at a classic Cole Valley spot. She didn't order spaghetti. She didn't balk when he ordered veal.

But something happened as the evening wore on. Not something terrible. He didn't reveal himself to be a closet Republican (which, for this librarian, would have been a problem). He didn't bemoan the amount of tax money spent on public transportation. He didn't talk about how he didn't have time to read for pleasure and it just didn't interest him.

Despite all of this, he probably wouldn't be getting a second date.

There was no spark, the librarian reported. On paper, he was great. IRL, he was just fine.

Spark, or lack thereof: it's sunk a thousand relationships. But what if there never is a

spark? What if you're just not a spark-y
person? Do you sit around waiting for your
spark to come along, or do you settle for
the great-on-paper, fine relationship?

And if she wasn't part of this experiment,
would our Undateable Librarian have settled
for Mr. No Spark?

BERNIE TRIED HER HARDEST not to punch a hole through
her monitor.

Settle for no spark. What year did Colin think this
was? She'd bet he'd never asked himself if he should continue seeing someone with no mutual spark, just for the
sake of being in a relationship.

Not that she had done that. Not that she would do that.
She had never seen the point. Relationships were such a
pain that she never understood why people went through
them if there wasn't something extraordinary there.

All of the delight she'd felt after last night's date had
long ago evaporated. But was her level of delight as
pathetic as people who tried to force themselves into un-
interesting relationships? Were her expectations really so
low that she was thrilled because he was a decent conversationalist who did not have terrible breath?

Yes. It was true. She'd been out of the dating pool for
so long because she thought there was nobody there for
her, and she had started to think that everybody was a vile
monster whose only goal was to subjugate his prey into
housewifely submission.

Maybe that wasn't fair to the men of San Francisco.

Or of the world, really.

Her last date, Parker, was a great guy. Not great for
her, but great. Which made her think there were other

great guys out there, and that one of them would be great for her.

Hence, the floaty feeling of delight.

Which Colin burst as soon as he published that story.

She should be glad. It was a reminder that while she was taking part in an interesting personal experiment, Colin was using it for his professional gain, which meant driving more people to Glaze.com, which meant asking interesting-ish open-ended questions like he was Carrie Bradshaw in 2003. They each had something they wanted from the experience. If she got the great love of her life out of it, that was just the icing on the cake. The cake was her participation in a series of activities meant to prove that the Disapproving Librarian and all of her cynical sisters were not actually undateable.

She pulled her hair up off of her neck and fastened the clip in place. It was almost lunchtime, and she'd gone all morning without putting it up, which was a new record for her. She had come to terms with the fact that keeping her hair down was not an admission that the patriarchy was right and she needed to spend more time on her appearance.

She was trying.

She wanted to tell Colin that.

After she punched him in the face.

This was not healthy. She should walk off some of her anger, preferably with Starr. Or maybe she'd just go see if Maddie had any cookies.

"There's our girl!" Al said when he opened the door, although Bernie could barely hear him over Starr's ecstatic barking. It was nice to be wanted, Bernie decided. Even if it was mostly from a ten-pound fluff monster whose second love was rawhide. "Come in, come in," Al said, ushering her around Starr, which was silly since

Bernie just bent down to pick her up. "I'm running out to the store. Do you need anything?"

"I can go for you," she offered, considering whether or not she'd be able to sneak Starr into Safeway. It hadn't worked last time. Too many tempting smells.

Al waved her offer away. "You and Maddie have your girl talk. I'll be back before you know it."

Bernie found Maddie seated at their tiny kitchen table, her face tight.

"Bernie!" She brightened a little. "Is he gone?"

"Al? Yeah, he said he'd be right back."

"Good. That man is wearing on my last nerve."

"What? Why? What happened?" Bernie sat down across the table from her, Starr in her lap, and reached for Maddie's hand.

"Oh, nothing. It's just this tiny apartment, and I can't get up and go anywhere without him. He gets so worried."

Bernie winced. "I'm sure it's just because he cares."

"I know he does. I just . . . well, you don't need to hear about this old lady's problems."

"Maddie, stop that. Anyway, we can go somewhere if you want. I was just coming to take Starr for a walk. We'll leave him a note."

"Aren't you going out with your nice young man tonight?"

"Uh . . ." Bernie had explained that Colin was not her nice young man, but she hadn't quite gotten around to the whole dating-thirty-different-guys-for-a-story thing. It wasn't that she thought Al and Maddie would judge her. Al was always telling her she should sign up for "that Kindling on the computer," which Maddie later explained meant Tinder. Which, yikes.

Al and Maddie were like her grandparents. She loved

them, and she knew she had their support, but talking about her love life just felt like too much. Even though, a few months ago, she'd walked in on them in flagrante delicto, so it wasn't like they didn't appreciate the finer points of romance.

Anyway, Bernie'd worked the whole thing out with their dog. She didn't need to bore Maddie with the gory details.

"Actually, I'm going out later this afternoon. But we have time to go grab a coffee. . . ."

"That's sweet, dear, but these old bones don't do anything quickly anymore. Anyway, Al's gone out, and by the time he gets back I'll be in love with him again."

Well, that sounded terrible.

"It's not terrible, you know. I can see that look on your face."

"No look," Bernie protested, even as she felt her facial muscles relax out of her patented look of unconscious disapproval. She focused her attention on Starr, who was focusing her attention on the plate of toast in front of Maddie.

"You're young and you have so many choices," Maddie explained, breaking off a piece of crust and feeding it to Starr. "It wasn't like that in my day. If you didn't get married, you were a suspicious old spinster."

Not so different from today, Bernie thought.

"I was against marriage, too, you know. I wanted to be an engineer."

Bernie felt her eyes go all wide with surprise. "Maddie, I had no idea."

"My parents didn't have the money to send me to college, and there were no scholarships for girls back then. I could have become a math teacher, I suppose. But the idea of spending all day with those monstrous little children . . ." Maddie shuddered. "And then I met Al and it didn't matter."

"So you gave it all up for him?" Bernie arched an eyebrow at Starr, as if to say, See? This is what women have been dealing with. Starr continued to chew on her toast.

"I wouldn't say that. I just didn't have the fight in me it would have required to break into the field. It was easier to do what was expected of me."

"Maddie, this is depressing."

"No, it's not meant to be. I made my choice, and I've been happy. I've spent sixty-three years with the love of my life, and the worst that happens is that he gets on my nerves sometimes. Yes, I didn't get to build rocketships, but Al and I have created a life together, a happy life. We take care of each other."

"And you never wanted to go back to school?"

"Oh, sure. I did, once. In the early eighties I enrolled in City College. I didn't last a semester."

"What happened?" Bernie asked, imagining Al missing coming home to dinner and a clean house.

"Do you know how much I hate school?" Maddie asked.

"But you wanted to be an engineer."

"During my first class, I realized that everyone in the school was younger than me, and most of my classmates were men. Boys, really. And I realized if I got this degree and got a job, I'd just be answering to boys my whole life, and I can't imagine anything worse than that."

"So you gave it all up so you could answer to your husband?"

Maddie let out a quick laugh, bright and sharp. "Is that what you think? No, no. I was a housewife, but I did not answer to Al. The home is *my* domain. If anything, he answers to me."

"True."

"But the truth is, nobody answers to anyone. We're a team. We take care of each other, and we love each other's dreams."

"That's sweet, I think."

"Yes, I know you're too modern for anything silly like love. But you watch out for that nice young man. I think he's the one who could capture your heart."

Bernie snorted.

Chapter Twenty-Two

Dear Maria,

I met my boyfriend at a wrestling match. I went there as a joke with a group of girlfriends, and I couldn't believe I'd met such a handsome, normal-looking guy. We've been going out for a few months now, and it's been great, except for one thing. He is really serious about how much he loves wrestling. Which would be fine, except that he thinks I'm super into it, too. I kept it up when we were first dating because I was interested in him, and I wanted him to be interested in me. But now we have a standing date at a wings place with pay-per-view, and he got us tickets to an arena match for our six-month anniversary.

Help!

Big Elbow to the Heart in South Beach

Dear Big Elbow,

I can see you've met your match, ha ha ha. You have two choices: you can fess up, and find something else you have in common, or you can keep on pretending. It depends on how badly you want to keep this man. It sounds like he's a little obsessed, and by a little obsessed, I mean that it sounds like you are dating a man-child. Your entire relationship is based on this lie. My readers know that I am not against a little white lie if it keeps the peace, but this lie is really pinning you to the ropes. Your choice is either to be happy and alone, or to live a lie with your man. If you choose the latter, keep in mind that wrestling is fake, and maybe he's into that sort of thing. Don't ruin the illusion for him unless you plan to break up with him.

I still can't figure out how to work in a full nelson joke, and for that, readers, I am very sorry.

Kisses,
Maria

COLIN WHISTLED AT HER and it took everything in her power not to smack him in his pretty face.

She couldn't believe Makeda had convinced her to wear leggings in public.

Bernie didn't even wear leggings in private.

Well, she wore them, sometimes. Under dresses, if her tights were all in the laundry.

Not with just a thin shirt that had a large hole cutout in the back (showing off her new sports bra, because apparently her old sports bras were only good for the incinerator).

Athleisure, it was called. "We've reached peak ridiculousness," Bernie had told Makeda.

"I can't believe you're complaining about a fashion movement that allows you to wear sweatpants in public," she'd flung back.

But Bernie wasn't wearing sweatpants. She was wearing tight leggings. And, yes, the shirt with the cutout back was long enough to cover her butt, and, yes, she was pleasantly surprised at how good her legs looked in the leggings, but still.

"You look hot."

She blushed. Blushed! God, she was turning into the kind of woman who wore leggings and blushed at male attention. What would Marcie say? What would Starr say?

Starr would probably say that she was responsible for Bernie's legs, on account of all that walking, and probably Bernie should give her some extra treats for that.

"I'd give a lot of money to know what just went through your head," Colin said.

"What do you mean? Nothing."

"Your face didn't say nothing. Your face said anger, then embarrassment, then more anger, then it got kind of soft at the end there."

"I was thinking about a dog."

"A real dog? Not a metaphorical dog referring to men in general or me specifically for whistling at you?"

"No, I was thinking of an actual dog. One that I actually like."

"Sick burn, Bernie."

But Colin didn't look offended at all. He had a crooked smile on his face that made her smile back.

Good God, were they flirting?

A cold wind blew off the bay, straight through the hole in her shirt.

Once again, fashion was making her a damsel in distress. Were backless shirts the new high heels? Probably not, but she reached for the sweatshirt she'd brought, despite Makeda's protestations that it ruined the lines of her outfit. It was cold out here at the entrance to the Golden Gate Bridge.

"I can't believe I'm walking across the Golden Gate Bridge. I feel like such a tourist."

"A tourist wouldn't have brought a sweatshirt," Colin pointed out, which was true. Lots of people came to San Francisco in the summer expecting summer temperatures. Ha ha ha, said the microclimates and the cooling breezes off the bodies of water that surrounded their little peninsula.

"At least it's a nice day," she conceded. She'd driven across the Golden Gate Bridge when it was so shrouded in fog that she couldn't see the car in front of her. Today was bright and clear and, miraculously, sunny. She was wearing an updated version of sweatpants, and had learned about a fashion trend that would enable her to acceptably wear this version of sweatpants in public without being shamed by her new clothing conscience. It was a great time to be a woman!

"Do you want to know about your date?"

"Don't spoil my good mood," she told Colin, tilting her head up to soak in the sun.

"He's not a software guy," he said. "So that's good, right?"

"Variety! Pia must really like me."

"He's a personal trainer."

"Oy," she mumbled.

"His name's Chad—"

"Chad the personal trainer? That sounds ominous."

"He's the head trainer at a gym in the Mission, and he coaches baseball with the Boys and Girls Club after school."

"That's nice."

"He said he wanted the chance to do an unusual date, and to show you a little about what his passion is."

"His passion is frequenting tourist attractions in high-end sweatpants?"

"No, he's a runner."

It took a moment for Bernie to understand what Colin had said. She was so dazzled by the sun and the ath-leisure. . . .

"Did you say 'runner'?"

"Yeah."

"So we're running?"

"He promised to take it slow."

"I don't run!"

"More of a jog, with lots of walking. He's a well-respected running coach."

"I'm wearing athleisure! Running isn't leisure!"

"You walk all the time, right? This is just . . . a little faster."

"We couldn't just have casual sex?"

He raised an eyebrow at her.

"What, I have casual sex!" Sometimes.

Rarely.

But she wasn't against the idea.

It was certainly preferable to running across the Golden Gate Bridge. On a date.

"There'll be a car at the other end to take you into Sausalito for a drink."

"And where will you be?"

"I'll meet you guys at the restaurant."

"What if he tries to throw me off the bridge?"

"He's not going to throw you off the bridge."

"What if I trip and fall over the railing?"

Colin turned to look at the bridge, probably seeing the very high railings that it would be virtually impossible to accidentally fall over. "Um . . . I hope you can swim?"

"Glad to know you've got my back."

Colin gave her a sarcastic bow.

"Melissa?"

She turned from the top of Colin's head to see a man, about her height, with gelled hair and the hugest biceps she'd ever seen.

"Hi," she said. "Chad?" She was almost afraid to shake his hand. He looked really strong.

Chad surprised her by leaning in to kiss her cheek. "I'm so pumped we're doing this. You ever run across the bridge before?"

"Nope. I haven't even walked across."

"Sweet. We'll take it nice and slow. Less than two miles, no problem. You pumped?"

Two miles? "Um, yes. Pumped." Bernie fought off flashbacks to high school gym class. She must have survived the mile run because she was here, wasn't she? But it hadn't been pleasant. This would be twice that.

"That's what I want to hear." Chad turned to the bridge and let out a cloud-splitting *whoop*. "Let's do it."

"No small talk first?"

"We can talk while we run. That's how we know we're at an optimum heart rate."

"Wow, we're really running, huh?"

He just gave her a toothy grin.

"I have to warn you, Chad, I'm not much of a runner."

"That's what everybody says. Then they get a little time with Chad."

"And then they really want to run?" she said with a laugh. Chad smiled, but he looked puzzled.

She turned to give Colin a wide-eyed look, to let him know he was a dead man, because not only was he making her go on a date that was really a workout, but also with a guy who did not appreciate her lame jokes. One of those things she could handle, but two? All she saw was Colin walking away. Probably to take a car to Sausalito. Where he would meet them at the restaurant. If she didn't fall off the bridge.

"Have you stretched?" Chad asked.

"Oh, uh. No." *Because I thought we'd just be taking an athleisurely walk, not training for a marathon.*

"Gotta stretch, get good and limber. Let me help you."

And before she could say anything, she was in Chad's arms, being bent and twisted in ways that were a little alarming. Truth be told, it didn't feel terrible. She did feel good and limber when he was done. Almost like she could run two miles (less than two miles, really) with a guy who didn't laugh at her lame jokes.

"Ready?"

She was not ready. But she didn't think she had much of a choice. Especially when Chad pressed a button on his watch, then grabbed her hand and started jogging for the bridge.

Chapter Twenty-Three

COLIN WATCHED BERNIE HOBBLE off the bus and up the sidewalk to the café the next evening. He felt a little bad, putting her through that running date. In his defense, he'd thought Chad would be a catch.

That wasn't true. He'd thought Chad seemed nice and very enthusiastic and the complete polar opposite of Bernie. He knew Pia had picked him out because she had some sabotage in mind. That just proved to Colin that Pia didn't know anything about finding a good story. Two people who got along okay but didn't have any kind of spark was boring. Two people who had nothing in common and were forced into an uncomfortable situation together: that's where stuff got interesting.

Unfortunately, Bernie did not fall madly in love with Chad on their trot across the bridge. She did admit that his tips on proper running form made the activity less immediately terrible than she expected it to be. Any good will earned on the Golden Gate Bridge, though, was ruined when Chad threw a fit that the bar didn't have low-carb beer on tap.

It had ended up being a great story.

Still, Colin felt a little bad as Bernie winced every time she bent her legs. She should have stretched afterward, like Chad told her to.

After Chad left in his carb-induced huff, Bernie insisted on Colin buying her a beer. She'd earned it, she said, and Colin agreed. It ended up being a really quick beer, because almost as soon as she started drinking it, her eyes began drifting closed. Colin ended up having to practically carry her to the car to take her home. He offered to take her inside and help her get to bed, but she punched him (weakly) in the arm and muttered some very unladylike curses that made him laugh. Then her neighbors came out—the cute old couple—and brought her inside and promised to feed her, so Colin felt he'd done his best by her.

Of course, today she was a little stiff.

"Shut up," she said, when she got close enough to see him. "I hate you."

"Not feeling too great?"

"I feel fine, thanks. Just as long as I don't have to move." She flopped heavily into the seat across from his.

"Good thing I didn't schedule a dancing date tonight."

"I would kill you."

"You'd have to move to kill me."

"I'd find a way."

"Has anyone ever told you that you have anger issues?"

"Yes, and that person is dead now."

Colin tried not to smile. "This date is much more low-key."

"Then how come I couldn't wear sweatpants?"

She was wearing an outfit Colin suspected Makeda had picked out for her—ankle-length pants with a funky paisley pattern that were even more appealing than the leggings yesterday, not that he would tell her that—a cream-colored blouse, and a big chunky necklace. "You look good," he told her. "I like your necklace."

"It's a statement necklace," she informed him. "I feel very trendy."

"Are those shoes on trend?" He looked down at her feet, which were shod in her crappy old clogs.

"You're lucky I changed out of my bedroom slippers. I could barely get these pants on. Do you know how many muscles it takes to put on a pair of pants?"

He admitted that he did not.

"I should send you a bill for Epsom salts. And my water bill. I've taken three baths so far today."

His mind immediately went to what he now knew were her great legs barely covered by a thin layer of bubble bath.

He'd definitely keep that to himself.

"So what fresh hell do you have for me tonight?" she asked, leaning against the brick wall of the café.

"You'll like it. It's boring."

"Can't wait."

Since she'd been such a good sport—mostly—about the jock date, he'd decided to reward her with the kind of date that he himself would rather slit his wrists than participate in. In other words, the perfect date for Bernie. "Poetry reading."

She didn't say anything, so he looked up from his phone, where he was pulling up the info on her date for the evening. She didn't look happy. Not mad, precisely—nothing like she looked when he'd mentioned running across the Golden Gate Bridge—just sort of . . . neutral. It made him nervous.

"Do you like poetry?" he asked, hesitantly. Not that they could do anything about it now. This was the date. The guy was on his way.

"I do."

"Good, right?"

"I know we've only had four dates together, but I already don't trust you."

"What do you mean?"

"It's not going to be naked pudding poetry or something, is it?"

"Now that's an idea. But no, alas. Just regular old poetry."

She looked relieved. Nerd.

"And your date is a poet," he added.

"I can do a poet."

"That's the goal."

"I'm ignoring you."

"Good, because your poet's here."

The poet, Alex, nodded at him, then kissed Bernie on the cheek. Colin did his fade-into-the-background thing, and watched the date unfold.

She could kiss Colin.

When she'd woken up this morning, barely able to move, her first thoughts were of the quickest way to dispose of his body. Then, like an idiot, she logged onto Glaze.com and read his article about yesterday's date, and decided that a quick death was way too good for him. Clearly she'd been set up with Chad because she was bound to have a bad time. Bad time, good story.

Poor Chad, she thought, as she read through Colin's gentle skewering of her date's fitness obsession.

But really. Low-carb beer? That was like low-fat cheese. What was the point?

Now she was sitting in a dimly lit café next to a very handsome guy who was smart and interesting and seemed genuinely interested in her life. She was actually talking to him. It was like Parker all over again, but with the added spark of desire. Alex had a square jaw and strong shoulders and long, dark hair pulled together at the back of his neck. He was even making a scarf work. She was starting to understand why people liked dating.

"So, what have you been reading lately?" he asked. If she hadn't been so sore, she would have jumped across the table onto his lap.

Instead, she talked about the novel sitting on her bedside table that she had been staying up way too late to read because she could not imagine how the characters were going to overcome the insurmountable odds the author laid out in front of them, but she also could not imagine them not overcoming those odds.

"I hope you don't take professional offense at this," Alex said, "but I've thrown books across the room before, when an ending really upset me."

Now she wanted to jump across the table and rip his clothes off.

Instead, she smiled and tucked her hair behind her ear. "I've done it, too. Not with this book, though. I think this book is definitely going to give me a book hangover."

"Book hangover?"

"Yeah, where you finish reading something so good and so engrossing that you can't really handle being back in the real world."

"Nice. I've had that before. I didn't know there was a word for it."

"Librarians have a word for everything."

"Well, I'm glad I caught you prehangover."

"I guess there's still a chance this could be a wall-thrower.

There's a possibility the author will tear them apart and keep them apart just because she can."

"Ah, so you're a sucker for a happy ending."

She took a sip of her drink. "I just think these two have earned it after all they've been through."

"So you're a romantic, huh?"

"What? No. Definitely not." She snorted. Definitely not.

"Then why would you get upset if the characters don't get the happy ending you think they deserve?"

"Because they're characters. I want them to be happy."

"Face it. You're a secret sucker for a happy ending."

"Am not," she said, but she smiled when she said it.

"Your secret's safe with me," he said, and crossed his fingers over his heart.

She melted a little. Dating. Who knew?

Well, everyone else in the world knew. And now she was starting to know.

"Poets and poetesses, welcome!" The woman on the stage introduced herself as Elvira, the hostess for the evening, and explained that she'd call the poets up one by one. Then she closed her eyes and went into a riff about the ocean and birds and heartache and Bernie thought she might cry. This was so much better than running.

Then Elvira produced a fishbowl full of scraps of paper. With a flourish of her wrist, she picked out a scrap and read it. "Hold on to your seats, ladies. Our first poet is Alex Bacon!"

That was her date! She looked over at Alex, surprised, and he gave her a crooked smile that made her a little more melty. "I'm glad I'm going first so I can focus on you the rest of the night."

If their earlier conversation had not involved his entire focus, she was in for . . . something. She'd never felt like this on a first date. Maybe she'd take him home with her, see what kind of focus he could lay on her there.

As he threaded his way through the crowd, she clapped with the rest of the audience, throwing in a whistle at the end. This was her date. He winked at her from the stage, and she smiled back. He pulled a pair of reading glasses out of his pocket, and she smiled even wider. Hot and smart and cute. She could definitely kiss Colin. As soon as she was done kissing Alex.

He pulled a tiny moleskin notebook from his back pocket and started to read.

And totally burst Bernie's bubble of attraction.

Clearly, Alex was a man who had been burned by past girlfriends. Or else the vicious women he described who were all attempting to stomp down his creative spirit were metaphors for something else. But then there were metaphors about poison flowers and teeth and Medusa and she was pretty sure he was talking about an ex. Then his tone and his posture changed and he seemed to be reminiscing about a beautiful woman; she radiated peace and light and Bernie thought, Hey, that's sweet, until she realized that he was talking about his mother in a way that could be interpreted as not entirely platonic. Which. Um.

She looked around the room for Colin, hoping to throw him some sort of distress signal, but the romantic atmosphere made it too dim to see. Besides, he wouldn't save her. He'd let her run across a bridge yesterday. Anyway, even if he wanted to rescue her, she didn't think she could get up and leave, her muscles were still so sore.

Then the room was clapping, and Bernie turned toward the stage and added her own polite applause. But good gosh, she was ready to be done with this date. As Alex walked back to the table, giving hugs and high fives to the audience, she couldn't help but notice that everything looked affected—his posture, his smile, his ridiculous scarf. She'd been under his spell. Now that she knew how he felt about women, the spell was off.

And this was why she did not like dating. The disappointment. Although at least Alex had been efficient about it. Usually it took weeks to reach this level of disappointment in a man.

"You okay?" he asked when he finally made it back to her.

She realized that she had her face on. Her Disapproving Face. She schooled her features into a smile. "Wow, that was really brave," she said. Which was not a lie. She imagined it took a lot to get up in front of an audience to read something really personal like that. Especially if it was really, really personal. Like, too personal.

"Thanks," he said, skootching his chair closer to hers. "Fortunately I get a lot of material from my exes."

And your ponytail looks stupid too, she wanted to say, but instead she just smiled politely until it was not unforgivably rude to leave, insisted that he should stay and talk poetry with his friends, and hobbled to the bus stop. Alone.

Chapter Twenty-Four

DATING DISASTROUSLY
(SPOILER ALERT: THIS TIME,
IT'S NOT HER FAULT)

By Colin Rodriguez, Staff Writer

You shave your legs, do your hair, take time with your makeup. You pick your outfit with care, discarding piles of rejects on the bed that you think, if things go well, you'll be using later. You send pictures to your friends, asking for emergency opinions. You put on uncomfortable shoes. You try to time it so you arrive not too early, so you don't look eager, but not too late, so you don't look rude.

And then the guy's a total dud.

As a guy, hearing sentiments like these used to make me defensive on behalf of men everywhere.

Then I started Dating with the Librarian.

Since I know our readership is primarily female, I'm going to make a list that I want you all to share with the men in your life. It'll be real simple so they can understand.

Men:
When you're dating, do not:

—Show up wearing a shirt that looks like it was the cleanest thing on your dirty laundry pile.
—Monopolize the conversation. If you end the evening knowing nothing about your partner, you don't deserve the kiss you probably didn't get.
—Talk about your ex. Or your ex's new boyfriend. Or your mother. For the love of God, do not talk about your mother.

These things seem like common decency. And they are. So, please. Post and share. For the sake of all the single ladies out there: Fellas, step up your damn game.

THE PROBLEM WITH THIRTY DATES in thirty days was that she had to actually go on thirty dates in thirty days. It was only date ten, and already Bernie was exhausted.

"Think of it like a volume discount," Marcie said to her over the bubbling of the water in the pedicure machine. "The more dates you go on, the greater chance of having a good date."

"I'm still waiting for the good ones," Bernie said.

"Everyone is, honey," Dave said. "You're just playing catch-up."

She leaned back into the neck massagers on her chair and groaned. She was tense. Dating stressed her out.

For example, instead of spending a lazy Sunday puttering around her apartment or taking Starr on a leisurely walk or lounging in the park with a book, she was making beauty preparations.

At least Dave and Marcie had agreed to join her for the mani-pedi. Jeaneaeane had set her up with an appointment at a very chic spa in the Marina, and when Bernie told her she'd like to include her friends, Jeaneaeane had exclaimed, "A girls' day?" like a proud mother and agreed to pay for all three of them. Well, to have Glaze.com pay for all three of them.

So she was getting a new wardrobe, a cabinet full of makeup she'd probably never wear again, and unheard-of access to beauty procedures, which, so far, were turning out to be pretty amazing. All she had to do was spend every night of her life with someone she wasn't interested in.

Did that make her a whore?

No. At least whores got laid.

"They haven't all been bad," Marcie said. "Some were just boring, right?"

"Boring is bad," Dave chimed in.

"No, but not aggressively bad."

"Nobody was aggressively bad," Bernie said.

"What about the poet with mommy issues?" Dave asked.

"Or the teacher who cried?"

"Or the guy who made artisanal Worcester sauce?"

"That guy wasn't bad. Just a little weird."

"What about the model/actor who wanted you to use him for his body?" Marcie asked.

"Wait, I didn't hear about this one," Dave said.

"Bernie has his headshot. He gave it to her."

"Oooh, what about the guy who got sick at Dim Sum?"

"He didn't get sick. He just refused to eat anything he hadn't eaten before."

"Never trust a man who won't stick unfamiliar things in his mouth," Marcie warned.

"That's my line, baby," Dave said.

Bernie burst out laughing. This was what she needed. Some time away from the pressure of dating. Some time away from Colin. She was starting to forget who she was.

"Lift," said the woman at her feet scraping years of dead skin off her heels.

"So what are you doing tonight?" Dave asked.

"Let's see. She's done the casual dinner, the adventurous dinner, the artsy date, the sporty date. . . ."

"Ugh, too many categories," she said. "Don't you people ever go on regular dates?"

"Who's 'you people'?"

"You dating people."

"Honey, you're one of those people now, too."

"Ugh. Just what I wanted."

"You signed up for it," Dave reminded her.

"Under threat of death from you guys!" And all of her other friends. And neighbors. And coworkers. She would bet if she had polled random people on the street she would have gotten the same threats.

The whole world wanted to see Bernie matched up with someone.

Including herself. She really really hated to admit it.

Or at least see Bernie capable of getting herself matched up with someone.

Ugh.

"We're going to that new fusion place in SoMa."

"The one run by the yogi or the one with drag queen waitresses?"

"I'm not sure. Colin and Pia do all that stuff. I just show up."

"And who's your guy?"

"Again, Colin knows."

"Someone who can afford a trendy, overpriced restaurant in SoMa."

"Remember when we first moved here and there were still abandoned warehouses in SoMa that held illegal raves?"

"Those were the days," Dave said. "When building code violations meant nothing."

"I hated those raves," Bernie said.

"That's because they were fun."

"No, because they were loud and late and everybody was on drugs."

Marcie just shrugged, neither confirming nor denying.

"You really are a party pooper, you know that?" Dave said. "But we love you anyway."

It was tricky to dress for San Francisco weather, or so Colin had been told. Depending where you were in the city, it could be hot and sticky or foggy and windy, no matter what time of day it was. He'd never had a problem with it. But then, he'd grown up here. Maybe he was born meteorologically flexible.

He sent a quick text off to Steph, telling her that no, he was not going to get her a doggy bag from Gastrique. He wasn't even going to be eating. His plan was to get Bernie set up, then find a spot at the bar and nurse an eighteen-dollar beer until the date was over. With the way things had been going, he didn't think it would be that long.

Bernie really wasn't very good at dating. She was clearly nervous, she constantly fiddled with her new clothes, and when she wasn't thinking about it, her face defaulted to that Disapproving Librarian look that had gotten her into all this trouble in the first place. Well, he supposed he had gotten her into this most recent trouble. But she started it.

But to be fair, it wasn't entirely her fault. On paper, the guys that he and the girls had picked looked good. They mostly had jobs, they had interests, they were good-looking. Fine, so Chad the Personal Trainer wasn't going to work out. That one was kind of mean, Colin could admit to that. But the other guys . . . after hearing Bernie talk about why the guy was no good, and taking out the sixteen thousand grains of salt needed to decipher a Bernie complaint for the rest of the world, he could see what she meant.

Makeda told her that he just hadn't set her up with the right guy yet, because Makeda was one of those silly people who believed in the *zap* of true love. When the right guy came along, Bernie would know and that would be it. Magic! Oh, she'd still go on the rest of the dates— Clea had made it clear that quitting early was not an option, even for true love. Especially not since the stories were making Bernie something of a celebrity. Not Bernie, per se, but this ferociously independent librarian who had been swept aside by romantic society because she refused to play by its rules. And now she was a champion to the underdog. Also, she brought in a lot of ad revenue. The fact that it was a daily story helped.

What didn't help was Pia breathing down his neck to take over the story. She wanted to take it in more of a *Bachelor*-style direction, turn the focus to finding Bernie's Prince Charming. Finding the man who made Bernie *zap*.

The idea was laughable. If Bernie met Prince Charming, she'd feed him to the dragon.

Besides, the idea that there was just one man for one woman, or one woman for one woman, or one man for one man, or whatever, that was a myth perpetuated by greeting card companies and women's magazines. Kind of like the one he worked for. But the idea that, at some point in your life, you'd meet the last person you'd ever sleep with . . . that did not inspire good feelings in Colin. Steph said he was cynical. He thought his little sister was delusional. If he believed her every time she came home in love with a new girlfriend, Steph had met The One at least six times since college.

But their parents, she always pointed out. Yes, their parents had been together since middle school. But their parents were not normal. They still held hands in public. He had yet to see any other couple still madly in love after thirty-five years like that. He still didn't understand how they stood each other all the time. What did they do all day at their condo down in SoCal? Just stare lovingly into each other's eyes?

Never mind. He didn't want to know.

The point was, to assume there was some divine hand playing matchmaker for each individual in the world was ludicrous. How did that account for the high divorce rate in this country? And what if your perfect match lived on the other side of the world, and you weren't destined to meet until you were too old to enjoy any of the fun stuff that people in love got to do? Especially when you could be doing those things with people you weren't necessarily in love with?

The whole system was messed up.

But that didn't mean people should stop dating. They should stop trying to force this idea of destiny and love into what was just good old-fashioned chemistry. And they should put on their nicest clothes and go to expensive restaurants and try to get laid.

"Is this it?"

And then Bernie was standing in front of him, wearing a flowy dress that hit just above her knee, and sandals revealing toenails painted bright turquoise.

Painted toenails always did something to him.

He looked up into her face.

She looked good. He didn't know why he was always surprised by that. Probably because he was always half expecting her to show up in one of her old sack dresses and give the finger to him and his story. Which wasn't fair at all; she'd been a surprisingly good sport this past week or so.

Her hair wasn't straight—it would probably never be straight after she'd washed it, or so Jack said—but she'd managed to tame it into soft waves that fell around her face. Whatever tricks Jeanaeane had given her were working, because her brown eyes popped, and her lips looked eminently kissable.

Not that he wanted to kiss her.

"Hey," he said, and leaned in to kiss her cheek.

That was weird. He didn't normally kiss her cheek.

And she smelled good, too.

Damn.

"Hi," she said, accepting the kiss and then stepping back without biting his head off.

Progress.

"Are you sure this is the right place?"

He understood her confusion. Gastrique had a door that was designed to look like part of the brick facade. There were no windows that faced the street. In any other town, that would be the sign that it was a dingy strip club. In San Francisco, it was hip.

"It's here," he said, and pointed out the discreet door handle.

"Weird."

"I believe the word you're looking for is *cutting edge*."

"That's two words."

He rolled his eyes. He should have known he couldn't get through an evening without an argument.

"Is the date going to be able to find it?"

"I hope so. He's one of the investors."

"Oh. A fancy guy."

"Well, I was going to try to find a fishmonger to take you here. . . ."

"What's wrong with fishmongers?"

"Seriously?" The woman had a fight for everything.

She shrugged.

"Oh, ha ha, you're joking. I get it."

She smiled at him. She was even sort of laughing. He had no idea what she'd been doing with her afternoon, but it had worked some kind of magic. She seemed relaxed. She seemed actually happy.

"Okay, Amy Schumer, let's talk about your date."

"Yes, please. What does my date do when he's not doing laps in a swimming pool filled with hundred dollar bills?"

"His name is Salvatore Kristofferson, and I'm pretty sure I know him from somewhere, but I'm not sure where."

"There are so many Salvatore Kristoffersons out there."

"He's twenty-five, runs a venture capital firm." Colin soldiered on over her newfound comedy routine. "He says he works too much and he needs to be reminded that it's important to take time for dating. Hence the date with you."

"That's it? That's all you've got for me? That he works too much?"

"Sorry, babe, you're just going to have to get to know him the old-fashioned way."

"Ah yes, the old-fashioned way. Become the subject of an unfortunate meme and then become the subject of a human interest series on the dating life of the modern spinster. That old-fashioned way."

"You're really on fire tonight, aren't you?"

"Besides, what's the point of getting to know him? He's clearly not very memorable. You didn't even remember where you remember him from."

"Yes, but unlike you, I meet a lot of people. I probably interviewed him for a story."

"I hope it wasn't 'Help! I'm attracted to a serial killer!'"

"Oh, so you do know my work?"

"It was very insightful. Tell me, where do you keep your Pulitzer?"

"Save your charming banter for the date," he warned her. His phone dinged, and he pulled it out. "Even though he's going to be late. Come on. He said to meet him at the bar."

"Do you know the password to get in?"

"Ha ha." He pushed in on the palest of the red bricks and a door handle popped out.

"Whoa," she said.

"Impressive, right?"

"Mmm . . . more like excessive. Do they serve state secrets in here?"

He figured if he ignored her bad comedy, she'd get it out of her system. He was pretty sure Salvatore Kristofferson didn't want to date someone who sounded like she came straight from the Reno nightclub circuit. Instead, he ushered her inside what was the smallest restaurant he'd ever seen. They might as well be eating in his kitchen.

Except it smelled a lot better.

There was no hostess—there was no room for one—so he put his hand at the small of her back and guided her to the bar. There was one open stool on the corner, and just enough space for him to stand next to her if he didn't breathe.

He had no idea where he was going to go when Salvatore Kristofferson showed up. There didn't seem to be an available square foot anywhere. At least he wouldn't have any trouble spying. Observing. Reporting.

Whatever.

"Hi," Bernie said to the bartender, who nodded at them, which Colin supposed was the signal for them to place their orders. Bernie asked for water, and Colin wanted to kiss her because he was pretty sure he was paying for this round himself. In the time it took her to pick from a list of artisanal waters, both fizzy and flat, he'd ordered his beer and prepared to nurse the hell out of it.

"This is . . . this is quite a place."

He watched her look around the restaurant. He could see her taking it in with sardonic interest. He could just imagine her inner monologue, skewering the faux-folksy decor that kind of looked like one of those home-style chain restaurants, but with higher ceilings. It was painfully hip. But the food was supposed to be amazing, and apparently the water selection was unmatched.

The small space was a mixture of large, community tables in the center with smaller, two-person tables tucked into the corners. The dim lighting did make it romantic, although the dull roar of bright conversation diminished that somewhat. He wondered if it was quieter out on the patio. A wide bank of windows, which looked left over from the building's previous life as a warehouse, looked out onto a large brick patio, lit with tiny white lights and a generous number of outdoor space heaters. It was no less crowded out there, but maybe the sound carried up the walls of the courtyard and disappeared into the night.

He was aware that they looked like two suburban bumpkins, out in the big city to take in the fancy eatin' places. Although he supposed an actual bumpkin would be even more bewildered by the rough-cut wooden tables and the artfully shaggy decor. It was a five-star restaurant dressed up like a crappy dive. Very San Francisco.

A waitress walked by with a plate of food and Colin was immediately impressed and jealous. Unlike other overblown fancy places he'd been, Gastrique seemed to have actual, reasonable portion sizes. His stomach growled. He wondered what he would have to do to bribe Bernie into snagging him some leftovers. Maybe when Salvatore went to the bathroom, he'd sneak over and raid the bread basket. Maybe he could afford an appetizer.

The bartender returned with their drinks, and actually smiled as he put them on the steel-and-concrete bar. "Mr. Kristofferson!" he exclaimed.

Ah. So the smiles weren't for them, the common people.

Geez, he was starting to think like Bernie.

They both turned to face the man who could make hipsters smile. He was a good-looking guy, with dark eyes and neat, dark hair, and a very expensive-looking suit. Colin snuck a look at Bernie. She looked pleased.

"Call me Salvatore, my man. I told you," he said to the bartender, shaking his hand. He ordered a drink Colin had never heard of, and almost before he finished the order, the drink was in front of him.

Finally he turned to them. "Melissa, right? Salvatore." She stuck out her hand, presumably to shake, but Salvatore took it and turned it and kissed the back of her hand.

Colin managed to hold back a snort. Especially when he saw Bernie with stars in her eyes. That must be some magical water.

He wanted to fade into the background, both to watch the date and to figure out where he knew this guy from, because he did look familiar. The problem was, there was no place for Colin to go. If he took a step back, he'd be sitting on the long table behind him. If he took a step to either side, he'd be sitting in someone's lap. He supposed he could just sit under the bar. That would be totally inconspicuous.

"You want this seat?" Colin came back to life as he realized Salvatore was offering him Bernie's bar stool. So they were going to get to actually sit at a table. While he nursed his full-paycheck beer at the bar in his regular-guy clothes.

"I always feel overdressed when I come here," Salvatore confessed, nodding at a few of the diners who were all wearing casual clothes that Bernie now recognized as very, very expensive. "Is outside okay?"

It took Bernie a minute to catch up. Her senses were kind of on overload. The constant thrum of conversation made it hard to hear, and trying to weave through the packed-in tables was making her feel self-conscious about the size of her hips. But Salvatore led her confidently to the back of the restaurant, where an inconspicuous big guy opened the door to the patio for them.

The night was chilly, and Bernie was glad she'd brought a cardigan, even though Makeda had said it was a major fashion no-no. But this was San Francisco. Dressing in layers was key. And hadn't she already compromised by wearing sandals? So she could show off her pedicure? Surely that was enough.

Salvatore steered her toward an empty table at the back of the courtyard that was somehow, miraculously, unoccupied. And it was close to one of the tall space heaters, so, really, she didn't need the cardigan. So there, Makeda, she said to herself.

"You look beautiful," he told her when they were seated and drinking.

"Thanks," she said, and tucked her hair behind her ear. Compliments still made her self-conscious, though she was doing better at not taking them as veiled insults. Maddie would be proud.

"So, have you eaten here before?"

Bernie managed not to snort. "Nope." She also managed not to add, "It's a little out of my librarian price range, dumbass." Because he wasn't a dumbass. At least, he'd given her no evidence of dumbassery. A little bit of a frat bro, but nice enough. As much as she hated to admit it, she was impressed with the restaurant and with him. The hipness of the restaurant was painful, but Salvatore seemed genuinely kind to the people who, essentially, worked for him. Of course, the night was still young.

She gave herself a mental headshake. Give the guy a chance. Be in the now. Practice normal dating habits.

"Everything looks delicious," she said into the menu, where everything looked unfamiliar and there were no prices listed. Still, if her artisanal water was anything to go by, it would be delicious.

"Thank you," Salvatore said to the waitress who brought them a plate of crudités. Ooo . . . vegetables. "Tell Marco to send us whatever is good tonight."

"Yes, sir," she said, and scooted back inside.

"Marco is a genius. You won't be disappointed." He indicated the plate, and she took a carrot. Ooo . . . carrots.

"You don't have any eating restrictions, do you?" he asked, just when she had a mouthful of carrot. "Not a vegetarian or gluten free or . . ."

She shook her head. She'd eat anything. And this was somehow the best carrot she'd ever eaten.

"Good. Try the dip," he said, and she picked up a slim cracker and dipped.

"Holy shit." Which was not meant to come out of her mouth. But holy shit, that dip was good. She wondered if it would be rude to ask for a straw.

Salvatore laughed. "It's very popular. Some people come here just for this appetizer."

Maybe because that's all they can afford, she thought. But maybe not. The dip was amazing.

"So are you a chef as well?" she asked. And do you have the recipe for this dip?

He laughed again. "No, no. I just recognize talent when I see it. Or when I taste it, I suppose."

"Yeah, you do." She put her hands on her lap, to keep herself from licking the bowl clean. Besides, she wanted to save her appetite for whatever Marco was going to send them next.

And for good table manners. Yes, manners. Dates. Manners. All of it.

God, that dip was good.

"So, you're a librarian?"

"Yes, although I'm taking some time off at the moment." Not by choice, she wanted to say. I'm on a colleague-ordered dating sabbatical.

"It's always good to take a break," he said. "Although I'm not very good at that."

"I hear you're a workaholic."

"Guilty as charged. I was very interested to see this . . . project you're working on. It was a reminder that I hadn't had a break in . . . well, I don't know how long."

"Well, I'm glad I could help."

Their waitress returned with two plates piled high with noodles. It smelled amazing. Bernie wanted to stick her face in it. As the waitress explained what everything was, Bernie half listened and half took a mental picture to tell Al about later. He would be very interested in this meal. Maddie would be very interested in the date.

So far she had only good things to report. He was a good conversationalist, like Parker, and she felt a little spark, like Alex. Part of her kept waiting for the other shoe to drop, but as he told funny stories about traveling around the world, he didn't once bring up his no-good exes or his mother, or anything else that set off red flags.

She looked through the plate-glass windows to try to catch Colin's eye. He was still at their spot in the corner of the bar, chatting to the attractive woman next to him. Of course he was.

Well, if she was going to have a good date, she didn't see why he couldn't have fun.

Just then, Salvatore's phone rang. "I'm so sorry, I thought I turned it off. Ah, this is work. I have to get it."

"Go ahead. I'll just hang out with the carrots."

He leaned in and kissed her cheek. "You're funny. Don't wait for me. Eat."

She ate.

It was delicious.

To be honest, she was glad Salvatore wasn't there to watch her slurp noodles into her mouth. Noodles were definitely not first-date food. But they were so, so good. Surely the gods of dating manners would understand.

Maybe they were the ones who called Salvatore away so she could slurp in peace.

Unfortunately, they did not keep Colin away.

"Your boyfriend's been gone awhile," he said as he kept Salvatore's seat warm.

"Shut up, I'm eating."

"I figured out where I know him from."

"Where?"

"Woody's."

"Woody's? The crappy gay bar?"

She watched the smug smile spread over Colin's face. "What were *you* doing in a gay bar?"

"It's my neighborhood dive. I go there all the time."

"Well, maybe it's Salvatore's neighborhood bar."

"Maybe. But how do you explain him sticking his tongue down another man's throat?"

"Hmm. Maybe he's bi."

Colin shook his head. "You really do have an answer for everything."

Bernie just shrugged. She didn't care if he was bi. Hell, she didn't care if he was gay at this point. She'd gladly be Salvatore's beard if it meant she could eat here every night.

She saw, around Colin's head, Salvatore working his way back through the tables. "He's coming back," she told Colin. "You should go."

"Can I have a bite?"

"No."

"Bring me leftovers?"

Bernie was starting to get nervous that Colin wouldn't be gone by the time Salvatore got back. How would that look? Her date was only gone for a second, and Bernie had filled his seat with another man? That just seemed rude, even if the man was only Colin.

Except that Bernie saw Salvatore greeting people, taking a moment to chat. It really was taking him forever to get back to her. Colin could probably eat the rest of her entrée and order another one before her date returned.

Not that Bernie would share.

Then Salvatore sat down at one of the tables. That was cozy of him, she thought. So was the way he was passing food around. And spreading his napkin on his lap. And ordering a drink from the waitress.

"He's not coming back, is he?" she asked Colin.

Colin turned. When he spotted Salvatore, he turned back to her.

"Can I have his dinner?"

"I should say I'm too upset to have an appetite, but this food is really really good."

"Sorry we can't say the same for the date."

"I'm going to pretend he's gay. That way it's not my fault he wasn't attracted to me."

"That doesn't explain his rudeness."

"Yes. This does seem kind of pointless, doesn't it?"

"Would it make you feel better if we ordered a whole bunch of food and ran up a huge bill?"

"You know, I think it would." She smiled at Colin and picked up her menu.

Chapter Twenty-Five

Dear Maria,

I'm nervous that my boyfriend is way out of my league. He's so much smarter than I am, and he's done so much more stuff. He's traveled around the world and he knows all these cool bands. Sometimes it's exhausting just keeping up. But I love him! How can I hold on to a guy like that?

Simpleton in Twin Peaks

Dear—I'm not going to call you Simpleton,

I'm just going to say this. If a guy makes you feel like you are less smart or less accomplished or less interesting than he is, you better run. He is not better than you; he just needs you to feel that way to make himself feel better. And those guys turn out to be serial killers.

Kisses,
Maria

"ALCATRAZ IS A NATIONAL RECREATION AREA."

Bernie looked at Colin like he was crazy. He wasn't. True, Alcatraz was a terrible place for a date. But Pia had given him a list of possibilities for today, and Alcatraz was the least likely to get Bernie to run off screaming. It was that or bungee jumping, and he didn't think Bernie would let him take her anywhere near the Golden Gate Bridge again.

Besides, a tour of Alcatraz was educational. Bernie liked boring educational stuff. He'd thought she would probably find it totally romantic to learn stuff.

The look on her face told him otherwise.

That's just her face, he reminded himself.

"So, what, we go for a hike?"

"It's not that kind of place. You're going to take the audio tour."

"We can't talk through an audio tour. Why couldn't we just go to the movies?"

"You went to the movies last night."

"Hmph."

"And, as I recall, your date did talk through the entire thing."

Bernie rolled her eyes. "Nothing makes a movie more fun than a guy whispering in your ear about how the main chick was so much hotter in the comic book."

"See? This is way better. No chicks on Alcatraz."

"Great."

"And it's educational. You like that, right?"

"I have been wanting to do this tour. . . ." Of course she had. And who was Colin to stand in the way of Bernie's secret tourist dreams? First the Golden Gate Bridge, now this. Afterward, they could take a cable car along the Embarcadero and then drive up Lombard Street.

He took in the line of tourists, all decked out in shorts

and San Francisco sweatshirts that they had to buy at the price-gouging tourist shops because June in San Francisco liked to trick tourists into thinking they weren't in California at all.

Bernie stood out, if only because she was dressed for the weather (a cashmere sweater that made her eyes pop and a bold-printed scarf that had Makeda written all over it), and wasn't wearing either a San Francisco sweatshirt or shivering in crazy high heels. He'd never noticed how many women wore heels in impractical situations before. Not until Bernie pointed it out, that is.

She was wearing her sensible clogs again, which Makeda had banned from use on dates; she'd even threatened to confiscate them. Colin had half a mind to send Makeda a picture, but since Bernie was following the other rules—well, her version of following the rules—he decided to let her off the hook.

Besides, they were going to a national recreation area. That called for sensible shoes. Or so he could imagine her arguing with him.

"I bet some of these people are on first dates," he said, indicating the crowds lining up for the ferry.

She rolled her eyes. "At least it's a nice day for a ferry ride."

"See? A ferry ride. Totally romantic."

"Yes, a ferry ride to a prison."

"Hey, it's also a designated historic landmark."

She rolled her eyes again. At this rate, she was going to strain something.

"So who am I meeting today for this terrible date?"

He pulled up his phone and his List of Dudes, as Steph called it. He wasn't crazy about carrying around a List of Dudes on his phone, but it was all in the service of professional development.

"Angus is a puppeteer," he said, and watched her face for signs of approval or dis-. She seemed a little interested. "Not that a person should be defined by his job," he added. She scowled at him. Hey, it wasn't his fault she'd fallen into his trap.

Leave it to Bernie to be impressed with a puppeteer.

"He's had several serious relationships and he says he's always ready to fall in love. His interests are fighting for animal rights, puppets, and Shakespeare. I guess in that order."

"Huh. Shakespeare."

"I'm hoping he talks in rhyme."

"I won't be impressed unless it's iambic pentameter."

Ha ha. Smart people jokes.

"Is that him?" Bernie asked, pointing to a guy walking toward them. He was wearing jeans and a T-shirt—not very impressive—and a hat. A knit hat. With ears.

"Oh, God, he's dressed like a puppet," he said.

"I'm giving him the benefit of the doubt," she said. "Maybe that's just the shape of his head."

Colin looked at her, not believing what he was hearing. This girl would give even a weirdo a chance to adjust his first impression. Anyone but him.

"Hi!" Ear-hat man said when he got close. "I know that face!"

"Angus?"

"That's me!"

"Hi. You can call me Bernie."

"Oh, do I have to? Just kidding. Great name."

"Great hat."

"It's not a hat. That's just the shape of my head."

Good God. They were perfect together.

"Why do you look so sad?" Angus asked Bernie.

"What? I'm not sad."

"No, I mean in your picture."

"Oh, geez. Nobody's brought that up in a while. I had almost forgotten it even happened. Hey, thanks for bringing it up."

"Don't you worry. Angus is here to turn that frown upside down!"

Bernie didn't say anything, but she didn't have to. The way her eyes flew wide open told Colin that he was wrong, that she was not amused by Angus. There was hope for her yet.

"I promise you won't be sad when Angus is around." Angus and his hat stepped closer and put his arm around her. He licked his lips. She inched away.

"'Shall I compare thee to a summer's day?'" Angus asked, and Bernie looked as puzzled as Colin felt. This guy. Comedy whiplash.

"You call this summer?" Angus said, but it didn't sound like Angus. Probably because his voice had gone all squeaky. Which could probably be explained by the fuzzy squirrel puppet he'd pulled out of his back pocket.

The guy kept a puppet in his pocket.

"Hey, Colin, remember we have that thing?"

Colin tore his gaze from the pocket puppet, which was now making kissy noises at Bernie. "What thing?"

"Oh, did you forget, too? Yeah, it's really important. I can't believe we forgot about it. I'm so sorry, Angus. We have to go."

"You do?" the squirrel asked.

"I'm really sorry."

"Yeah, I'm really sorry, man," Colin told him. "And, uh, squirrel. It's a really important thing."

"Fine. If you want to be sad," Angus said with an exaggerated frown.

"I don't really want to be sad, but I think if I stay on

this date and miss this thing, I will be sad." Bernie took a step back into Colin. He took her arm. He wasn't going to stop her if she bolted, but he wanted to be prepared to keep up.

"How about a kiss good-bye?" the squirrel squeaked.

"Absolutely not."

"Fine. Maybe some other time."

"Maybe."

Angus turned and walked away. Before he had gone two steps, he turned back. "I should have known that someone who wears leather shoes would be a coldhearted snake. No offense to snakes." Then he stepped away and, no joke, cartwheeled down the sidewalk.

"What . . . what was that?" Bernie asked.

Colin watched tourists stumble out of Angus's way. "That was you blowing off a date."

"These aren't even real leather shoes. They're vegan leather."

"Of course they are."

"I feel kind of bad. Do you think he knew I was lying?"

Colin thought about how to answer. Bernie's face was not built for subterfuge, and there was no way that a person who had such important "thing" couldn't even remember what it was, let alone when it was.

But then, the guy had a squirrel puppet in his back pocket.

"I think you fooled him," he told her.

"Can we still go to Alcatraz?"

Chapter Twenty-Six

AFTER MUCH DEBATE, and by debate he meant him reiterating the rules of their arrangement for the story and her pushing back on everything before he even finished saying it, Colin let Bernie pick the next date. They were halfway done with their thirty dates, and he was feeling magnanimous.

She wouldn't tell him much about it, which made him nervous. But that was only because he had no trust in Bernie's judgment about what was fun and romantic.

Of course, they hadn't had much luck with more traditional fun and romantic dates, so maybe she was right that it was time to try something different. Just one date on my terms, she argued, then we can go back to your regular boring stuff.

He remembered her having fun on some of the dates, dammit. She smiled a lot with that guy at the *Musée Mécanique*, even though James was a total goofball. Knowing Bernie, she only liked James because he was exactly the person she wasn't supposed to like. Colin couldn't decide if she had strong principles or if she just lived to be contrary. She certainly seemed to like arguing with every single thing he said.

His Uber dropped him off at the address Bernie'd given him, which turned out to be a hole-in-the-wall performance space wedged between the dodgy end of the Mission District and Portrero Hill. It reminded him of the kinds of places he used to sneak into in high school, where he and his friends would see some post-punk rock show, then two or three years later, the band would be huge and have a hit on the soundtrack to a show on the CW. He hadn't seen a place like this in a while. He felt a wave of nostalgia for the scrappy creativity that was the San Francisco of his youth.

Then someone muttered "sellout" and spit on the sidewalk in front of him. The guy was wearing an outfit that looked held together by safety pins. He had probably been at all those shows Colin and his friends went to. The difference was, Colin had moved on.

He ignored the guy, who was muttering and spitting his way down the sidewalk. So maybe the Safety Pin Superman wasn't aiming at Colin. Maybe it was just a generalized anger brought on by speedy gentrification.

There were a few people milling about outside the theater, sucking down last-minute cigarettes and greeting each other wildly. He spotted Bernie walking toward the venue from the Muni stop. She smiled when she saw him. She actually looked happy.

Huh. All he had to do was let her get her way, and she was happy. Good to know.

She was wearing an oversized scarf wrapped around her neck, and her hands were shoved in her pockets out of the wind. She was wearing riding boots that went just about to her knees, and a skirt that did not. He took a moment to admire the majesty of Bernie's legs.

"Hey," she said, brushing her wind-blown hair out of her face.

"Hey," he said, leaning in to kiss her cheek. Because he'd decided they kissed cheeks now. "You look good." Because he'd decided he would tell her when she looked good.

"Thanks," she said, sounding a little surprised. "So," she said, looking around. "Where's my guy?"

Phil Ulbrick was a dentist in the East Bay. He'd gone to art school first, though, so Colin thought he would be sufficiently weird for Bernie. Colin hadn't seen him yet. Of course, he hadn't looked very hard.

"Melissa?" A guy in a suit and the whitest teeth Colin had ever seen approached them.

"Phil?" When he nodded, Bernie stuck out her hand. "Call me Bernie." She was smiling. She liked guys with teeth like this? "This is Colin from Glaze." Colin shook Phil's hand. "Thanks for setting this up, man," Phil told him. Colin didn't like this guy.

"Sure, no problem. See you guys later," he said, then faded into the smoky background.

He strained to hear their conversation over the exclamations about hipster bands and such. "So, what are we going to see?" Phil asked.

"It's a friend of mine. Her show is opening tonight," Bernie explained. Colin got a bad feeling in his stomach. "It's an exploration of the societal implications of rejecting conventional gender norms as told by a woman who escaped a polygamist cult."

"Oh," Phil said. Colin mentally slapped his head. He was never letting Bernie pick the date again.

"So you went to art school?" Bernie asked.

"Yeah, but I gave that up. Now my palette is teeth." Colin gave Bernie credit for not rolling her eyes.

Their scintillating conversation was interrupted by the opening of the doors to the theater. Phil paid for their tickets, though Colin saw Bernie protest, as usual. Colin followed them in and took a seat toward the back of the theater, which wasn't that far from where they sat toward the front. There were probably a hundred seats—folding chairs, he was not surprised to discover—and by the time the lights went down, the house was about half full. So much for sneaking around. If Phil so much as stretched, he'd see Colin. Maybe he'd be so riveted by the performance he wouldn't notice, Colin thought. And hoped. Then the stage lights went up and Colin sat back to watch the show.

Bernie wished that Marcie had told her that the show would be so . . . graphic. Not that there was anything wrong with Marcie's naked body, but this was a lot, even for her. Even Bernie knew that wasn't the kind of thing you sprang on a guy on the first date. Poor Phil. He looked a little shell-shocked.

"Do you want to grab a drink or something?" she asked him. She really didn't want to send him home like this. She doubted he'd be able to find the BART station in his condition. Marcie's performance art was one of the rare instances when drinking made your judgment better.

Phil nodded, and she started to guide him into the crappy dive bar next to the performance space. But then she spotted Colin, blinking heavily in the street lights, and he shook his head vehemently and inclined his head up the street. Fine. She took Phil's arm and pointed him in the direction of the very nice-looking wine bar on the next corner. Before they made it in the door, though, Phil stopped her.

"I'm sorry," he said, and she had a sinking feeling the date was over. "I can't do this. You're really nice, but I think I need to go home and just . . . process."

"Okay," she reassured him. "Sure. Um." She wasn't going to go out with him again. Even if she wanted to, she had a feeling Phil was going to lose her number.

"That was your friend?" he asked in a small voice.

Bernie nodded. "She's very creative."

"And . . . flexible." He shuddered.

"Do you want me to walk you to the station?"

He shook his head and turned to walk away. Before he got too far, he turned back and kissed her on the cheek. "Thank you for a nice night. It was . . ." He trailed off. Poor guy.

And then she was standing outside of a pretty nice wine bar all by herself. She wasn't ready to go home. She, like Phil, needed to process the evening. And she needed to find Colin to make sure he wasn't too terrible to Marcie in his next article. The performance wasn't awful. Incomprehensible and bawdy, but not awful.

And now she knew Marcie played the clarinet. So that was exciting.

She looked around for Colin, since he wasn't where she'd last seen him on the sidewalk, and then there he was, right in front of her. How did he keep doing that? Showing up exactly when she needed to find him?

"Don't tell me you're traumatized, too," she said when he was close enough to hear.

"No, I was going to ask you for Marcie's number. I've never seen the clarinet played like that before."

She smacked his arm a little harder than she meant to.

"I'm just kidding!" he protested. "What happened to Phil? Couldn't handle a little menstrual poetry?"

Bernie sighed. "You're never going to let me live this down, are you?"

He just shrugged. "I'm definitely never going to let you plan a date again. Although it wasn't just going out to dinner, I'll give you that. In fact, I might never eat again."

"That's too bad. I was going to see if you wanted a drink."

"Drinking, yes. Definitely."

He held the door for her and they walked into the dimly lit bar together. They found two stools at the far corner of the bar, away from the door, away from the noise of the other customers. And away from the bartender.

She was about to ask Colin if he wanted to go somewhere else when the bartender appeared before them, holding two glasses of wine.

"Hi," she said, starting to order her own drink.

"From the table up front," the bartender said, indicating a couple at a shadowy table beneath the window. She squinted, but she couldn't see who it was. Then the couple moved and caught the light, and she groaned.

"You know them?" Colin asked, indicating the two of them waving frantically and way less subtly than they probably imagined they were.

"My friends." She started to get up to talk to them, but Dave and Marcie waved her back to the table, mouthing "no!" and "date!" and "hot!" Bernie rolled her eyes and shook her head. "Not my date," she mouthed.

"What?" they mouthed.

She started to get up again, but they put hands up to stop her. Marcie grabbed her giant shoulder bag and the two of them made their way through the narrow bar to Bernie and Colin's corner.

"How'd you get out of the theater so fast?" Bernie asked Marcie when they were close.

"Dave texted me."

"Since when do you come running when Dave calls?"

"Since you are finally doing something exciting and I didn't want Dave to be the only one to witness the hot gossip."

"Great." Why were these people her friends again?

"Well, we'll let you go," Dave said, looking Colin up and down.

"No, stay," Bernie said. "This isn't my date."

"It should be," Dave said.

"This is Colin, the writer."

"Ooohh . . . hello, Colin the Writer."

"He's straight."

"Oh." Dave actually pouted. Great, as if Colin's ego wasn't big enough already.

"Great show," Colin told Marcie. "I almost didn't recognize you with your clothes on."

Marcie laughed. Bernie made a face at her. That wasn't funny. Why was she laughing?

"So how's our girl doing with all of these eligible bachelors?" Dave asked.

"Yeah, I'm just beating them off with a stick."

"You're not supposed to beat them off," Dave said. Then he looked at Marcie and they burst out laughing. They ran out of the bar, hand in hand, giggling.

"Sorry," Bernie said. "They get a little punch-drunk after a show."

"Was Dave in it?"

"No, he's the director. He directs, she performs, they both produce and write and all the other stuff. When they're doing a show together, they get this weird twin-language that's a little nuts."

And you're on the outside, Colin thought.

"How do you guys know each other?"

"College. They moved out here right after. I did after library school."

"They seem nice."

"Don't make fun of my friends."

"I'm not! They seem like a lot of fun."

"Good. They are."

"Good."

"Good."

"Are we arguing over whether your friends are fun or not?"

Bernie just took a sip of her wine, because she was pretty sure they were.

Colin shook his head. "So, tonight's date was a bust, huh? You think it would have been any different at a different venue?"

Bernie shrugged. "He doesn't seem to have much of a backbone."

"You need a strong constitution to date the Undateable, Disapproving Librarian."

"Ha ha."

"Seriously, what kind of guy do you like?"

"None."

"I'm beginning to see that."

"No, I mean, I don't have a 'type.' I either like them or I don't. It's not fair to reduce a person to one small aspect of their lives."

"But you won't date stockbrokers or corporate lawyers."

"Because the life choices that led to those fields represent a fundamentally different worldview from mine."

"A money worldview."

"Yes, valuing money over creating meaning."

"So you don't like money?"

She raised her eyebrow at him over the tip of her wineglass. "You know that's not what I mean."

"So, okay. You want someone who's poor."

She rolled her eyes. "Someone who's not driven by money."

"Even if it would make your life more comfortable."

"No, because it wouldn't be comfortable because I'd be with someone so fundamentally different from me that there's no way I could be happy."

"You really think these things through, huh."

"What, I should just throw myself into things? I've done it. It only leads to getting hurt."

"You're right. It's much better to already decide that it's not going to work out before you really get to know someone."

She laughed at him. And he called her argumentative.

"So what about your type?" she asked.

"No, uh-uh. We're still talking about you. You've got to have some ideal guy."

"Not really. I'll just know him when I see him."

"Like porn?"

"Yes, exactly like porn."

"Close your eyes."

"What? Why?"

"Just close them." He put his hand over her eyes, so she didn't even have a choice. "You're coming home from a long day at the library, checking out books and stuff."

"I don't check out books. That's the circulation department."

"Shhhh . . . it's been a long day of . . . librarianing. Don't—you don't have to give me a lecture on what a librarian does. Just pay attention."

She huffed out a breath.

"You open your apartment door, and there he is. Your dream guy, waiting for you. What does he look like?"

"I don't know. He looks like a guy."

"Okay, what has he been doing all day?"

She tilted her head a little, thinking. "He's been work-ing on something for the good of humanity."

"Very specific."

"Okay, he's a teacher."

"Your teacher is tired from a long day of giving out bathroom passes. How does he greet you?"

"Uh. He says hello?"

Colin took his hand away. "Do you just have no imag-ination?"

"Of course I do! I just haven't envisioned my perfect 'Lucy, I'm Home' moment." She took another sip of wine. "Okay, if you're so creative, what's it look like for you?"

"The woman I come home to?"

"Yeah."

"You're not gonna like it."

"I'm sure I won't, but tell me anyway."

"She's naked."

"Of course she is."

"And she's made dinner."

"Of course she has."

"Not because she's the woman, but because she loves to cook. See, I hate to cook, so my ideal partner loves it. And I do the dishes."

"Fair."

"It's worked in the past. So she's working on dinner—"

"Naked."

"Okay, in an apron, but nothing else. High heels. Heels and an apron."

"Remember how I said I'd know porn when I saw it?"

He wagged his eyebrows at her. She rolled her eyes.

"Okay, fine, for real. Here it is: I don't even come home from work alone. I go meet her at her office."

"What does she do?"

"Um, something in an office. I don't care what. She wears pencil skirts."

"Okay."

"I meet her at the office, and sometimes she's waiting out front for me, or sometimes I have to go in and drag her away from her work, which is what she wants me to do, otherwise she'll be in there all night. So I go in, kiss her on the neck—"

"Porn."

"A gentle kiss hello, and she turns and her face lights up and she grabs her coat and I take her briefcase and we walk hand in hand to the MUNI together. We stop at the market on the way home and pick up something to make for dinner."

"Naked?"

"We get home, and I let her in, and I give her a real kiss hello."

"And you get so caught up in it that you forget all about dinner?"

"Something like that."

"You're ridiculous," she told him. "Sounds codependent." But damn, that sounded kind of nice.

Chapter Twenty-Seven

Dear Maria,

I've made a terrible mistake. I met this guy, and he was nice enough, but when he asked me out, I turned him down. I just thought I could do so much better, you know? But we stayed friends, and hung out a little. The more I get to know him, the more I like him. And when we first met, I thought he was just okay-looking, but now I can't stop looking at him. How did I not notice that he has the most perfect mouth?

Except now he has a girlfriend. I think they're getting serious, but I want another chance with him. What should I do?

Sloppy Seconds in Russian Hill

Dear Sloppy,

Karma, am I right? I'm sorry to tell you that that ship has sailed. He's got a girlfriend. Attempted home wrecking is not going to endear him to you, unless he is an asshole, in which case

you should probably not throw away your
reputation for him anyway.

Maybe one day he'll break up with his
girlfriend and you can try again. But maybe by
then you'll be married, unhappily, to the first guy
who asked. And it will be your own fault because
you wouldn't go out with him when you first met
because he wasn't cute enough.

Kisses,
Maria

THE PALACE OF FINE ARTS was a very romantic place for a date. It was picturesque, it was public, and, even though it was a pain to get to on public transportation, Bernie appreciated that Colin had listened to her and scheduled a low-key date. It wasn't like she didn't enjoy big events that were crowded with people and made it impossible to hear a conversation (which, in some cases, she was actually grateful for), but it was exhausting. Besides, if she kept eating all that rich date-restaurant food, she wasn't going to fit into her clothes.

And now she was the kind of woman who worried about her waistline.

If she didn't have so many people in her life telling her this was a good idea, she would be worried. But Marcie and Dave had promised—promised!—to tell her if she turned into even a little bit of a Bernie-bot, and since she'd had brunch with Marcie that morning, and Marcie hadn't said anything, Bernie figured she was still Bernie.

Still, she was glad to be going on a non-eating date.

Especially since she'd had a big brunch with Marcie this morning.

But that was only because she knew she was going on a non-eating date this evening.

She thought fondly back to a time when she had been certain of everything. She couldn't pinpoint exactly when that time was, but she was pretty sure it ended about the time she met Colin Rodriguez.

Humph, she thought.

"You okay?"

And there he was, standing in front of her with a puzzled look on his face.

"A lot of our conversations start with you asking if I'm okay. Have you noticed that?" she asked him.

"It's because you always have an inscrutable look on your face."

"Inscrutable how?"

"I don't know, like you're in pain or something."

"Pain?"

"Yeah, or some kind of mental anguish."

"I'm not in mental anguish," she lied.

"Your face tells me otherwise."

"Leave my face alone," she told him. "It's just my face."

He didn't say anything else, just held the car door open for her.

"You look nice today," he said, once they were safely buckled in.

"Thank you," she said, because she was good at taking compliments now. And she liked her outfit—score one thousand for Makeda. Her dress had a retro vibe, with bright buttons down the back and a hemline that went right below her knee. And it had thick straps so she wasn't flashing her fancy new bra straps everywhere, and Makeda had paired it with a funky silk motorcycle jacket. She was so pleasantly surprised that she even wore the shoes that went with the outfit, cute navy Mary Janes with a two inch heel. She was wearing heels! Training wheel heels, but they were heels, dammit.

She felt girly and good, and she did her best to ignore the part of her that said only a Bernie-bot would enjoy feeling girly and good.

She turned and caught Colin looking at her legs. He must have sensed her laser glare, because he looked up at her and just shrugged.

"Cute shoes," he said.

"Shut up," she said, like the mature adult that she was.

"Today you're going out with Ben," he told her. "He's a hairdresser. And yes, he's straight."

"I didn't suggest that he wasn't."

"Well, that's how he introduced himself on his application, so I thought I'd just throw that out there."

"Sounds defensive."

"He's a straight male hairdresser in San Francisco. Can you blame him?"

"Fine. What else?"

"He plays the viola in an art-punk band in Oakland."

"Hip."

"But I looked them up and the band just broke up last weekend. Apparently the lead singer stole a bunch of money and fled the country."

"Yikes."

"Yeah, so maybe don't bring the band up."

"What if he brings the band up?"

"Then you can talk about it."

"Thanks, boss."

As usual, Colin's annoying debrief made the ride seem short, and they were pulling up in front of the entrance to the park before she felt like she had adequately purged her system of her daily requirement of male-induced snark.

"Oh, good, there he is."

Ben was tall and slim and wearing a narrow black tie that dressed up his well-worn boots. His face was clean-shaven and his hair was slicked back and hip, but not oppressively so. She could see tattoos peeking out of the sleeves of his long-sleeved dress shirt.

Good work, she said to Colin. But not out loud. She didn't want him to get any ideas about her having a type.

Besides, he'd set her up with handsome guys before. She didn't want to get her hopes up.

"Kind of a hipster," Colin said.

"Don't be jealous. Not everyone can pull off tattoos, you know."

"Hey, I have tattoos."

"You do?"

He just winked at her and shoved her out of the car.

It was crowded at the Palace of Fine Arts. Bernie thought that was because it was a nice day—any sunny, relatively warm day tended to drive San Franciscans outdoors in droves—but it turned out that was wrong. Well, it was a nice day, but it was also someone's wedding day.

"Oh," she said as they approached the pond that the giant, domed palace overlooked. "So much for a walk."

She tried not to look too disappointed, especially since she knew every minute feeling she ever had showed on her face. But she and Ben were having fun together. He was funny and smart and he told her all about the absconding lead singer, but he made it sound like one of those life experiences that a guy feels grateful for in retrospect. He had a pleasantly chill outlook on life, but not so chill that Bernie thought he was one of those hipster slackers that Marcie liked to date.

He could be a good match for her, she found herself thinking.

Which was the first time she had thought that in the dozen or so dates she'd been on.

Huh, she thought. So that's why people do this stuff.

All of this in the first ten minutes of the date.

And now it was over. Or at least they'd have to revise the plan. She wondered where Colin was. Surely he'd help them come up with a backup plan.

"Well, should we find a coffee shop or something?" she suggested. She didn't really want to find a coffee shop. It was a sunny day, and almost even warm out. The swans that swam in the pond were reflected in the still water.

"I don't know. It's a nice day for a wedding."

"Yeah, they're lucky."

"Seems a shame to miss it."

"Yeah . . . wait, what?"

Ben had a devilish grin on that handsome face.

"No," she said. "We can't."

"Why not? This place is always open to the public."

There were people milling about, walking through the architecture. Most of them were clearly not dressed for a wedding. Unlike Bernie and Ben.

"I'm wearing a tie," Ben pointed out. "And you look gorgeous."

"But we weren't invited. We don't even know these people."

"You don't know that. We don't even know whose wedding it is."

"I'm pretty sure I don't know anyone who can afford a wedding at the Palace of Fine Arts, do you?"

He shrugged. "Who knows? This city is full of secret trust fund babies. Just be cool, act like we belong."

"But—"

"Come on, it will be a great story to tell our grand-children."

Grandchildren. Bernie wasn't even sure if she wanted children, but when Ben said it, she felt warm and gooey inside. He took her hand, and she didn't resist as he pulled her toward the empty chairs at the back of the wedding.

Colin watched Hipster Ben and Bernie walk toward the wedding. Oh, no, he thought. They're going to make a scene. Or Bernie's going to run away and break her legs on those heels. They were nice legs; he didn't want them to break.

Where had that thought come from?

They were nice legs, but this was Bernie. He didn't think about Bernie's legs. He didn't think about Bernie holding hands with another guy and how lucky that guy was. Sure, she was great—most of the time—but his whole point was to exercise her dating muscle and prove to the world that there is no such thing as undateable. Watching them take their seats—well, not their seats, but the nearest empty seats—at the back of the wedding, he should have been happy. He was doing his job. This would be a great story, provided they didn't get arrested for trespassing. Actually, that would make a *great* story. He wondered if events here were open to the public. He pulled out his phone to look it up, while the ceremony began.

Bernie had never laughed so much in her life. At least that's how she felt as Ben led her off the dance floor after the DJ played a particularly rousing chicken dance. She was crashing a wedding. With a handsome guy who knew how to chicken dance.

"Do you want something to drink?" Ben asked.

"Yes, but don't leave me here alone."

"You're fine," he said, and before she could protest, he disappeared into the crowd at the open bar.

Look natural, she told herself. Look like you belong at this wedding.

"Hi!"

She turned to face a woman, much younger than she, with blond straight hair and lots of eye makeup who was wobbling like she was a little drunk. A bridesmaid. Oh, God, Bernie thought. We're caught. Be cool, she reminded herself.

"Hi," she said, totally cool.

"Who are you?" The bridesmaid squinted at her.

"Um, I'm a cousin."

"Ooooh, are you Diana's cousin from Oregon?"

"Yup."

"That's so weird. Diana said you were a bitch."

Well. There you go.

"No, I'm the other cousin. That one is totally a bitch."

"Oh my God, thank God! You totally don't look like a bitch! I love your dress."

"Thanks. I, uh. Yours is nice, too."

"Psh, it's terrible. Diana is all 'It's totally worth the investment because you can wear it again!' When am I ever going to wear a violet dress again?"

It did look a little . . . elderly. Bridesmaid looked like she had one of those figures that would look good in anything, but even she wasn't quite pulling off the giant bow at the waist.

"It's Fritz Bernaise, as if that matters. It's ugly, and it was really expensive. My parents were pissed."

"That you had to wear such an ugly dress?"

"That they had to pay for it. I'm not a trust fund baby like Diana."

Uh-huh. Secret trust fund babies.

"And"—bridesmaid leaned in uncomfortably close to Bernie—"the bow is supposed to go in the back, but Diana made us wear them in the front. Even though we look pregnant."

"Bitch."

"Yeah, she's the one who's pregnant!" Bridesmaid gasped and slopped her drink. "Don't tell her I told you."

"I won't."

"I'm so glad I met you, Diana's cousin. You are so not a bitch."

"Thanks."

"I'm going to tell Diana that."

"No, no. Let's not tell Diana I'm here. We'll just keep my niceness a secret."

Bridesmaid threw her head back in laughter. "You are so funny!"

Bernie looked around nervously to see if anyone had caught the fact that this drunken bridesmaid was talking to someone nobody recognized. But before she could make even a small scan of the room, she was enveloped in a bow-crushing hug.

"I love you, Diana's cousin. I wish you were my cousin."

Bernie patted her back. "Okay."

"Will you come to my wedding?"

"Uh, sure."

"I love you."

"Okay. I love you, too."

"You're so pretty."

"Thanks."

"You smell so good."

This was getting weird.

"Can I cut in?" It was Ben, back to save her from the clingy bridesmaid.

"Oh my God, you're hot. Diana's cousin, is this your boyfriend?"

Ben put his arm around her and said, "Yup."

"Oh my God, I want to rip your pants off!"

Bernie looked up at Ben with a mixture of alarm and amusement. He looked back at her with mostly alarm.

"Hey, maybe later," Bernie said. "We're gonna dance."

"Oh! Yes! I want to dance!"

"Um, this is a two-person dance," she said gently.

Bridesmaid stood there, staring at them, for what felt like two whole minutes.

"You know what, Diana's cousin? You are a bitch. You are uninvited from my wedding." And she stormed off in her dyed-to-match shoes.

"What was that all about?" Ben asked, not taking his arm from her shoulder. She didn't make any move to get out of it.

"Just making friends."

"With the bridal party? Damn, girl, you're more adventurous than I thought."

He put their drinks on a nearby table and turned into her so they were front to front, ready for the DJ to stop playing nineties nostalgia music so they could slow dance.

The DJ did not comply.

Bernie looked over Ben's shoulder, where her bridesmaid was crying to the bride and a woman who looked over at her with a pinch-faced grimace. Uh-oh, she thought. That must be the bitchy cousin.

"Hey, do you want to get out of here?" Ben whispered in her ear.

"Yes, definitely," Bernie said. This was enough adventure for one night.

Chapter Twenty-Eight

Dear Maria,

I went out with this really great guy last weekend, and it was the best first date of my life. There was instant chemistry. We like the same bands and the restaurant was really romantic and we went out dancing afterward and he is not a total idiot on the dance floor. So when he asked me if I wanted to come over for a drink, I said yes. And then I slept with him.

Now he hasn't called me. My friends say it's because I slept with him too fast. But he was so cute, and we had such a great time! Is it okay to sleep with someone on the first date?

Horny in the Lower Haight

Dear Horny,

I get this question way more often than seems reasonable to me. The reason I think people should stop asking me this question is that it is the

21st century, and, no matter what Congress says, women have control of their own bodies. So, if a woman wants to sleep with a consenting adult, even if she hasn't known said adult for very long, then yes, it is okay. The reason it is okay is because adults can make decisions and can express their attraction to each other by getting naked, and it hasn't ended the world so far, so we're probably fine.

So, to answer the first question that I think you are really asking me, no, it is not slutty to sleep with a guy on the first date. The reason it is not slutty is because there is no such thing as slutty. There is sexually active, and there is the label that society unfairly pins on young women who express their natural sexual activeness by having sex. I could go into the whole thing about how women are sluts but men are studs, but we've all been there, done that, got the T-shirt, as the kids used to say. (I don't remember when kids used to say this, but surely there was a time?)

The second thing you are really saying is that what you've done—naturally and consentingly— must have been wrong because your slutty date has not called you for a second round of mutual sluttitude. That, my dear, is not a matter of your doing something wrong. That is a matter of managing expectations. Having sex with someone does not induce instant monogamy. I'm sure your vagina is magical and that this is what you expected, but the fact of the matter is, you had a lovely time with your young man, but there was no deeper conversation about relationship expectations. If you slept with him because you

*thought it was the only way to get him to call you
again, well, my dear, you are stupid.*

*Now, does this mean that this man is not rude?
No, it does not. It's not very nice to put one's body
parts into a virtual stranger's body parts without
so much as a how do you do afterward. Does this
mean that he should be tarred and feathered and
shamed on social media? No. Please see above,
vis-à-vis two consenting adults. Does this mean
that, should you run into said young man again,
you should go home with him again, expecting
him to call the next day? No. But did you meet a
nice guy and get your world nicely rocked? Yes.
You should leave it at that.*

Kisses,
Maria

MARIA WAS STARTING TO GET STRANGE.

She'd always been a fiery, independent-minded old
broad, but this . . . Maria was starting to talk like Bernie.

He should rewrite the column. But he didn't have time
because he had an Undateable deadline and he had barely
written a word of the story that was his actual work that
he actually got paid for. It was Bernie's fault. She was
supposed to have met him twenty minutes ago to debrief
and to get ready for tonight's date, but she hadn't shown
up yet. She'd replied to his text this morning, so he knew
she wasn't dead. She was probably just busy bonking that
hipster band loser.

No, wait, the hipster hairdresser ex-band loser.

Not that Colin knew for sure that Bernie had gone
home with him. He'd just lost track of them, that was all.
He didn't know how she and what's-his-name had snuck
into the reception, but Colin hadn't gotten past the front

door. It didn't help that his beat-up jeans and T-shirt sort of pegged him as not a wedding guest. That still didn't take the sting out of it.

He was cool, dammit. He could get in anywhere.

So he waited outside like a creep, but then the sun went down and he got cold, so he went into a bar down the street for warmth and beer. He texted the name of the bar to Bernie, telling her to meet him there when the date was over. He drank two beers before she wrote back, and all she said was that she could get home on her own. Which was fine, because she lived out of the way. He could just walk home from here. But then he saw her and Ben walking down the sidewalk, Ben's arm all cozy around her shoulders, and it was all he could do not to chase her down the sidewalk and ask her what this was all about.

He knew what it was all about. He'd been on dates before. The way they were smiling at each other, they had that good date vibe that meant they weren't quite ready for the night to end. Maybe they were going into a different bar for a drink. But then they hopped into a cab. So either they were taking a cab to a different bar, or she was going home with this guy.

If he'd been on a date with a girl who put a smile like that on his face, he'd want to take her home, too.

But he wasn't even mad about that. He didn't care what she did with her body parts. She could sleep with the whole city of San Francisco. He didn't care.

He didn't care.

He totally didn't care.

No, what he cared about was that she was late. Didn't his time mean anything to her? Did she think he would just wait around all day for her? That he had nothing better to do? Just because he didn't, that didn't mean she should think so.

Just when his righteous indignation was reaching its boiling point, the bell above the café door dinged and she walked in. Her hair was pulled up in a messy bun and she was wearing jeans and an oversized sweater and a bright grin on her face.

He did not care.

"Sorry I'm late," she said. "Is it okay if I get a coffee? I'm dying for one."

"It's two in the afternoon. You haven't had coffee yet?"

"I'm just pooped," she said, and popped over to the counter where he heard her cheerfully order a latte with an extra shot.

"That's fine. I don't want anything," he said.

"Sorry, did you want something?" she said and there was definitely a gleam in her eye. Great, now she was laughing at him. She was late, and she was laughing at him.

He so did not care.

"No." He picked up his empty coffee cup and put it down again. Well, he didn't need more coffee. It was two in the afternoon. What did she think he was, some kind of writer?

Maybe he could start drinking whiskey.

Maybe that was what it was about Bernie. She made him want to drink. Maybe if he drank more around her, she wouldn't be so annoying. Then he could be like a real writer. Like Hemingway.

Yeah, Hemingway.

"Mmm. Yes. Caffeine." Bernie sat across from him at the table. She was probably going to burn her mouth on that latte.

Good.

He didn't care.

"Are you okay?" she asked him. What kind of question was that? he thought.

"Yes."

"Okay. You look like maybe you ate something bad."

"How come you're in such a good mood?"

She stretched her arms out over her head and smiled. "I had fun last night. When I saw the wedding, I thought for sure the date was over, or at least it was going to turn into a boring coffee date."

"What's wrong with a coffee date?"

"I never in a million years would have thought that I would crash a wedding! So crazy."

"Yeah, so fun to ruin someone's perfect day."

"Psh, they barely noticed. You're just mad because you couldn't get in."

"I am not!" Ha, what did she know? He didn't care at all. "Anyway, I'm glad you had fun with Ben. I thought for sure he'd be too much of a loser for you."

"What do you mean?"

"I mean, with all those tattoos and the hair and he's in an art rock band! He's trying a little hard, don't you think?"

"That's not very nice, not when you don't even know him. Whoa, do you think we switched bodies last night?"

"I hope not."

"Well, I'm sorry I wasn't able to catch up with you after the wedding. But I had fun. And now I'm ready for my next date."

"What about Ben? Don't you want to see him again?"

She shrugged. "I thought this was a one-date-only situation."

"Yeah, but—"

"Anyway, he's moving to Berlin."

"Germany?"

"Yeah. At the end of the month. So there's no sense getting involved."

"Should've thought of that before last night."

She picked up her mug, then put it down before taking a sip. "I know you're not trying to slut-shame me right now," she said.

"What? No!"

"What's your problem, then? Are you jealous or something?"

"No! No, I don't even care, come on. I just—I have a deadline, that's all. And you wouldn't return my calls."

"You only sent me one text."

"I sent two."

"And I responded. And now I'm here."

"So, okay. Great. Let's do this. Are you ready for the interview? Great. What were your first impressions going into last night? Did you think you'd end up sleeping with this loser?"

Bernie stood up so fast that Colin was surprised the table didn't flip over. But it didn't, and before he knew what was happening, she was halfway to the door.

"Hey, wait! Hold on. Stop, I'm sorry." He grabbed her elbow, and she shook him off, but she did stop her mad dash for the exit.

"Is it out of your system now?"

"Yes."

"You're done shaming me for doing the totally normal thing that millions of dating Americans do every night?"

"Yes."

She didn't say anything, just turned and sat back down in front of her abandoned latte.

"You know, you don't even know if I slept with him,"

she said, once he was situated back in front of his open laptop.

He looked up in surprise. She hadn't slept with him?

Good thing he didn't care.

"So . . . what did you guys do all night?" he asked, despite not caring. He just needed to know, for journalistic reasons.

"I'm not letting you put that in the article," she said.

"But it's part of the experience."

"No way. You can write about the parts of the date that you saw, but that's it."

"Fine. No overnight details. But off the record?"

"We had fun. The end. Don't worry, I'm sure this next date will be terrible and I'll be mad about the whole thing again."

"Can't wait."

He so did not care.

Chapter Twenty-Nine

DISAPPROVING LIBRARIAN ON FIRST IMPRESSIONS

By Colin Rodriguez, Staff Writer

What does it take for a guy to make a good first impression?

I can tell you what informs my first impressions of my dates. Wait, no, I can't. It's more of a general package deal, and once the elements are broken down, it seems wrong. Will I notice if she has nice legs? Sure, if she's wearing a skirt. But will I notice if she didn't shave her legs that day, or will I be turned off if her legs aren't that nice? No. Will I notice if her hair looks good? If she's wearing a lot of makeup? If she's smiling? If she's scowling into her phone? If her earrings match her shoes? (Actually, I've never noticed that. Sorry, ladies.)

But what about the first impression that a guy leaves? I've never thought about that.

"Your privilege is showing," says the librarian as we sit down to talk about her last week of dates. Which is her cute way of saying I'm a self-centered asshole. But what does she notice about a guy when she walks in to meet her date?

Especially since she has notoriously said that appearances don't matter.

"Stop twisting my words," she tells me, and I ask her to clarify, because I am a dummy.

"It's not that appearance doesn't matter," she explains over a gigantic latte. It's going to be a long afternoon if she has to drink that whole thing, which is good, because it will probably take a while for her to talk herself out of this conundrum she's caught in.

"Appearances matter, but there are no requirements for how a guy is supposed to look before I'm attracted to him. Does he have to look like he's wearing clean clothes? Yes. Does he have to be tall? No. It's just in the—" And here she flaps her arms around for a bit, explaining the "the" that has a guy leaving a good first impression.

Now might be a good time to throw it out to the readership.

So, Glaze.com readers, what is it? What do you look for in a guy that makes you say, yes, I'll walk into the restaurant and go on this date.

"ARE YOU SURE you have permission for this?"

Colin turned and gave Bernie an eyebrow, which Bernie took to mean that she shouldn't ask any more questions. She held up her hands in defense. "Just making sure."

Colin unlocked the door to the carousel building tucked away in Golden Gate Park and walked around, out of sight, until the carousel came to life. Bernie couldn't stop the gasp that came out when she saw the carousel, glowing with electric light.

"Wow."

Colin stepped out from inside the mechanism and came toward her, weaving between exotic shellacked carousel animals.

"How do you know how to work this thing?"

"I would tell you that it has something to do with my little sister who works with the Parks Department, but that could put her job in jeopardy."

"And then you'd have to kill me."

Colin didn't say anything, just held out a hand to her. She grabbed it—quickly, before it carouselled away—and let him pull her onto the ride.

She found her sea legs while Colin checked his phone. "He's late."

Bernie shrugged. She was in no hurry.

"Would you care to pick your mount, milady?" Colin asked with a grand flourish and a bow.

"You know, chivalry is an outdated notion that posits that women are the weaker sex, incapable of functioning without a man."

"So, no being nice?"

"No putting women on a pedestal. It makes us helpless. Pedestals are for objects and prizes, not people."

She waited for his smart-ass comment, but it didn't

come. Instead, it looked like he was actually thinking about it. She'd let him think it out, she figured, and started a slow perusal of the carousel's creatures. It was a flamboyant, majestic masterpiece, with horses, sure, but also a tall proud giraffe, a ferocious dragon, a rooster. She settled on the goat.

She climbed on, mindful of the full skirt of her dress, though she supposed it didn't really matter. As she was settling in, Colin climbed on the tiger next to her.

"I can't ride while we wait?" he asked in response to her raised eyebrow.

"It's a big carousel, you know."

He just shrugged.

Carousels were really slow.

It gave her time to appreciate the bright illustrations on the panels in the center, scenes from the old-timey Bay Area surrounded by ornate gold leaf frames. Again and again, as they turned and waited. It was a weird combination of thrilling and boring. That was kind of a metaphor for this whole dating experience.

"What are you thinking?" Colin asked.

"Just metaphors and stuff."

"Uh-huh."

Colin leaned past her to wave to someone outside the building.

"Is that him?" she asked against the sudden onslaught of butterflies in her stomach. She wasn't used to feeling butterflies before a date. She supposed it was an improvement over the old predate panic she had felt at the beginning of her month of dates. This was less painful, and more ticklish. Maybe dating could be fun.

"Never mind."

They circled around again, and Bernie noticed the

person seemed to be wearing all the clothes he owned at once.

"Why do you say that?" Bernie asked, even though the guy looked homeless and she was secretly relieved. But whatever, she reminded her liberal brain. Maybe he was just a really committed hipster. She shouldn't judge his sartorial choices just because she looked fabulous now.

They circled around again, and this time her not-date had pulled up his shirt and pressed his naked torso against the glass of the carousel building.

Her date was a flasher. She had veto power, right? She wondered if there was another way out of the carousel building.

On their next go-around, her not-date was gone.

"That was a quick show," Colin commented, and Bernie immediately wanted to defend the homeless flasher who had interrupted her peaceful ride. Because that was her reaction to everything Colin said—to firmly claim the opposite.

Colin checked his phone again. He swiped through a few things, then sighed and put it away.

"He's not coming, is he?"

Colin looked at her with pity. She didn't really care that she was getting stood up. This was the first time it had happened, and she'd been on eighteen dates so far. Still, something about that look made her want to cry. And then punch him in his pitying face. This Colin, he provoked strong reactions in her.

She didn't give in. Instead, she rested her cheek against the pole of her goat and let the carousel carry her up and down, slowly in a circle.

"I'm sorry," he said, and she squeezed the pole because the urge to punch was coming on stronger than the urge to cry. Or maybe the urge to punch was trying to overpower the urge to cry.

"At least you'll get a story out of this, right?" she asked him. "Spinster Gets Stood Up?"

He didn't laugh, despite the smile pasted on her face.

Colin wasn't sure when this had stopped being a story. All he knew was that some rando from the Internet had stood Bernie up, and he wanted to punch that dude in the face. Even though Bernie was right; the no-show would make an interesting story.

"I am really sorry," he told her, and he thought he saw a murderous rage in her eyes, but that couldn't be right. He was being nice. She looked away, and he watched her bob up and down on her goat.

"Are you okay?"

"I will be if you quit looking at me."

"Hey." He reached out for her arm. She didn't turn. "Are you crying?"

She whipped her head around so fast, Colin felt the breeze. She wasn't crying.

She'd really meant it when she said she didn't need him to be nice. But this wasn't holding the door for her. This was being a friend.

No, no, not a friend. They weren't friends. They hated each other. Disliked. Preferred the company of others.

Still, she was his story, and his responsibility. He had a professional obligation to try to get it right.

"Are you mad because you got stood up?"

"Can you stop trying to guess how I feel?"

"How can I make it better if I don't know what's wrong?"

Her head tilted back in shock. "You don't need to make

anything better. God, you're so patronizing. You know that?"

"Patronizing? For wanting you to feel better?"

"Yeah. You want me to be this nice, quiet little receptacle for all of your feelings of inadequacy and helplessness. Guess what. I'm pissed that I got stood up. And I'm pissed that I'm pissed. And I'm pissed that you keep looking at me like I'm a delicate flower that will shrivel up and die at the first disappointment. I'm still trying to process all this, okay? And I don't see why I have to be pleasant while I'm doing it."

"No one ever accused you of being pleasant," he muttered.

Then she did the last thing he ever expected Bernie to do.

She started laughing.

Oh, he'd heard her laugh before. She laughed on her date with stupid Ben. She laughed when she talked about the hilarious, hilarious patriarchy. She'd even smiled at him a few times, which was usually a prelude to laughter.

Normal people smiled, then laughed. She ranted at him, then exploded in a full-belly, tears-streaming-down-her-face, silent, red-faced laugh attack.

At least he thought she was laughing.

"Are you laughing?" he asked, just to make sure.

"Your face—" she gasped. She tried again. "Not pleasant—" She didn't get very far before choking on another laugh.

"I don't get it," he said. He had a feeling that he might be pouting, but he was a grown man so he definitely wasn't pouting because grown men don't pout. Although she did seem to be laughing at him. But why? For calling her not pleasant? He insulted her and she laughed?

Apparently their relationship was evolving.

"Oh, crap," she said with a mighty sigh, wiping her eyes. "Sorry," she said, but he didn't believe for a second that it was a sincere apology since she followed it with a giggle. Bernie did not giggle.

She also did not hide her face with her hands. Bernie never hid from him. It was always all out there for him to see, whether he wanted to or not. That was her face. That was how she got into this mess in the first place.

"Are you crying?" he asked, just to make sure.

"Shut up," she said, the words muffled by her hands.

"Hey." He leaned across to her goat and pulled her hands away. She turned her face away from his, but not before he saw her lips pinched tight and her wet cheeks.

"I'll kill him," he said. "I'll track him down and put a flaming bag of poop on his doorstep."

She let out a watery laugh. That was good. A laugh was good. Well, a less maniacal laugh was good. He'd have preferred a sincere laugh, but it was better than abject weeping.

"Don't worry about it," she said.

"Don't worry about it? You're crying!"

"No, I'm not," she said, wiping her cheeks. She turned and bared her teeth. "See? I'm smiling."

"Yikes."

She took a deep, shuddering breath. "Ugh, dating is the worst." She rubbed her chest. "I don't even know why I care. I didn't even know this guy."

"Maybe he had a work emergency."

"Maybe. What does he do?"

"Uh, he's a professional sign painter."

She snorted.

"There could be a sign emergency," Colin suggested.

"No, it's fine. He just changed his mind."

"Or chickened out."

"Yes. He chickened out of dating me because I'm so intimidating."

"You are intimidating, you know."

"Why, because I have such a mean face? The face that broke a thousand Internets!"

"You don't have a mean face."

She turned and looked at him.

"Okay, sometimes you have a mean face. But that's not it. You're intimidating because you're confident."

"Oh, so I should look vulnerable and fluffy so a man feels more comfortable with his ability to dominate me?"

That was his Bernie back, the one who wouldn't let anything go. He almost smiled, but he was afraid she might kill him.

"It's not good for a man's ego to be with a woman who doesn't need him."

"Which is exactly why I don't date."

"No, I'm not explaining myself right."

"Okay, yes, please do a better job explaining to me why I need to be meek and desperate in order to attract a man."

"Men are fragile."

She snorted.

"We are! We need to feel needed!"

"So I need to make myself incompetent to get a man?"

"I thought you didn't want to 'get' a man?"

She sighed and bumped her head against her goat's pole. "How many times are we going to have this argument?"

"It's our shtick, baby. It's what we do."

She laughed against her goat. "You don't find it exhausting?"

He shrugged. "I like to have something to strive for."

"To strive to change my mind about diminishing myself to make a man look good?"

"To convince you that making yourself vulnerable to love doesn't diminish you."

She looked over at him. She looked surprised. "Wow."

"I know. I'm not just a pretty face."

"I never thought about it that way." She looked out the glass windows, at the city slowly spinning by.

He watched her thinking. He'd never done that before—really watched someone puzzle something out. But with Bernie, it was a daily, fascinating occurrence. Had he really never gone out with anyone who was this thoughtful before? Or had he just not been paying attention?

Also, he wasn't going out with her.

But it was too late. The thought was planted in his head. What would it be like to go out with Bernie? It wouldn't be peaceful, that was for sure. It would be a lot of walking on eggshells to make sure he didn't say the wrong thing.

Except he didn't feel like he had to walk on eggshells. He kind of liked it when she argued with him. He found himself saying things he didn't even mean, just to watch her hackles go up. He didn't really agree with her—he still thought she took everything way too seriously—but he was starting to understand her point of view.

He wasn't really sure how he felt about that.

He just knew that he liked being around her, and he was not going to think about how glad he was that her douche bag date hadn't shown up tonight.

She tucked her legs up underneath her, somehow managing to stay balanced on the goat's back. She still looked sad. Thoughtful and sad. Emo girl, she would call herself if she wasn't so in her own head.

Now he was reading her mind. It was starting to get weird on this here carousel.

"So," he said, needing to break up the heavy silence around him. "Should we talk about tomorrow?" Tomorrow's date was going to be at a roller derby bout. People busting heads in a controlled environment seemed like the perfect thing for her. He sort of couldn't wait to tell her.

"Is it okay if we don't? Just for a little bit?"

"Sure." He could not talk. He could just sit here on his tiger while she sat over there on her goat and he could watch her hurting and not do anything about it. No problem.

Gah, feelings. This was really annoying.

Before he could talk himself out of it, he had climbed off his carousel animal and was standing next to hers. He rested one hand on the goat's rump, feeling the up and down motion, up and down. Bernie turned and looked at him, surprised, and he put his other hand around her waist. He didn't even feel her hesitate, she just wrapped her arms around his neck and leaned into him. But then the goat rose again, and she almost lost her balance and she leaned back, laughing a little. "Scooch up," he said, and before she could say anything else, she was twisted around, her back to the pole, and he was climbing into the seat. He pulled her close again, pulled her head to his shoulder, and rubbed her back. She hooked her legs over his and they both hung there, riding the carousel waves and breathing together. He closed his eyes and took her in. She smelled nice. Sort of like strawberries. The longer he rubbed her back, the more she melted into his chest. He rubbed her arms and her neck and, with his eyes still closed, he ran his hand up her cheek and he didn't even open his eyes as he bent down to her mouth.

* * *

Bernie was drunk. She must be drunk, except this felt better than being drunk because she didn't have that out-of-control, vaguely nauseated feeling and the ominous foreknowledge of a headache in the morning. She just felt sort of floaty and soft and warm as Colin rubbed her back and her arms. Her head rested on his shoulder, and she could hear his heart beating in his chest. She wrapped her arms loosely around his waist. She thought she might fall asleep, but she didn't.

She just knew that she didn't feel bad about being stood up anymore.

She wasn't sure what shifted, but something did, and suddenly she felt the closeness and maleness of Colin, how gentle his arms were, how good he smelled, how strong his back felt. Then his hand moved up to her cheek and she instinctively moved into it, off of his shoulder, and watched his face, his eyes closed, until she couldn't watch anymore because he was kissing her.

Well, this was unexpected. She should acknowledge that, think about the terrible ramifications of kissing a guy who was writing a story on her and whom she didn't even like at all.

But who could think at a time like this? Who could think when his lips were soft on hers and all she wanted was for them to not be quite so soft? So she pressed closer to him and opened up, and his arms came tight around her, pressing even closer. She let out a little groan when she felt his tongue against hers and he started to pull back, but no, she wasn't done with this yet. She pulled on the fabric of his shirt and he got the message, changing his angle so he could go deeper and hotter. She lifted her arms so they were around his shoulders and his hands moved up to the sides of her breasts and just rested there, driving her mad.

Finally, eventually, they had to come up for air. Stupid air. He didn't move, just rested his forehead against hers while she breathed and breathed with her eyes closed.

"Bernie?"

"Shh."

She rubbed her lips together, savoring the taste of him. They felt thoroughly kissed. She liked it.

"Can I talk now?"

"No."

He huffed out a quick laugh. Finally, she opened her eyes and looked at him. Her hands had done some damage to his hair, and he looked just as flushed as she felt. Dang. That was some world-class chemistry.

There were probably some terrible ramifications. They should discuss them. But she didn't want to. They didn't even like each other. This was just a kiss.

"I know we should talk about this," she said. "But I don't want to."

"Okay."

"Okay, good."

"Should we talk about it later?"

"This is probably going to shock you, but how about if we never talk about it?"

"You don't want to dissect what this means for society?"

"The societal implications of your tongue down my throat? No."

She leaned into him again and rested her head on his shoulder. His arms came around and rested loosely on her hips.

"You're okay?" he asked quietly.

"Yes."

He shook his shoulder a little so she sat up and watched him examine her face.

"Okay." Then he pulled her head back to his shoulder, and they rode around the carousel.

Chapter Thirty

"SHE WAS STOOD UP?"

Pia looked like she wanted to punch a wall. Colin hadn't thought she had it in her. Judging by the looks on everyone's faces around the table, he wasn't the only one.

"It wasn't much of a story," Clea said. "But the comments are through the roof."

"And most of them were nice," Jeanaeane said. "Very low troll ratio."

"Because everybody loves Bernie," Makeda said. "She's every woman."

Colin rolled his eyes.

"But she really wasn't that upset about it?" Pia asked.

Colin thought about Bernie, looking forlornly over the spinning city. Then he thought about her falling into his arms, her body wrapped around his as he comforted her. Then her mouth under his. Her fists clenching his shirt. His hands pulling her closer.

Yeah, she got over it.

Or did she? Had he just taken advantage of her vulnerable state? Bernie wasn't used to being vulnerable. Maybe he shouldn't have kissed her.

But she was into it. He knew what it was like when a woman was responding to him.

Maybe he was just comforting her with his body. Hell, if she wanted to comfort herself with all of him, he wouldn't argue.

Whoa. Where did that come from?

"We need to take advantage of this."

He realized Clea was talking to the group, not to him. Not to his inner thoughts, which were venturing into uncharted territory. He didn't want a woman like Bernie. He liked women who were quiet and polite and spent a lot of time at the gym. He didn't like women who argued with everything he said and didn't spend hours on their appearance. She was so not his type.

He just liked her, that was all. They'd been spending so much time together. It was a proximity thing. A proximity thing he'd have to get a hold on, because it was totally unprofessional.

Get a hold on her, Rodriguez.

He adjusted himself in his chair.

"I love it. What do you think, Colin?"

And he totally hadn't been listening. Great, another thing Bernie was messing up for him. She was supposed to be saving his job, not messing it up. Although, to be fair, he didn't always pay very close attention in these meetings. It usually didn't matter.

"I'm not sure. Can you explain it again?"

Clea rolled her eyes. Pia didn't seem to notice that Colin had checked out for a minute there, bless her naive little heart.

"I think it's great," Pia was saying, her eyes lit up in excitement. "We'll make it a real event. We can get sponsorships. We'll do it up, have all the guys there."

"It's only a few days away," Makeda said. "What kind of space can we get?"

Pia dismissed her with a wave. "I'll give you some names to call."

Makeda looked annoyed—it was not her job to call venues—but Pia soldiered on.

"Alcohol sponsors, we'll get beauty sponsors and people to do her hair and makeup. And a dress. Where can we get a dress?"

"Well, when I'm done calling your people, I can call my people."

"Wait, what dress?" Colin really needed to pay attention.

"The thirty days are almost up. Thirty dates in thirty days, right?"

Colin nodded. His palms started sweating. He didn't like where this was going.

"It'll be a huge event," Dali said. "People are clamoring to find out who she chooses."

"But wait, hold on." He really needed to get control of this situation.

"I'm kind of holding out for Pete," Jeanaeane said.

"Pete? That was so long ago! Nobody remembers Pete!"

"But wouldn't that be poetic? If she chose the first guy she met?" Jeanaeane sat back with a dreamy sigh. He hadn't known Jeanaeane could do a dreamy sigh.

"But what about Ben? He was hot." Now Clea was weighing in on this? What was wrong with these people?

"It would do her good to date a hairdresser," Pia said.

He hated to rain on the first time in history that Clea and Pia had agreed on something, but this was getting out of hand.

"It's not about her choosing someone," Colin interrupted. "It's about proving that she's not undateable."

"Pft," Clea said. "If that was it, we could have ended this series a week ago. Proving her dateability was just the first step. Now we have to go big."

"It could become an annual thing," Makeda said. "Every year, we pick the most undateable woman in San Francisco and set her up. Oh my God, I'm going to get to throw out so many Birkenstocks."

"Real women are in right now," Pia said. "We'll have people chomping at the bit to dress them."

"Real women are in?" Colin powered through the incredulous crack in his voice. "What does that even mean?"

"June thirtieth is a Friday. Perfect. We'll run it like a date night. Or a mixer! Bring your single friends and find hope for the future!" Clea was standing up now, reaching for the projector and furiously making notes.

It was happening. They were throwing a huge, attention-seeking party. For Bernie. To choose a man.

Bernie was definitely going to kill him.

Bernie promised herself it wouldn't be weird.

It would be totally fine. No big deal. "No big deal," she muttered as she got off the bus at the Cow Palace.

"Excuse me?"

She turned and looked at the guy next to her. He was handsome. Before Colin's stupid story, she barely noticed handsome men.

She gave him a vague smile and headed toward the entrance. He wasn't the handsome guy she was looking for. Her handsome guy was named Marc-with-a-c and he had brown hair and a beard and would be wearing a green shirt. This handsome guy had brown hair and a beard and was wearing a black Misfits shirt. And a fedora. If Marc-with-a-c was wearing a fedora, she was going home.

She checked her phone. No messages from Colin. Just

some more words of encouragement from Dave and a
picture of Marcie in a tiny tube dress asking if she looked
too much like a drag queen to meet a potential producing
partner. Bernie had no idea how much was too much like
a drag queen, but she told Marcie she looked fine. She
looked like Marcie. Marcie had a look.

Bernie used to have a look. It wasn't much of a look,
but it was hers. It involved wearing whatever clothes were
clean and whichever shoes would hurt her feet the least.
Tonight she was wearing boots that pinched her toes,
which Makeda had made her wear because she wouldn't
be walking far and the boots didn't have heels, which was
as far as Makeda would compromise, shoewise. Bernie
was also wearing skinny jeans and a flowy top that was
just long enough to make her feel slightly less uncomfortable with the fact that she was wearing skinny jeans. She
had on mascara and eyeliner and lipstick and her hair was
down, or at least it had been down when she left the
house. But it was windy and she'd had to wait at the bus
stop for a while because she was being stubborn and insisted on taking the bus, so now it was up. She thought
about finding the ladies' room to fix it. Which was definitely not ever part of her former look.

But hey, she was getting dates.

And it wasn't like she didn't kiss on the first date.
She'd kissed a few of the guys on earlier dates. Jamal,
who made her laugh, and Mark-with-a-k, who took her to
a trendy gelato place in Cole Valley.

And Colin. She'd kissed Colin. No, she'd straight up
made out with Colin. But only because she was feeling
crummy and he had been so sweet and smelled so good
and even though she disagreed with everything that came
out of his mouth, she still liked him. And his mouth.

"Focus on Marc-with-a-c," she reminded herself.

"Who?"

Because she had been thinking about him, Colin magically appeared before her. He had a talent for that. It was annoying.

"Hi," she said, tucking her hair behind her ear like a girl who did stuff like that.

"Date's not here yet?" he asked, totally not fazed by the fact that, less than twenty-four hours ago, her tongue was down his throat.

"Nope. Hope I'm not getting stood up again!" Did she sound frantic? She thought she might sound frantic. Then she thought she sounded like she was expecting Colin to make out with her again because that was what had happened last time she was stood up. "Not that I want to make out with you again," she said, totally not awkwardly at all.

"Ah." He rubbed the back of his neck. Great, she'd made him uncomfortable.

Well, why shouldn't he be uncomfortable? She was uncomfortable. And it wasn't like she'd been making out with herself. They were in this uncomfortable situation together. They should both feel weird.

That, oddly, made her feel better.

"So," she said. "Marc-with-a-c."

"Marc-with-a-c," he said, pulling out his phone. "He's a graphic designer for a small firm in the East Bay. He drives a Prius."

"Well, I'm sure I'll love him."

Colin gave her a crooked smile. Her heart totally did not do a little flip. Not at all.

"He went to Stanford, and he's lived in the city for about five years. He's never been married, but he was engaged to his college girlfriend. In his free time he plays disc golf and watches horror movies and—you'll like this even better than the Prius—he reads."

"Oh? What does he read?"

"Uh, it doesn't say. But he wrote it down, so . . ."

"So he can read."

"And he chooses to read for fun. Listen, don't grill him, okay? Just try to get to know him."

"I know. I'll learn something about him before I judge him."

"I appreciate you taking to your lessons."

"Thank you."

They stood at the door, looking for Marc, moving out of people's way as they headed inside.

"So."

"So."

"So . . . roller derby?"

"I thought it sounded fun." And Pia had insisted.

"Not very romantic."

"Sure it is," he said. "All that adrenaline gets the blood pumping."

She was sure there was something she could say about women beating each other up and adrenaline, but she couldn't quite put it into words that Colin would argue with. "Great," she said instead.

"Great."

And still, no Marc.

"Are we going to talk about this or what?" she asked.

"Talk about what?" She looked at him. "Oh, that. Right. Kissing. Sorry about that. It was totally inappropriate of me."

"It wasn't just you."

"I appreciate you saying that, but I should not have jumped on you like that. You're the story," he said.

"Right."

"It won't happen again."

"Good."

"Good."

"Okay, just wanted to clear that up." It didn't feel clear at all. If anything, she felt more muddled. She heard what Colin was saying—that it was a mistake and it wouldn't happen again, that he would maintain his professional boundaries—and she appreciated that. But she didn't feel better about it.

Stupid vulnerability.

"Melissa?"

Brown hair, beard, green shirt. "Marc?"

"Hey. Sorry I'm late. I was looking for parking. It's crazy out there. I didn't think roller derby was that popular."

"Actually, it's had quite a resurgence in the past few years," she started. Then she caught herself. Dates don't like to be corrected. Be nice. Don't judge until he gives you something to judge him for. "I'm glad you found a spot. This should be really fun." She turned to face Colin, to get some credit for course-correcting and acting like a normal dating person.

But Colin was gone.

She turned back to Marc-with-a-c and let him lead her into the stadium.

What kind of self-respecting adult played disc golf?

Actually, a bunch of Colin's friends played at the course in Golden Gate Park. But that didn't make Marc any less of a dope. And the beard was a little much. He was a graphic designer, not an artisanal brewer. Marc-with-a-c was trying a little too hard. And Colin didn't like the way he guided Bernie around by the small of her back. She hated to be led around. She could walk perfectly well on her own.

And Colin wasn't acting crazy at all.

It wasn't his fault that kissing Bernie had completely messed him up. Well, he'd initiated it, so maybe it was his fault. But he hadn't meant to. He'd just meant to comfort her. He hated to see her upset. And it felt totally natural to go from holding her to kissing her, and he'd thought she felt the same way. But clearly she had been waiting for him to redraw the line in the sand. They were back to writer and subject, which was good. That was how it should be. That was what he wanted.

He watched Marc lead Bernie to their seats, and took his own seat a few rows behind them. Then he unclenched the fist he hadn't realized he was clenching.

This was ridiculous. This wasn't any different from any other date, and here, he had the added bonus of watching tough chicks on roller skates kick each other's asses. There was not a thing in the world he should be complaining about.

A woman in pinup curls handed him a program, and he idly started flipping through it. Steph had dated a derby girl once, and Colin was amazed at the athleticism and toughness of the ladies, but he was less convinced by their ridiculous names. Who was he kidding, he loved them. Badass puns, Steph called them. He flipped to the team roster. Trixie Sticks. Ophelia Burn. Liz Vicious. AnaMurderPia. That one was a bit of a stretch. He looked closer at her picture. She looked vaguely familiar, though it was hard to tell since she was wearing her helmet and had stars painted over her eyes. AnaMurderPia, aka Li'l Smasher, was the newest member of the squad, and would be jamming tonight for the first time. He flipped over to the rules portion of the program. Dang, Li'l Smasher had her work cut out for her.

Oh, God, he thought, as the realization struck. Ana-MurderPia. That was Pia. The pain-in-the-ass, entitled, practically teenage woman who was trying to steal his job.

And he was about to watch her get her ass kicked by women twice her size wearing roller skates.

He wasn't proud of it, but the thought made him feel better.

Until he looked down in the stands and saw Bernie laughing with Marc and playing with her hair. Playing with her hair! She never did that. They were probably talking about books or hybrid vehicles or something equally dorky. Whatever it was, it sure sounded funny. She never laughed like that with him. At him, yes, but not with him. And once he told her that at the end of the month, she would be putting on a sparkly dress and choosing men in front of a room full of strangers, she definitely would not be laughing.

Colin had to remind himself not to care.

And then the lights went out and the music came on and the announcer called roll and the bout began.

Chapter Thirty-One

Dear Maria,

Why can't men be men anymore? Why do they always want to talk about feelings and use hair products? Where are all the men who want to take care of their women?

>   *Proud Cavewoman in Western Addition*

Dear Cavewoman,

I realize that dating in the Bay Area can feel like a politically correct bubble. San Francisco has a proud history of nonconformity and free thinking, embracing radical ideas like women who can take care of themselves or that the societal suppression of man's natural emotional response is bad for both men and women. However, those men most assuredly still exist. Some of them even exist around here, recent transplants from redder pastures. You can find them at overpriced cigar clubs, bemoaning the fact that women express

*opinions and want to be paid equally for doing the
same work as men. Go on and find yourself a
caveman, but don't come crying to me when your
hands hurt from rubbing that stick against a rock
all day, trying to get some warmth.*

And yes, that is a metaphor.

*Kisses,
Maria*

MARC-WITH-A-C HAD NEVER been to roller derby before.

"I'm kind of surprised you're into it," he told her,
stretching his arm out behind her seat. She could
barely hear him over the din of the bout, but she was
doing her best.

"I wouldn't say I'm into it. I mean, I enjoy it. Women
kicking ass and all. But I don't actually set any of these
dates up."

"Oh, that explains it."

"What do you mean?"

"Nothing. You seem like one of those empowered types.
I can't imagine you'd want to watch women skating
around in skimpy panties."

"They're not strippers."

"Still."

Bernie bit her tongue. She wanted to argue with him,
to say that these women were wearing athletic gear that
they gussied up for themselves, not for the arbitrary male
gaze. But it was no fun arguing with these dates. Not like
it was arguing with Colin. Arguing was kind of their thing.

No, she reminded herself. They didn't have a thing.

"Who're those people down there?" he asked, pointing
to a small cluster of fans sitting on the floor at the curve
of the track.

"Those are the suicide seats. Good view, but slightly dangerous."

"You wanna go down?"

She'd never sat in the suicide seats before. She preferred watching the action from a safe distance away. But where had that ever gotten her?

"Sure." She looked back at Colin, who nodded when she pointed down to the track. He didn't get up to follow, but he seemed to get the message.

Marc-with-a-c was a roller derby convert. His "shut it down" was as loud as any of the pierced, funky-haired folks sitting with them in the suicide seats. Bernie was almost too caught up in the speed and adrenaline to be bothered by it.

"Yes! Cut that bitch off!"

It wasn't that Bernie was a prude about cursing. She believed in freedom of expression like a good San Francisco librarian should. But something about the violence in Marc's tone was making her not love this festive evening out.

"Aw, come on, Ref! Get your head out of your ass!"

That got the ref's attention, and Bernie saw some of the other track judges look at Marc and confer amongst themselves.

"Come on, baby! Shake that little thang!"

"Okay, Marc, that's a little much," she said, even though he probably couldn't hear her.

He was acting like he couldn't hear her; that was for sure. He kept hurling suggestive comments at the smallest member of the squad, calling out her small stature and her short shorts.

Then she stopped skating.

Right in front of them.

She spit out her mouth guard. She looked sweet and delicate, except for that murderous look in her eyes. "You got something to say to me?"

"Get back out there and skate, Tinkerbell!"

"You think you're a big man?" the woman shouted back, then made a gesture so vulgar that Bernie was momentarily impressed and distracted from the angry misogyny of her date. Still, she tried to keep Marc from jumping up, but he was quick for a big man. And then he was charging at the tiny, murderous woman on roller skates.

That was a mistake. Almost before he got close enough to touch her, Tinkerbell pulled back and socked him in the jaw. The arena was dead silent as she made contact. As Marc stumbled backward, the audience burst into a deafening roar, drowning out Bernie's shouts for Marc to calm down, sit down, and they should go. The crowd must have given Marc some energy, because he shook the punch off and went for Tinkerbell again. This time, he was stopped by her padded elbow.

Bernie scooted back, trying to get out from under Marc's stubborn rush of testosterone. Before she could get very far, she was hauled up to her feet and shoved out of the way. It was Colin. Colin, who was now pushing his way in between Marc and Tinkerbell. The crowd around them chanted and hollered. Tinkerbell yelled, "Let me at him, Colin!" Marc started to yell back, but whatever he was about to say was cut off by the two security guards who wrestled him out of the stadium.

The crowd went wild. Tinkerbell raised her arms in victory. Bernie thought she might vomit.

"You wanna get out of here?" Colin asked, and she nodded and grabbed his hand and pulled him outside.

"Are you okay?" he asked once they were out of the arena and it was quiet enough to hear.

"What the hell was that?" asked Bernie, feeling a little dazed.

"Bernie, are you hurt?" Colin had a firm grip on her forearms and had her pinned against the wall with his intense glare.

"No. But did you see that? He went psycho!"

"Sorry about that."

"You didn't do it."

"Well, I appreciate you not blaming my entire gender for one loser's 'roid rage."

"Seriously. That was weird, right?"

"Yeah."

"And look at you, all manly and stuff, breaking up the fight."

"Impressed?"

"He was twice the size of that skater girl. Is it wrong that it felt good to watch her kick his ass?"

"No," he laughed. "Definitely not wrong."

"Hey, that girl knew your name."

"Yeah, we work together."

"At Glaze?"

"No, at my sideline job in a fight club."

"Dang. You fashion people have layers and layers."

"I'll say."

"Should we find Marc?"

Colin hesitated, thinking. "We *should* find him."

"Hmm. But what if we didn't?"

Colin smiled at her and it made her think about last night when she'd cried and he'd comforted her and then kissed her. She wondered what it would be like to kiss him when she wasn't in emotional distress.

So she leaned in to him and found out.

It was still great.

When she pulled back, Colin looked surprised.

"Adrenaline," she said.

"Okay."

"You okay?"

"Definitely."

"Should we go?"

She heard sirens and Colin must have heard them, too.

"Yup."

Chapter Thirty-Two

DAY MAKEUP WAS DIFFERENT from night makeup.

Bernie had learned that from a makeup tutorial video Jeanaeane had sent her before her very first afternoon date. Bernie had hoped day makeup meant no makeup, but no. It meant the same amount of makeup, just applied in a completely different way.

Bernie ignored the video and just put on some mascara. But as she looked in the mirror, she felt a little bland. God, what was she becoming that her practically naked face looked bland to her. That probably wasn't a good sign.

Also, she liked lipstick now.

So she put some on.

She would wait outside for her Uber—Sunday bus service was a little wonky, which meant she'd either be two hours early or an hour late for the date. She supposed she could have asked Colin to come get her, but he hadn't offered, and after the weird way the roller derby date ended, she couldn't blame him for wanting to keep his distance. They didn't even like each other. Why the hell did they keep kissing?

She renewed her determination to Not Be Weird. They'd been spending a lot of time together, and the carousel ride at night had been romantic. It was a moment; they shared it. Last night they both had a lot of adrenaline running through their systems. Another moment. No big deal.

He was a real good kisser.

She shook her head. Good for him, he was a good kisser. So was she, dammit. She'd received many compliments on her kissing. Well, not many, but several. And surely for every compliment she received there were several people who just didn't offer feedback?

Okay. Now she was clutching at straws. But whatever. She was a good kisser. And so was Colin.

Gah.

"Got another date?"

There was a distinct twinkle in Maddie's eye as she squeezed out the door behind her. Al had her walker folded up in one hand and was holding the door open with the other. Starr barked from the front window. The dog had serious FOMO. Bernie smiled at her neighbors and moved out of the way. She took Maddie's arm and, between her and the railing, they got down the five stairs to the sidewalk.

"Picnic in the park," Bernie explained as Al unfolded the walker. "How about you guys?"

"That sounds like a good idea. What do you think, pet?"

Maddie patted her hair. "We're getting haircuts. And then you're taking me to lunch. Don't try to get out of it. I'm not sitting in the dirt when you promised me Thai food."

Al shrugged. "I tried."

"You look very pretty, Bernie." Maddie squeezed her

arm, and Bernie felt a surge go through her. What was it? Pride? Happiness? Or just the general warmth of being appreciated?

Being appreciated for her looks. Hmph.

"You're scowling," Maddie scolded her.

"Sorry. Poker face. Got it."

"Or just learn to take a compliment."

She did have a point.

"Let's try again. Bernie, dear, that lipstick is very fetching."

"Fetching?"

"No, you say, 'Thank you, Maddie.' That's it."

"Thank you, Maddie," Bernie said, obediently.

"Next time, try to sound like you mean it," Al said.

Bernie laughed, at the couple and at herself. She really couldn't take a compliment, could she? When someone complimented your looks, it wasn't an insult to every other part of you, she reminded herself. Maddie liking her lipstick didn't mean that her naked lips looked monstrous and it was about time she finally learned to cover them up. It just meant that Maddie liked her lipstick.

Huh. Epiphanies.

"Okay," she promised. "Thank you, Maddie. I mean it."

"Now, are you going to be nice to your date?" Al asked.

"Oh, don't get her started on being nice," Maddie warned. "Just be yourself, dear. Not fake nice, and not defensive. Just your beautiful self."

"Oh," Bernie said. She kind of felt like crying. That might have been the nicest thing anyone had ever said to her. "Thanks, Maddie."

"There you go!" Maddie said, clapping her hands. "That didn't hurt, did it?"

Bernie laughed and gave Maddie a gentle hug. She waved them down the street just as her Uber pulled up.

The ride to the park wasn't long, but it was enough time for her Maddie-high to fade and those old first-date jitters to come back.

Her phone buzzed, and she read the message from Colin.

Running late.

Her stomach flipped. What was she supposed to do now? She didn't know what her date looked like. She couldn't even remember his name. Bob? Johann? Sanjit? It could be anything!

Here's today's guy:

Attached was a picture of a square-jawed guy with a buzz cut who was, she had to admit, very cute. Not that it mattered.

His name is Matt. He's in sales. I forget what. He's normal.

Blergh, normal. She thought back to the vegan puppeteer. He hadn't been that bad.
Yes, he had.
But normal? She didn't do normal.

Be there in twenty. Didn't want you to think I stood you up. ;)

Ugh.

Don't think your winky face is getting you out of trouble. See you soon, unless Matt sweeps me off my feet.

Too normal for you.

Why are you setting me up with guys you know I won't like??

Quit texting. You're on a date.

She wasn't on a date yet, she thought. But then they were pulling up to the entrance to the Presidio, and there was a guy with a buzz cut pulling a blanket out of his trunk. Maybe Matt. If so, she liked what he was doing to his pants, bending over like that. Not that she judged him on his physical attributes. He squinted over at their car and she gave him a little wave, figuring she could just dive down to the floor if this wasn't her date. Because that would be totally smooth.

It wasn't necessary, though, because as he walked closer, she recognized his face from her phone. She grabbed her purse and went to open the door, but he got there first and held it open for her.

"Melissa?" he asked.

"Hi. Matt, right?"

"Wow, you're so much more beautiful in person."

"Thank you, Matt."

So that's how it's done, she thought as Matt helped her out of the car. That's how you start a blind date.

The Presidio was a wonderful park with some of the best views of the city and the bay. It was one of her favorite places to walk, and she'd spent many hours there when she first moved to the city. And the sky was clear, which meant they could actually enjoy the view.

Well, she would have been able to enjoy the view. If only the wind would leave her hair out of her face.

"More wine?" Matt asked, holding up the bottle.

It was a lovely wine, and she would love another glass. But the wind. So annoying. Also, she wished she was wearing pants. She wasn't sure if she could juggle another glass of red wine while holding her dress over her knees.

She gave up and crossed her legs, tucking her skirt between her legs. Not the most ladylike way to sit, but it was better than flashing her underwear.

Although she was wearing some new Makeda-required underwear. Maybe it would be good to flash it. See if she could get some more compliments out of this guy.

But right now she didn't think Matt was interested in her underwear. He was telling her about the amazing vineyard in Napa that he'd bought this wine from, and how there was another vintage that was better, but he was saving that for his wedding day. And how he'd visited a vineyard in Argentina over the winter and he was really thinking about going into business with them.

"Wow, Argentina. That'd be something," she said. "Do you speak Spanish?"

"Un poquito," he said, and she spoke just enough Spanish to know that he meant "a little." "There's a foreman who takes care of a lot of that, though."

"A lot of the speaking?"

"With the workers, that kind of thing. I won't really be involved in that."

"But you'll be a partner."

He smiled at her. "An investor. I'll supply the capital. I won't have to get my hands dirty. That's not how business works."

He winked at her.

That made her want to toss his subpar vintage wine in his smug, patronizing face. But then what would Colin say when he showed up and she was sitting alone in the wind? Instead, she took a deep breath. He wasn't that bad, this Matt. And he was right; she didn't know anything about business. She'd never worked for a for-profit business. And he really was very handsome.

"So have you always been interested in wine?" she asked, politely.

"Nah. I mostly got into it as a way to impress women." He chuckled. How very charming he was. "I was strictly a beer guy—and domestic beers." She thought she saw him shudder. "But I figured if I wanted to impress a better class of women, I needed to cultivate better taste."

She bit her tongue.

"So tell me about yourself. What are you into?"

She took a sip of her wine. It actually was good. It made Matt's condescension seem a little more bearable. Or it would once she had another glass.

Sigh. She needed to try, at least. "You know, this experience has been so strange. I feel like I can hardly remember what I was into before I was dating all the time. I read a lot. I still read a lot, just a little less. I saw my friends a lot more."

"But now you're really into dating?"

"I wouldn't say I'm *really* into it." More like contractually obligated to complete it. Even if it wasn't as terrible as it had been at the beginning of the month. And she didn't technically have a contract. But she couldn't leave Colin in the lurch.

Not that he didn't deserve it, pushy as he was.

Ah, who was she kidding? She couldn't even muster up the energy to be mad at him. She'd agreed to his scheme. He was following the rules.

Well, most of the time he was following the rules. There were also the times when she broke the rules, and he followed along.

So, he was following along while she rewrote the rules?

"What are you thinking about?"

"Huh?"

"Your face. You looked like you were confused about something."

"Oh, that's just my face. It's nothing." Just Colin. And how you can think you know someone, and then they surprise you.

And wasn't that the truth. She looked at Matt with fresh eyes. So he gave off a strong whiff of patronizing. There were worse things than trying to be nice, right?

"You hungry?" he asked, pulling containers out of the brown shopping bag he'd carried into the park.

"Starved," she said, and meant it. She'd woken up too late to eat a real breakfast, and then she'd been running around trying to get ready for her date so she skipped lunch. She did not, as a rule, skip meals. She sort of wished Matt would hurry the hell up unpacking that bag.

"Thanks for bringing the food," she said.

"Hey, when I take a girl out, I take care of her."

He's being nice, not patronizing, she reminded herself.

"Wow, this looks great." Her stomach growled. "Do you cook?"

"No, it's from this great little market in my neighborhood. My girlf—" Matt stopped, container of pasta salad frozen in midair.

"Your what?" Bernie asked. Surely she'd misheard. Surely he didn't just start to say girlfriend?

"Nothing. It's a great little market. Everything they have is delicious."

Maybe he meant ex-girlfriend. She needed to give him the benefit of the doubt. He's not patronizing, and he doesn't already have a girlfriend, she told herself.

"Olive?" He passed her a jar. She didn't take it.

"Matt."

"Hmm?"

"Do you have a girlfriend?"

"What? No! What? That's crazy! Come on. No way. Okay, fine, yes."

Bernie blinked at him a few times, soaking in the newest twist in her ridiculous dating life.

She did her best to stand up without flashing her underwear at him—he didn't deserve it, the jerk—and she stomped down the hill to the parking lot.

"You owe me lunch."

Colin checked his watch. He'd pulled up to the park five minutes ago, which meant Bernie had been on her date for about half an hour.

He'd been planning to wait five more minutes before doing a casual walk-by to see how the date was going.

And now here was Bernie, adorable skirt and nice hair blowing in the wind, looking like she was going to kill him. At least they were back to normal.

"What happened? Where's Matt?"

"He's up there," she said, pointing up the hill to where Matt was sitting alone on a blanket. "He's probably on the phone with his girlfriend."

"His what?"

"Don't you screen these guys at all? First a walking psychopath, now a guy with a girlfriend?"

"I didn't think I would have to ask if a guy had a girlfriend when he's signing up for a dating story!"

She snorted at him. He wanted to protest her unfairly low opinion of men, but he couldn't. He should have screened for girlfriends.

"Let's go." She brushed past him and started walking across the parking lot.

"Where're we going?" he asked, rushing to keep up with her.

"I'm starving. You're buying me lunch."

Chapter Thirty-Three

"You must be sick of it."

Bernie put down her beer and picked up the container of takeout noodles. He watched, fascinated, as she dangled them into her mouth.

"Of what?" he asked. He'd lost track of the conversation.

"A whole month without dating."

He took a swig of his beer. He hadn't really thought about it. But he'd been out of the game for a few weeks before he started this story, and Bernie was right, he hadn't been on a date since. Not that there would have been time. But until she mentioned it, he hadn't really missed it.

Of course, now that he'd had the realization, it should have been a blow to his pride, to go this long without even a first date, but he felt fine about it.

"I guess I'm just living vicariously through you."

She snorted. "That doesn't sound very satisfying."

"No, I guess it's not." And yet, he was fine. "I'll get back out there once we're done."

"Women of San Francisco, beware!"

"That's right. Beware of all of your dreams coming true. Ow!"

She hit him on the shoulder. It didn't hurt, but he rubbed the spot like it did.

"I'm still not convinced that dating is fun," she said.

"Has it really been that bad?"

"No, I guess not. I mean, some of them have been bad. . . ."

"Are you saying you're not into vegan puppeteers?"

"No. And I could have fallen in love with that poet, gosh, if only he had talked even more about his mother."

"Hmm. That would have been very sexy."

"Very sexy."

He watched her, slouched back into the couch in her living room, her feet up on the coffee table surrounded by cardboard containers. She looked different. It wasn't the makeup or the hair—the hair was the same, thanks to the wind. No, he realized it was because she looked relaxed. He'd known her for almost a month now, and this was the most relaxed he'd ever seen her. No fancy dinners, no raucous nightlife, just kicking back with a beer.

He liked that. Hell, he liked her, even though she annoyed the shit out of him.

"It has been interesting, though," she said.

"Interesting? That's not exactly how a guy wants to hear a date described."

"No, I just mean in general. I know you think I'm a total hermit—"

"No, I don't," he lied.

"But I do like meeting new people. And I can't imagine another situation where I would meet a disc golf-playing graphic designer."

"No, I suppose not."

"People are interesting, you know?"

"Just not necessarily for dating."

She sighed. "Mostly, yeah."

"Well, unfortunately, the story was not thirty friends in thirty days."

"I'd be into that story."

"I don't think I could sell my editor on that one."

"Too bad."

"Besides, don't you like the energy and tension of dating?"

"Maybe. Sort of. Not really, no."

"Are you sure?"

"No. I mean, the nervousness I used to feel is getting less debilitating. It's kind of pleasant now. And I have had some good times, even though they're not necessarily romantic times. But it hasn't been really sexy, you know?"

"I tried my best to find hot guys for you," he said, and felt immediately ridiculous. "Well, the girls at the office tried their best to find hot guys for you."

"Maybe I'm just a little frustrated."

"But I thought you were having fun."

She turned her face to him without lifting her head off the couch. "That's not what I mean."

"Oh," he said. "Oh. That kind of frustrated."

"Yeah, that kind of frustrated."

"Well," he said, hedging. "What about Ben? He didn't rock your world?"

She sighed. "No. We stayed up all night listening to music."

"So not . . . ?"

"Is it terrible that I only pretended we slept together because I could see it bothered you?"

"Hey, it didn't bother me. But I guess that's not a good idea on the first date, right?"

"Psh," she said. "You've never slept with someone on the first date?"

"Well, sure, but . . . oh, I see. Double standard."

She smiled at him. "You're learning! Anyway, none of them really felt right. Not even Ben."

He felt relieved. He wasn't sure why.

"Of course, it didn't help that you were always there."

"Are you saying I cock blocked you?"

She shrugged into the couch.

"Well, you haven't exactly been great for my love life. As you just pointed out."

"Hmm," she said around a mouthful of beer.

"Hmm," he said, wondering what she was thinking. Whatever it was, he enjoyed watching her think it. He'd miss that face when this was all over.

"We could fix that," she said.

He smiled noncommittally, still enjoying the view.

Then his brain caught up.

"Wait, what?"

She shrugged again. "I'm just saying. We're two red-blooded Americans."

"Americans?"

"You know, the expression."

He had no idea what she was talking about.

"I mean we're two moderately attractive straight people. . . ."

"What do you mean 'moderately'?"

"Okay, we're two superhot straight people who are not totally repulsed by each other." She looked at him for some sign of agreement.

"Sure," he said, because he was not repulsed by her.

Quite the opposite.

In fact, he was pretty attracted to her. Physically, in a way he hadn't been the first time he met her. He didn't think it was because her looks had changed. Maybe. Maybe it was because she was wearing better clothes now. But he didn't feel attracted to her when he first saw her makeover. Which might have had something to do with the permanent scowl she wore that day in the office.

Now she only scowled when she wasn't laughing at herself.

And he liked that about her. Sure, she had some unfortunate battle-ax tendencies, but she always seemed conscious of the ridiculousness of any situation, and she was just as willing to laugh at herself as she was to laugh at anybody else. More so.

None of that, however, had anything to do with the fact that, if he was not mistaken, his librarian project was propositioning him.

"I'm just saying," she went on, inching into a more upright seated position, "we both have an itch to scratch, so why not?"

Why not? He could think of many complications if they slept together. Like the fact that he was writing a story about her. But it wasn't as if he was her doctor or her teacher. He was a writer. He wasn't even really a reporter. Being unbiased wasn't really a consideration in his pieces.

So . . . why not?

She sat up all the way, then leaned toward him. "Right? No big deal."

No big deal, he thought, and he couldn't really think of anything else because she had put down her beer and was coming toward him, unbuttoning her blouse and leaning over him.

"If you have an objection, now would be the time to voice it," she breathed in his ear.

Objection. He should object. Why? He forgot. It was

taking all of his brain power to remember how to breathe. But when he breathed, all he got was the scent of her, sweet and citrusy, and then his beer was out of his hand and on the coffee table next to hers, and her shirt was on the floor, and her hands were on the arms of the easy chair and he tilted back, but not away from her because she was right there with him.

Colin growled.

She'd never heard a man growl before. Not at her. Not for a reason she wanted to be growled at.

But oh, she liked this growl. This growl had Colin surging off the chair and sweeping her up with him, dropping them both on the couch with a bounce.

"Sorry," he gasped. "That bra affects me."

She smiled up at him and squirmed under the pleasant weight of his body covering hers.

"It's new," she told him.

But she didn't give a crap about the bra. That wasn't true. She liked the bra. It was surprisingly comfortable, but that was not her main consideration when Colin's mouth was an inch from hers and all he was doing was smiling down at her.

"Are you gonna kiss me?" she breathed.

"Uh-huh," he said, but he didn't. He just pinned her down with his eyes, examining every part of her face.

If her face ruined this for her . . . she wasn't going to let that happen. She wanted this. She wanted him. Maybe it was just a month of pent-up sexual frustration, but she didn't care. There was a man on top of her, and he was the man she wanted. So she picked her head up and closed that pathetic distance between them.

And then it was on. She'd kissed him before—twice—

but nothing matched the ferocity of this kiss. She felt it, too, like they had to get at each other *now* or it would be too late. Too late for what? She didn't care; she just kissed and kissed and wrapped her legs around his while his hands went exploring all over that new bra.

And then he broke the kiss, but she wasn't mad because he trailed hot kisses down her neck. She shivered and unwrapped her legs so she could get the leverage she needed to pull his shirt off without dislodging that tongue from doing whatever it was doing to her skin. But he was distracting and buttons were hard, and she couldn't get the damn thing off.

"Help," she urged, and he sat up and tore his shirt over his head, which was a mistake because the wrists were still buttoned.

"Crap," he growled as he pulled at the inside-out arms of his shirt.

"Stop," she laughed at him, then shoved him back so she could sit up and help him get out of the damn shirt.

The process was made infinitely more difficult by the fact that, while she fought with the buttons, he was continuing his exploration of all the sensitive spots on her neck. And sternum. And through her bra.

Finally, finally he was free and his arms were around her, but she didn't let him push her back down. Instead, she pushed him back so she was straddling him on the couch and had a chance to admire shirtless Colin.

"I hope you're not objectifying me," he told her.

"I'm not," she said as she ran her fingers over the ridges of muscle on his chest and his stomach. "Your personality is really hot."

He threw his head back and laughed, and there was all that gorgeous skin for her to explore, so she did. He was hard and smooth except in places where he wasn't, like the smattering of hair across his pecs, or the line that led down into the waist of his pants. She was really getting into it—and so was Colin, if the rise and fall of his breathing was any indication—when she felt his hands go around her back and the clasp on her bra sprang open.

"Hey." She started to tease him about . . . well, she wasn't sure what because he was looking at her with such intensity, with such want, that she just sat up and let him take in her breasts with his eyes and his hands and his mouth.

"Bernie," he said after a few minutes of her squirming helplessly on his lap while his tongue did wicked things to her. "Bernie, can we—"

"Bedroom?"

"Yes, please."

He had excellent manners.

He also had excellent core strength, which he demonstrated by squeezing his arms around her waist and hoisting both of them off the couch. It was a blatant show of masculinity and it was also a testament to his talented mouth that she did not even consider saying out loud the gender dichotomy joke that raced through her brain and right back out again as he took her mouth and she held on tight.

Their blind, conjoined shuffle took them a little longer to get into the bedroom, but once they did, it was so worth it. Colin tossed her on her unmade bed, and she retaliated by tearing off his jeans. So it was only fair that he reach up under her skirt and pull her panties off. It was her turn to get him more naked, but she made the executive decision that a condom was a more urgent need, so she scrambled up to her bedside table and rifled through the drawer. She knocked a few books over in the process, but that wasn't entirely her fault. Colin was all growly again and up behind her, pushing her skirt over her hips and leaning his chest into her back. She could tell that he had taken the initiative to remove his underwear, which made the dig through hair ties and bookmarks and all the junk that had accumulated in her bedside table all the more difficult.

"Hurry up, please," he growled into her ear, both demanding and polite. She wiggled back against him, just to see what would happen, and what happened was he bit her earlobe and cursed and Bernie thought that if she died right then, she would die happy.

But not as happy as she would die if she found the damn condom.

And then there it was, a whole row of them, and she turned in victory, but Colin was not interested in sharing her triumph. Well, he was, but his involved less "ah ha! Hooray!" and more tearing the foil wrapper and sheathing himself and untwisting her legs so she was open to him.

"Ready?" he whispered as he hovered over her, his whole body poised.

"Yes, yes," she whispered back, urgently, and pulled him closer. She arched up as he entered her, cruelly slowly, and she looked up to see the wicked glint in his eye so she squeezed and the glint turned less teasing and more growly, and she wrapped her legs and arms around him and held on.

Chapter Thirty-Four

THE BEST EVER.

That was the most articulate way he could think of to describe making love to Bernie. She was perfect. She was equal parts teasing and hot and daring. She was lying out, resplendent in her naked glory, and Colin wasn't thinking about how he'd never had sex with a woman like her before, a woman who thought like her or acted like her or looked like her. He was just thinking about her, and how he wanted her again, and how he might probably love her.

Which was clearly just the sex talking.

The best sex ever talking.

Colin idly picked up a wave of Bernie's hair and ran his fingers through it. "Your thirty days are almost over."

"Mmm," she said, and snuggled into his chest. He'd miss this, burning off this energy together.

It was just forced proximity, he told himself. He'd spent every day of an entire month with her. That was more time than he'd spent with anyone in his life that he wasn't related to. Just look at how he didn't even like her when they first met. How else could he explain the warm feelings except that he'd gotten used to her?

Except that he didn't really not like her when they met. He thought she was weird and prickly and that she would be terrible to work with, but he didn't dislike her. He had the feeling that she disliked him, but he didn't dislike her.

She definitely didn't dislike him now. She might not want to hang out and be besties after next week, but she'd stopped giving him that mildly horrified, completely puzzled look that said, "I know we are both human beings but I do not understand at all how you operate."

Man, he could even interpret her facial expressions.

She did make a lot of facial expressions. It was what got her here in the first place.

He was pretty grateful for the facial expressions. He dropped her hair and twisted so he was lying on his side, facing her. Even with her eyes closed, she made a face of displeasure as she was dislodged from his chest to the pillow.

"Stop looking at me," she muttered.

"I'm not."

"I can feel it."

"It's just because you're so cute when you're asleep."

She turned and buried her face in the pillow. He thought he heard her mumble something, but he wasn't sure that he heard right. Surely she didn't want to do that to him, after he had so clearly rocked her socks last night?

Just to make sure, he ran his hand up her hip, feeling the skin still warm from sleep.

She sighed, and he let his hands explore a little more.

This time, when she turned to look at him, she gave him a sleepy smile. "Remember when we hated each other?"

"Nope."

"Me, neither."

He pulled her a little closer, kissed her gently.

"This is weird."

That was not what he liked to hear when he was trying to get a little morning nookie.

"Don't you think it's weird?" She put her hand on his chest and looked up at him. "Think about the circumstances that got us to this point."

"I don't really want to think about circumstances." He lifted her hand and kissed the pulse at her wrist. Then he leaned in and kissed the pulse at her neck.

She put her arms around him, but she kept talking. "Sometimes I think I really do get in my own way too much." She sure did. He nipped her neck, let his hands get a little creative under the sheets. She gasped a little. But she kept talking. "Left on my own, I never would have done any of this. I had to get a push from Marcie and Dave and Starr—"

"The dog?"

"She's a very persuasive dog."

Clearly, he needed to work on his persuasiveness, if she was still thinking about a dog.

"I even got a push from Maria."

Colin's hands stopped their explorations. His heart might have stopped, too.

"Maria?" Surely not *the* Maria.

"Don't laugh, but you know that advice column, Take a Letter, Maria?"

Yeah, he knew it.

"I wrote her a letter. When I was contemplating your offer."

"Was that before or after your heart-to-heart with the dog?" he asked, hoping he sounded light and breezy. He sure didn't feel light and breezy.

"She told me I should live in the gray areas. That's where all the interesting stuff happens."

Oh, God. He remembered that letter. It was someone trying to decide between dying on the sword for her principles or seizing an unexpected opportunity.

Of course that was Bernie.

Of course she listened to Maria. Maria was contrary and ornery. She could be Bernie's sister.

"She was right," Bernie said softly, then draped her leg over his hip and started to explore his pulse points. He hoped she didn't notice that his heart was about to beat out of his chest.

He had to tell her.

This was definitely going to ruin any chances he had of morning nookie.

"Bernie."

"Mmm."

"I have to tell you something."

"Are you married?" she murmured into his neck while her hands slid under the covers.

"Uh . . . no."

"Then it can wait."

"It'll just take a second."

She turned her face so the pillow muffled her groan, then propped up her head, her face pasted with a falsely bright smile.

"Good morning, Colin. What is so urgent that it couldn't wait until after morning nookie?"

He put his hand on her naked hip under the covers. For some reason, he thought that skin to skin contact would make the news go down smoother. Like a spoonful of sugar, but skin.

Why was he doing this now? Why was he ruining a perfectly good afterglow with confessions? He couldn't explain it, like he couldn't explain anything about his relationship with Bernie. He just wanted her to know him.

"You know how you wrote that letter to Maria?"

"You mean the letter I just now described to you? Yes, I do. That feels like forever ago. God, that was back when I was just a meme. That was before I was a dating sensation."

"Sensational." He kissed her nose. He couldn't help it.

"I shouldn't have been embarrassed about writing that e-mail," she said, her eyes drifting closed. "I love Maria. She always gives good advice."

This was promising, he hoped. Maybe he was just desperate.

"Do you ever wonder who Maria is?"

"Mmm-hmm."

He couldn't decide if this was easier with her eyes closed. On the one hand, he didn't feel like she was looking into the depths of his soul. On the other hand, he wasn't sure if she was listening.

"I always pictured someone like Maddie," she said sleepily. "But like, Maddie's wild older sister. Someone who's seen it all and done it all and is now content to just grace womankind with all of her hard-earned knowledge."

Bernie was the only woman he knew who could form complete sentences when she was half-asleep.

Another thing he liked about her. Was that a weird thing to like?

"I know who she is," he said, and watched, fascinated, as that statement registered behind her closed eyes.

She opened them, and he saw that she was dying of curiosity.

"You do?"

He nodded, suddenly very, very nervous. She thought Maria was a wise old lady. Well, why shouldn't she? That

was what he was going for. But now that it was too late
to turn back, he was afraid that she would be mad. That
she would feel like he'd betrayed her by doing this. That she
would think that he was trying to pull a fast one on all of
womankind. Why was he doing this to himself? Why did
he have to tell her? He hadn't told anyone, not even Steph,
and he told her everything. Mostly.

He should keep this a secret.

But he didn't want to keep any secrets from Bernie.

Well, he thought. It was fun while it lasted.

"It's me."

"Hmm?" She still looked curious, but now also confused.

"I'm Maria." There. That should clear it up.

"You're . . . what?" Everything ran across her face so
quickly, he couldn't even properly read it all: anger,
maybe. Definitely more confusion. Surprise. And a lot
more that he couldn't figure out.

"I write that column," he said, banging that final nail
into his coffin. "I'm Take a Letter, Maria."

She turned her face into her pillow again and he heard
muffled snorts, and he thought maybe she was having a
stroke.

When she turned back to him, her eyes were wet with
tears. "You?" she asked him, and he saw that she was
laughing. She was laughing at him.

Well, at least she wasn't mad.

He shrugged, running his hand up to her waist, then
back down her hip again. "I was trying to figure out
women. It was just kind of a lark. Then somehow someone found it, and people started sending in actual questions and . . . you're not mad?"

"Why would I be mad?"

"I've been leading a secret double life. Most women would be mad."

She put a hand on his chest. "I think you know that I am not most women."

"No, you're definitely not." He pulled her closer and took a deep breath of that sweet spot at her pulse, then kissed her there.

"This is interesting, though," she said.

He almost hated to ask. "Interesting how?"

"Hold on, let me break this down. You're a man—"

"Yup."

"—giving women advice in the guise of an older, wiser woman. What does it mean that I thought your advice was really good?"

"That I'm a really smart guy?"

"Should I feel tricked? I mean, your sass was one thing when it was a fellow woman doling it out. But a man . . ."

"It wasn't to trick. It was just . . . it's just for fun."

"Hmm." She wrapped her arm around his neck and pulled him closer. "I don't know if I trust your idea of fun."

"Hey!"

"You told me dating was fun. What has been fun about dating so far?"

"Umm . . . it was fun to get yelled at by a puppeteer?"

"I don't know if that counts as fun. But it was definitely a special experience. Dear Maria, thank you for giving me the unique experience of being verbally abused by a militant vegan with his hand up a stuffed squirrel's butt."

"Is this going to be a thing now?"

"Me calling you Maria? Probably," she said with a smile.

"You have a really messed-up idea of fun."

"You're the one with a *Mrs. Doubtfire* complex."

She smiled even wider, but then she kissed him and rolled him onto his back and it turned out that they did agree on some things that were fun. Mind-blowing, sheet-grabbing, sweaty, naked fun.

Chapter Thirty-Five

"OH, GLORIOUS SUN GODS, we worship thee. Bestow thy blessings upon thy humble, worthless, melanin-starved servants!"

"Knock it off, you're blocking my sun."

Bernie smiled into her book. Dave and Marcie really were like an old married couple. Except Al and Maddie didn't bicker as much as these two did.

She'd woken up this morning to a long to-do list and heavy fog. Her plan was to spend the day doing laundry and getting organized for her return to work. She'd been off for a little more than three weeks, and really off—no e-mail, no professional journal reading; she hadn't even checked her favorite academic blogs. She wondered what had been happening in the world of academic librarianship. Maybe everyone had decided on open access journals while she was gone.

Maybe they'd turned to Maria for advice, and she'd . . . hmm. What could Colin tell them about libraries? He'd picked up some of her feminism; maybe he'd picked up some of her professional interests, too.

She still couldn't believe Colin was Maria. It made her

laugh every time she thought of it. Colin! Giving out all that good advice! Who knew he had it in him?

"Funny book?"

Bernie squinted up at Marcie. Her friend tilted the cover up and read the title. "*The Trial* by Franz Kafka. Sounds hilarious."

Bernie flipped the book over. Marcie was right. Huh. She thought she'd grabbed a much more fun book on her way out the door. Well, it was their fault, not hers. She was supposed to be spending her afternoon doing chores so she could be clear and focused on her movie date tonight and not thinking about the mountain of laundry she had to do or how messed up her sheets were because she and Colin left them in a tangled mess . . .

They didn't know about her . . . whatever with Colin. But she couldn't blame them for dragging her out in this weather. It was foggy in her neighborhood, as usual, but in the Mission it was hot and sunny, like an actual summer day. When the city's weird microclimates gave them a window of summer, she felt a moral and meteorological obligation to participate.

Dolores Park was packed, but enjoyably so. There were blanket farms everywhere, with families and friends and dogs all set up. Starr was having a field day letting everyone know where her territory was. Someone had a badminton tournament going. There were multiple Frisbees and soccer balls flying around. It was a good day.

"Bernie! Quit reading! We're celebrating!"

"I am celebrating," she said, tossing her book—which she hadn't really been reading—aside. She lay back and let the sun warm her face.

"We should celebrate with drinks and dancing!"

"I'm going to celebrate with knocking your lights out

if you don't calm down," Marcie told Dave. "And get out of my sun."

"Did you put on sunblock?" he asked her.

"Shut up."

"Uh-uh. I'm not nursing your pathetic sunburn again. And if you get skin cancer, I'm leaving you for another man."

Marcie grumbled something that Bernie couldn't hear, but she reached for the tube of sunblock and slathered it on her shoulders and nose.

"Thank you, my love," Dave said, and he flopped down on the blanket next to her. He pulled off his shirt and turned his back to her. She grumbled again, but squirted more sunblock into her hands and rubbed it into his back.

"Don't fall asleep, Bernie," he warned her. "I want to grill you on your romantic foibles."

"Ugh," Bernie said, and tossed her arm over her eyes. "I'm not asleep."

Someone, from somewhere in the park, was picking a ukulele. Bernie recognized the strains of a recent pop song and started humming along.

"Is she singing?" Marcie asked. "Dang, you better ask about those romantic foibles."

"There are no foibles to talk about," Bernie insisted.

"Then why are you so happy?"

"I don't know. Sun gods?"

"Get real." Marcie leaned over and pulled Bernie's arm away from her face. "You seem to have much less agita than usual."

"Agita?"

"Yes. Usually, you look like you're kind of having fun but you're always ready for the other shoe to drop. But now you're smiling. Quit smiling! It's weirding me out!"

"Stop," Bernie laughed. "I don't know. It's nice out. I'm happy."

"Must be all those pheromones," Dave suggested. "Being around all that man-energy."

"Hardly," she insisted. But maybe that was it. Her last few dates hadn't necessarily gone any better than her first week of dating. In fact, a few of them had gone decidedly worse. But somehow it seemed less dire. Less hopeless. That was it. Despite having absolutely no evidence that she was on some kind of path to romantic success, she felt hopeful.

Hopeful of what? That she'd end up with a relationship? That wasn't it. She didn't care about being in a relationship. That wasn't the goal of this experiment anyway. She just wanted to prove that she was not undateable. And she wasn't. She was totally dateable, and maybe, when this whole thing was over, she might go out on more dates. It might not be as much fun, without Colin to debrief to afterward . . . well, that wasn't always fun. Infuriating.

No, it was fun.

Damn, what was she going to do when this was over? What would she do when she didn't have Colin to argue with, to prove that she, while technically dateable, was not just one of those women whose primary goal in life was to pair off with the first guy who didn't totally repulse her? If Colin didn't offer his unsolicited opinion, how was she supposed to form her own opinion by arguing the exact opposite?

Ugh, she was totally one of those women.

Totally dependent on a man.

"Now she looks pissed," Dave said. "I swear, I would pay so much to hear what goes on in that head of yours."

"Why pay when you can see it on her face?" Marcie asked.

"Do you think I'm getting normal?" Bernie asked, sitting up.

Dave grabbed Starr as she started to run after an errant tennis ball. "Uh," Dave said. "How do I put this nicely? There's no way in hell you could ever be normal."

"Thank you," she said. She was pretty sure she meant it.

"What do you mean, 'normal'?" Marcie asked.

"I don't know. I'm going out on all these dates and it's making me happy. Am I just like all those other women out there?" She waved at the population of San Francisco, now happily frolicking in Dolores Park.

"Do you mean like other straight women? Other women with a healthy sex drive who pursue the means to sate their sexual appetites?" Marcie asked.

"I mean like all those women whose primary goal in life is to get a man."

Dave flopped back onto the blanket with a disgusted sigh. Starr settled happily on his stomach.

"Bernie, you have got to get this chip off your shoulder. You're going out on dates. You're making out with a few guys."

And sleeping with one, Bernie thought. She just hadn't told anybody about that yet.

"That doesn't mean you're signing a June Cleaver contract. You're not on a path to marriage, and even if you were, who cares? You're obsessed with being defined by your singleness. That's just as bad as being defined by a relationship."

"No, it's not."

"Yes, it is. You're sticking to some arbitrary, intellectual definition of who you think you should be, instead of being who you are."

"And who I am is in a relationship?"

"No! Grr, I'm going to hit you."

"Don't hit her, Marce. What she means is, you are you, whether you're single or in a relationship. Bernie is Bernie. Single Bernie is the same as Boyfriend Bernie. The constant is Bernie. Get it?"

She got it. She sort of got it. She got it in her head, anyway.

And, truth be told, she got it in her heart, too. That was probably what that happy feeling was about, way back a few minutes ago when she had allowed herself to be happy for no reason. Because she had a reason. The reason was that she was Bernie, and she was dating, but she was still Bernie. And she was sleeping with Colin, and she was still Bernie.

"I can't wait until you guys go through an identity crisis so I can console you about it," she said, but her bite didn't really have any bite to it.

"Hey, I'm just between polyamories at the moment. I have a date with two guys I've been talking to online tonight," Marcie said.

"Really?"

"We're going to the movies! Just like normal people do," she said, shooting a pointed look at Bernie. But a laughing pointed look, so Bernie laughed.

"I'll save you a seat," she said.

"Please don't," Bernie said.

"You're not supposed to date without me," a voice said from above Bernie. She knew that voice. She looked up.

It was Colin.

There was that happy feeling again.

Maybe there was something to those pheromones people kept talking about.

"Hey," she said, shielding her eyes from the blessed, blessed sun. "What're you doing here?"

"It's sunny," he said, as if no more explanation was needed. Which was true. "And I'm taking my sister for a walk."

He pointed behind him to a woman in shorts and a ponytail who was talking to a group of women on the blanket farm next to theirs.

"Steph! So good to see you!"

Bernie hopped up and enveloped Steph in a warm hug. She was all about the happiness today.

"What, no hug for me?" Colin asked.

"I'll give him a hug," Marcie muttered.

"Bernie!" Steph said, hugging Bernie back tightly. "I feel like I should apologize to you."

"Why?"

"If you weren't such a cool person, I wouldn't have recognized you in that meme and none of this would have happened." She waved at her brother, the "this" that had happened to Bernie.

"Oh, well." Did Bernie regret all that had happened? The meme and the dates and the makeover? And the Colin?

Must be the sunshine, because she didn't regret a thing.

"It's enough that you remember me as cool," she told Steph, and she meant it.

"You know you're the cool librarian at Richmond."

"What? No, I'm not cool."

"Yes! You're the only one under eighty—"

"Hey!" Liz was in her fifties. And Maxwell Dean was younger than that.

"Well, at least you're the only one who doesn't try too hard to be hip."

"It's the clogs," Dave said.

"Leave my clogs out of this," Bernie said. "Steph was just telling me that I'm cool."

"She said the cool librarian. There's a difference," Colin said with an arched brow.

Steph gave her brother a playful shove. "Listen, when I was a dumb college kid trying to figure out why I liked girls so much and also trying to pass my classes . . . you were good, Bernie."

"Well, you were good, too. Most of the time."

"Ha! I was terrible."

"But when you were good, you were good."

"And," Steph continued, turning to Dave and Marcie and Starr, "she helped me with my schoolwork and introduced me to Susan Sontag and bell hooks—"

"Okay, you're embarrassing me. What have you been up to?"

"And why are you blocking my sun?" Marcie asked.

Bernie rolled her eyes. "Are you guys in a hurry? Do you want to join us?"

Steph looked at her brother, then sat down on the corner of the blanket. Bernie sat, then scooched over to make room for Colin. She resisted the urge to lean into his chest and use him as a back support. Barely.

Steph talked about her job and meeting with the mayor and community groups and Bernie listened, mostly, but she was very distracted by Colin's smell. He smelled good. She wished they weren't here, in this crowd of people, so she could lean back on him and smell him and soak up the sunshine and Colin.

Whoa. That was unexpected. And kind of intense. You don't really like him, she reminded herself. You just like fighting with him and then sleeping with him. She looked over at him, admiring his strong jaw as he gazed out over the park. God, she really wanted to kiss that jaw.

Then he turned and caught her looking and gave her a warm smile that would have melted her insides if she liked him.

"Are you relieved that your dates are almost over?"

Bernie turned back to Steph, and she caught the glance that passed between Dave and Marcie. She made a mental note to remind them later that she did not like Colin.

Besides, the dates were almost over. Then she wouldn't have a reason to see him anymore.

That thought put a big ol' rain cloud over her happiness.

Even though it didn't matter because she didn't like him.

"Um, yeah," Bernie said to Steph.

"I can tell by your face that you're lying."

"That's just my face!"

"You're not relieved?" Colin asked.

"No! Of course I am! This has been the most exhausting three weeks of my life, and I have to go back to work next week. I can't imagine doing both."

"Dating and working? I can see you've learned a lot of valuable lessons from our time together."

"Shut up." She gave Colin a shove. "I mean going out with someone new every day. I'm glad tonight is just a nice, normal date."

"Because all of your normal dates have been so normal," Dave said.

"Oh, man," Steph said. "I've never been so happy to be gay in my life. Some of those guys really put you through the ringer. I want to hear about the stuff Colin left out of his articles."

"You read my articles?" Colin asked with obvious surprise.

"Shut up. Of course I did. They're about Bernie."

"Have you noticed the women in your life tell you to shut up a lot?" Dave asked.

"Shut up," said Marcie.

"I can't wait to see who you pick on Friday," Steph said.

"What?"

"All thirty of those guys in one room. Well, twenty-nine, unless Colin's inviting the guy who stood you up. Which you totally shouldn't, by the way."

"Steph—" Colin warned.

"One room?"

"Did Makeda pick out something fabulous for you to wear? She's kind of nuts, isn't she? I love her."

"Wait, what?"

"Do you have any idea who you'll choose? I'm voting for the wedding crasher. What do you guys think?" Steph turned to Dave and Marcie, who looked at Bernie for an explanation. But she didn't have one, so she looked at Colin, who was suddenly avoiding her gaze.

"Colin?" she said.

"Oh my God, wait. Colin! You haven't told her yet?"

"Told me what?"

"I was going to, today. When I picked you up for the date."

"Told me what, Colin?"

Colin took a deep breath, and Bernie braced herself.

"My editor wants to have a party to wrap up the series."

"Okay . . ."

"And she invited all of your dates—including the one

who stood you up—so you can choose one to continue seeing."

"Like a reality show?"

"No! Like . . . like a happy ending."

"But this was never about a happy ending! This was just about dating."

"Yes, but isn't that what dating's about? Finding the happy ending?"

"No! That's exactly the kind of narrative I did *not* want. Dating is for fun, remember? I never said my happy ending meant me being part of a couple."

"Then why did you do this whole thing? What was the point?"

"Because I thought I was undateable and you said you could prove me wrong!"

"And I did!"

"So now, because you guys bought me a bunch of clothes, I'm just going to be auctioned off to the highest bidder?"

"What? No!"

Bernie scrambled to her feet. "I've got to go." She felt panicked and out of control. This was *not* what she'd signed up for. She was so frustrated and angry, and she knew she was overreacting, she knew it, but she felt certain the next thing that came out of her mouth was going to be a sob.

"Bernie—" Colin got up and reached for her.

"I gotta get ready for my date," she said, and stormed out of the park.

"That went well," Steph said when Colin sat back down.

"You could have kept your big mouth shut," he told her.

"I didn't know it was supposed to be a secret!"

"I was waiting for the right time to tell her!"

"Colin! The party is in two days!"

"I know that!"

"When were you going to tell her?"

"I don't know!"

"We should go after her," Dave said.

"First we should kick his ass," Marcie said, nodding toward Colin.

"I'll take care of that for you," Steph said.

"No, I don't think he needs that," Dave said.

"Thank you," Colin said, gratefully, although Dave didn't look at him.

"You hurt our Bernie," he said, pulling the blankets up. Colin rolled onto the grass so Dave could grab the one he was sitting on. "But you can make it right."

"I can't cancel the party," he said, looking up at Dave.

"No, but you can help her make her choice."

"What's that supposed to mean?"

"You'll figure it out. Come on, Marce. Let's go take care of our girl."

Chapter Thirty-Six

Dear Maria,

I screwed up in a big way. I love my boyfriend, but I don't think he'll ever forgive me. What should I do?

Possibly Single in the Mission

Dear Possibly,

That's the problem with dating humans. They screw up. They make mistakes. Only he can decide if he's willing to forgive you. But consider this: do you want to be forgiven because you love him, or because you feel bad about hurting him and his forgiveness will make you feel better? If you love him, swallow your pride and give him some time. Then put those gloves on, girl, because it's gonna take some work.

Kisses,
Maria

BERNIE WAS WEARING A LOT of sparkles.

She stood on a box in the Glaze.com offices in front of a hastily thrown-up three-paneled mirror. Makeda was behind her, cinching the dress in at her waist while an intern sat at her feet, pinning up the hemline.

"We could go a little tighter. What do you think?"

Makeda wasn't asking Bernie. She was asking Marcie, whom Bernie had brought along for moral support in case Makeda tried to talk her into stilettos or some kind of floofy princess ball gown. Also, in case she ran into Colin.

Two days ago she was floating. No, she was soaring. It was because of Colin. It was because he made her feel good—really, really good—and she knew that she made him feel the same. How was it possible she hadn't noticed the sexual tension between them until they got naked?

And then a few hours later, her floaty feelings were shot down by Colin's cruel subterfuge. What was he trying to do to her, throwing a very public party like this? She'd been appreciating how his stories, especially lately, were less about her specifically and more about the difficulties of dating in San Francisco in general. Sure, she was the one who got set up with the guy who couldn't control his anger around roller girls, and the guy who was maybe secretly gay, and the guy who had a girlfriend. But the stories had an everywoman quality that made Bernie feel like she wasn't the one under the microscope, it was the whole city. Colin's stories didn't make her look sad or pathetic. They made her look smart and a little prickly but nothing like an object of pity or the butt of a joke. She liked the way Colin saw her.

This party would shift everything back on to her. Which was exactly what she didn't want.

Liz told her that Dean had gotten rid of all of the

Disapproving Librarian bookmarks. Then maintenance found a litter of feral kittens in the boiler room and someone had started a meme about Library Cats, so the Disapproving Librarian's brief infamy was forgotten.

"Ouch." A pin to the hip broke her out of her reverie.

"Hold still."

"It feels a little tight," she told Makeda.

"This makes a better line," Marcie said.

"You're supposed to be on my side."

"I am. I'm making you look good."

"I don't need—you know what, never mind. Pin away."

She'd lost her passion for the argument that she didn't need to look good. Maybe she'd changed her mind, that now she liked looking good. Or maybe she was just tired.

Just a few more hours and this whole thing would be over.

"How's our librarian doing?" Clea Summers, Colin's boss, came over and stood behind her in the mirror. "Looking fabulous."

"Thanks," Bernie said, because that was a compliment.

She didn't feel particularly fabulous. But she had to admit, the dress was great. It was not something she would ever in a million years wear of her own volition—strapless and sparkly and so long she was going to have to wear heels, dammit—but it was a good dress. It looked good on her.

Clea pulled Bernie's hair loosely off her shoulders, shaking a few strands artfully loose around her face. "We'll definitely have your hair up. Show off those shoulders. I don't know why you were hiding under all those frumpy clothes."

"I wasn't hiding," Bernie said.

"Well, I'm glad you took this journey with us. Your transformation has been amazing. And now we can finally get some good pictures of you. The before and after visuals will be terrific."

"You haven't had enough pictures?" They'd run a few with each story, but they were mostly taken by Colin's phone, candid shots of her with her dates, or pictures of the places they went. Nothing posed, nothing with too much of her face, just enough to show off the clothes in the wild.

Clea snorted. "Colin wouldn't let us send a photographer along on the dates. Said it would spook you. Can you imagine?"

Yes, she could. There was no way she could have been herself with a camera in her face. Colin knew that, even from the beginning.

"I almost sent Pia to do the story instead."

"Roller derby Pia?"

"Mmm-hmm. I've been looking for an opportunity for her. This story seemed like a good match for her."

"Colin did a good job." Bernie wasn't sure why she was defending him. He didn't even need defending. Besides, he'd gotten what he needed from her; he didn't need any more.

"He did. I sometimes wonder about the directions he took, though. Too quiet. Pia really knows how to make a splash."

Makeda snorted.

"This event is going to be amazing. Makeda, is everything set up for the step-and-repeat?"

"Pia's doing that," Makeda said.

Clea looked briefly panicked. So much for Pia knowing how to make a splash. "Great," Clea said, sounding like the idea of Pia being in charge of the step-and-repeat was the opposite of great.

Bernie wondered what a step-and-repeat was.

"I'm going to just go check on a few things," Clea said in a rush, then ran off. Like, literally ran, her heels making urgent clacks on the polished concrete floor.

Bernie watched her, wondering how she did that.

All this time, and she still couldn't walk in heels.

"The two of them are driving me crazy," Makeda said around a mouthful of pins.

"Your boss?" Marcie asked.

"No, Colin and Pia. I swear, the two of them are like cats." She pinned the last pin into the side of Bernie's dress and stood back to assess their work.

"Isn't Pia after Colin's job?"

Makeda dismissed the idea. "Colin's got it in the bag, thanks to you. Pia's still going all out on this party, though. Thinks she can pull through at the last minute. But one party does not make up for everything you and Colin went through together."

Ha. Together. That's why she was standing up on a pedestal wearing a totally non-Bernie dress, getting ready for a party she absolutely did not want to attend.

"I'm just saying it's a good thing you agreed to do this story."

"Sure," said Bernie. It was a good thing, even though it was hardly a conscious thing. She'd been raised to see things through to the end. That was why she kept showing up for dates when the odds were not in her favor of having a good time on any of them. That was why she was standing on a pedestal getting fitted for a dress that would involve her wearing heels in public.

She definitely wasn't doing it for Colin. Why would she do it for Colin? She didn't like him. She'd do this last thing to see the story through to the end; then she'd go back to her happily boring life, just with better clothes and the skills to handle a date or two. Maybe three in a year. Just enough to remind her that she didn't like dating, but that she wasn't totally undateable.

"Perfect. Be careful taking it off that you don't get stuck with a pin."

"Oh, now you're concerned about her getting pricked?"

"Honey, this whole thing was about her getting pricked." Makeda and Marcie laughed and Bernie smiled along with them, even though that wasn't true. It was about her proving that she could date. She could totally date. She didn't particularly want to, but she could.

"Are you sure it will be ready in time?" Marcie asked.

"That's what interns are for."

"I need an intern," Marcie said.

"Okay, I'll have Colin drop this off in a few hours. Then he can take you to the club."

"No! No, ah. Marcie can pick it up, right?"

"I can?"

"I'll give you all my makeup," she whispered.

"I can."

"That's good," Makeda said. "Surprise him with your fabulosity. I like it."

This had nothing to do with Colin, Bernie thought. And soon, neither would she.

When Pia had told him that they'd booked Ruby Skye for the big finale, Colin had assumed they'd be in one of the smaller private rooms of the notoriously huge club. They just needed a space big enough to hold thirty guys who weren't good enough for Bernie, the staff of Glaze, and a few visitors.

A few visitors turned out to be hundreds of people, PR reps from their advertisers, friends of friends, and what seemed like the entire under-thirty population of San Francisco.

Bernie was going to hate it.

The space looked great, although he did have to bribe a guy to take down the posters of the Disapproving Librarian that were next to the stage. He saw Pia running around looking for them, but short of throwing herself into the Dumpster and collecting all of the tiny pieces that the posters were now in, she wouldn't find them. It had been surprisingly cathartic, ripping up those posters. When Pia interrogated him, he just played dumb. He was good at playing dumb. Turned out, he was dumb.

How could he have agreed to this? He'd worked hard to keep Bernie out of the spotlight as much as possible in a story that was about her. For the readers, it wasn't about her. It was about the fashion and the dates and the hope and commiserating with a fellow sister trying to make it, romantically speaking, in a man's world.

"I hate to admit it, but the kid did a good job." Clea handed him a glass of champagne and clinked. "This is going to be huge."

"Huge," Colin repeated.

"You might have the grace to look a little worried, you know."

Colin shrugged. He wasn't worried about his job anymore.

"Have you seen Bernie yet?" Clea asked.

"No, her friends are bringing her."

"Makeda tells me she's going to knock your socks off. I saw the dress. Amazing. Who knew that underneath that frumpy little mouse was such a knockout?"

Colin knew. And he knew that Bernie didn't care about

being a mouse or a knockout. She just cared about being Bernie.

This whole thing was giving him indigestion.

"Should I regret letting Pia emcee?" Clea asked, although Colin got the sense she wasn't really talking to him. "I should be the emcee, right? I'm the editor."

"Mmm-hmm," he said, but he was mostly worried about getting the last drops out of his glass of champagne.

"She doesn't have the panache that I have. She doesn't have the experience. Maybe you should do it, Colin. This is your project." She turned to look at him. "No, never mind. You look like you're no fun tonight. Come on, Colin! This is it! The home stretch! Victory is within your grasp!"

"Yeah," Colin said with a smile that felt more like a grimace.

"Forget it. She can't emcee. She'll mess it up. Here—" She shoved her undrunk glass of champagne in Colin's hand and raced up to the stage. She really was fast in those heels. He downed her drink, then watched Clea and Pia briefly tussle over the mic under the stage lights.

Clea won. As she welcomed the audience and called out the sponsors and PR people and minor celebrities by name, Colin looked for another waiter and another champagne.

Instead, he found Pia, flushed and out of breath.

"Colin!" Pia was whispering desperately in his ear. "Have you seen Bernie yet?"

"I'm sure she's here somewhere. Her friends brought her." He pointed to Dave and Marcie, who were standing off to the side with Steph, champagne glasses in hand, whispering among themselves.

"Ugh, what is Clea saying? I've gotta go up there. Send Bernie over when you see her."

They were perfect for each other, Colin thought as he watched Pia snag the mic from Clea, then call up the thirty eligible bachelors who'd dated their librarian. Well, twenty-nine eligible bachelors, plus the one with the girl-friend, who'd actually had the nerve to show up tonight. So did the guy whom Colin was pretty sure was gay, and the puppeteer, wearing another stupid hat, and a guy he didn't recognize, whom Colin assumed was the one who'd stood Bernie up. Thirty men, of all shapes and sizes and varying degrees of interest in software development. Pia called out for Bernie, who did not respond. As Colin made his way over to Steph, who was standing with Dave and Marcie, he gave Pia credit for how she seamlessly stalled for time, making a joke about makeup, then intro-ducing each of the guys.

"Where's Bernie?" he asked Marcie.

"She said she was coming with you."

"No, Makeda said you were bringing her."

"Uh-oh," Dave said.

"No, she wouldn't do that," Steph said. "After all this work?"

No, she wouldn't, Colin agreed. She wouldn't let him down like this. But he dropped his empty glass on the nearest clear surface anyway.

Chapter Thirty-Seven

BERNIE WAS COLD. And she wished she knew how to turn on the carousel, so at least the passing view of the city would distract her from her thoughts.

She'd really, really screwed up.

When the car service had pulled up in front of her house, her hands were sweating. It was normal to be nervous, she'd told herself. You're going to have to talk to a bunch of people about dating. You're going to be the focus of attention. You're going to have to stand in heels for several hours. She took a deep breath and told herself that she could do it.

But as soon as she got in the car, she realized she couldn't. This wasn't her, the dress and the small talk. She wasn't the girl who could put on a happy face for strangers. Her face wouldn't let her. She wore her thoughts on her face; she always had. No amount of makeup was going to change that.

So she'd redirected the driver, and now here she was, cold and alone.

And Colin. Colin, whom she didn't even like and who was probably going to get fired after she ruined this for him. Colin would never forgive her.

She shouldn't have agreed to this if she didn't want to do it, she scolded herself. She should have just said, no, I'm happy with my dull little life where I can wrap myself in self-righteousness and pretend I don't need romance or intimacy to feel whole.

She didn't *need* those things. She just wanted them.

She wanted them with Colin.

And now she'd made a fool of him and lost him his job. Good thing she didn't like him.

She heard the door to the carousel building open and she tensed. She hoped it wasn't the police. She couldn't get arrested for sitting on a carousel, could she? Sure, she'd jimmied the lock open with one of her bobby pins, but that wasn't trespassing, was it?

She'd have to work on her get-out-of-jail speech. Sorry, Officer, but my face was turned into an unflattering meme and then I got swept up in a romantic fiction that was supposed to rehabilitate my self-image but it went too far and I'm wearing heels.

Yeah, that would work.

"How did I know you would be here?"

It wasn't a cop. It was Colin. The last person she wanted to see, ever again. So why did her heart do that stupid skipping thing?

"Hi," she said.

"I went to your apartment first. Maddie said you looked gorgeous—she was right, by the way—and she figured I was taking you somewhere special. So I thought about the places that are special to you and . . ."

He sat down next to her on the swan bench. She wished

she had tried a little harder to mount one of the other animals, but she hadn't wanted to rip the dress. She was pretty sure she was going to have to give it back, fabulous as it was. And now Colin was sitting next to her, close enough that she could smell him. She liked how he smelled, damn him.

"This is the part where you tease me because I found you using my oversized ego. I decided our first kiss was important to you."

She huffed out a sad little laugh.

"You're going to be late for your party," he said.

"I'm sorry," she said, and then, because she was frustrated and confused, she started crying.

"Hey, hey." He pulled her close to him and she gave in because he was warm and she was cold, but she shouldn't let him comfort her. She didn't deserve it.

"Don't be nice to me just because I'm crying," she told the lapel of his jacket.

"You're shivering." He pulled off his jacket and draped it around her shoulders. "What, no joke about how you can keep yourself warm without the help of the patriarchy? Bernie, you're losing your touch."

"Why don't you hate me?" she asked miserably. But at least she was warm. Colin made her warm.

"Well, I thought about it. Because on the surface, it looked like you were pissed about the party and just trying to screw with my career."

"I can see how it would look that way."

"Yes, but lately I've been overthinking things. I think it's because I started hanging out with this woman whose mind is a truly tiring maze of cross-examination."

Bernie sniffled. She knew she was exhausting. She exhausted herself.

"And so I realized that it wasn't about me. Can you believe it?"

She laughed, just a little.

"I know you better than that, Bernie. I know you're not vindictive or cruel. I knew if you ran away, there had to be a good reason."

"Is the fact that I'm a total chicken a good reason?"

"It's not a great reason." He wiped a tear off her cheek.

"I'm so, so sorry. I tried. I really did. I put on the dress and the shoes."

"Yes, I see."

"They hurt."

"I know."

"I was in the car and my feet were pinching and I thought about you and the story and the meme and I don't know how everything got so out of control when a few days ago it was fine. Weird, but fine. And then this big party and . . . it just isn't me, you know?"

"I know."

"I should have just gone to the party. I could have faked my way through it."

"No, you couldn't. Bernie, your face would have given everything away."

"I can't help it. It's just my face."

"I know. I love that face."

Bernie's heart stopped. "What?"

"It's stupid, right? You're my complete opposite. You have no social filter. You argue with everything that comes out of my mouth."

"No, I—Oh, maybe I do."

"I'm glad you didn't show up tonight."

"You are?"

He nodded. "I shouldn't have let you do this."

"Let me?"

"I was too chicken to tell you I didn't want you to choose one of those other guys. That I wanted you to choose me."

"Oh."

"You make me very confused, you know."

"Tell me about it."

"But here's the thing," he said, and he sat back and put an arm around her. "All of that stuff is true, the stuff that makes us so different."

"Yeah."

"And yet, you're the only person I want to argue with. You're the one I want to puzzle things out with, and have bad dates with. I thought I was doing you a favor, setting you up with all those guys to prove to you that you could do it. But I wasn't. I was doing me a favor, because I got to spend more time with you."

"That's . . . romantic?"

"No, it's stupid. I'm stupid. I should have just realized it sooner, but it made no sense, right? So how could I have known?"

"Known what?"

"That I love you."

"Oh."

Colin looked over to read Bernie's face. It was . . . well, she didn't know what her face was doing, she never really did. But she hoped it was conveying something like "that's nuts and ridiculous and the best thing I've heard in a very, very long time."

Instead, she said, "You do?"

"I do."

"Wow."

"Yeah."

"Huh."

"Right?"

"Let me process that for a minute."

"Go ahead. I'll be right here."

She looked out across the carousel animals at the lights of the city. Everything he said was true. They were a terrible match. They didn't agree on a single thing. He was totally normal and hot, while she was . . . well, she was abnormal and hot. Maybe it was just a physical attraction. Maybe it was just that they were both hot and they both wanted to bone so badly that he was mixing up love and lust.

But that other stuff he'd said, that was true, too. She loved picking fights with him. She loved that he pretended to be all mad about it, but that he still met every challenge she set down. She loved that he listened, and that he changed, and that he made her listen, too. She loved that he didn't require her to change for him to love her, but she did anyway, just a little, just enough to let that love in. Because she'd been doing that this whole time, without even realizing it.

"You're very sneaky, you know."

"Says the woman who skipped out on a huge party in her honor."

"That wasn't really a party for me. That was a party for the Disapproving Librarian-turned-Poster Child for Dating Misfits."

"That's true. In my defense, the party wasn't my idea. I tried to stop it."

"I know you did."

"I didn't mean for it to be a secret. I just couldn't figure out how to tell you."

"I forgive you."

"So what am I so sneaky about?"

She turned to him, and it was written all over his face. Uncertainty, fear, confusion. "Love," she said.

"I didn't do it on purpose," he said.

"I know. But you did it." She leaned forward and did what she'd been wanting to do since he'd rounded the corner and she realized he wasn't a cop. Well, since before then, really. But it didn't matter. He was here now, and she kissed him. "Thank you," she said.

"For letting you kiss me?"

"Yes, and for being so brave. I screwed up your life, and you tell me that you love me."

"You didn't screw up my life. Maybe just set my career back a little, but I didn't really like that job anyway."

"What would Maria say?"

"Hmm." He thought about it, his face tilted up to the roof of the carousel. She tried not to be distracted by the movement of his neck. Really, he was way more attractive than was necessary. "I think Maria would say that there are more important things in life than being able to afford to eat, and that I should follow my heart."

"Sounds a little sappy for Maria."

"Maybe she's getting sappy in her old age."

"I love you." She said it fast, before she could talk herself out of it.

Colin just smiled and took her face in his hands, and kissed the hell out of her.

Dear Maria,

    I met this guy who is totally not my type, but I can't stop thinking about him. What should I do?

        Confounded in Haight-Ashbury

Dear Confounded,

Cupid is a mean little cherub, but sometimes he knows us better than we know ourselves. If you're into this guy, don't worry about what you thought you wanted or what you imagined would be perfect for you. Just grab hold of what feels right and don't let go.

> *Kisses,*
> *Maria*

Epilogue

WHERE ARE THEY NOW?

By Clea Summers, Editor-in-Chief

Two years ago, a self-proclaimed spinster librarian took the city by storm when she agreed to our little dating experiment. Though she stood us up for the grand finale (we still don't forgive her for that, though the party was fabulous all the same), she still managed to capture the hearts of our readers.

She couldn't be reached for comment, but we do know that she is still working as a librarian. When we tried to track her down at work, we received a particularly nasty tongue-lashing from the director. Honestly, what kind of customer service is that!

We did learn, however, that she now leaves her ugly shoes at the bedside of our former staff writer, Colin Rodriguez. Yes, it turns out that the story took a *My Fair Lady* twist, and the two were married at city hall just a few weeks ago. I guess she really took the party right out of our once-notorious nightlife Lothario!

As for her Henry Higgins, Colin left us behind at Glaze, which we all got over very quickly, especially since our staff writer, Pia Wallington, managed to continue his series on setting the self-described undateable women of San Francisco up on their own thirty dates. Maybe we'll hear more from him in the future, but if he's anything like his new wife, probably not.

And Glaze has a baby! Well, sort of. Better than a baby: a book! Our fashion editor, Makeda Tiye, and our beauty editor, Jeanaeane Ng, collaborated on the gorgeously profound *The Real Girl's Beauty Bible*, which, according to the *New York Times*, is essential reading for any woman with a body or a face. They're in the midst of their book tour now, so be sure to check the calendar to see when they'll be near you. You won't want to miss it!

If you can't catch Makeda and Jeanaeane on one of their many live or TV appearances, you'll definitely be seeing them . . . on the bestseller list! Yes, *The Real Girl's Beauty Bible* was the only thing that could topple that grumpy, old *Take a Letter, Maria* from its fifty-three weeks on the self-help bestseller list—which is a little greedy, especially for a second collection of columns. I mean, the old bat didn't even do a book tour!

Read on for an excerpt from the next
Librarians in Love novel,

Falling for Trouble,

coming soon!

**The riot grrrl and the bookworm—just the pair
to get the whole town talking . . .**

Liam Byrd loves Halikarnassus, New York.
He loves its friendliness, its nosiness,
the vibrant library at the center of it all.
And now that Joanna Green is home,
the whole town sizzles.
A rebel like her stirs up excitement, action, desire—
at least in Liam.

Joanna never thought she'd have to come back to her
dull, tiny fishbowl of a hometown ever again.
She almost had a record deal for her all-girl rock band.
She almost had it made in L.A. And then her deal
went sour and her granny broke her leg . . . and now
here she is, running into everybody's favorite
librarian every time she heads to a dive bar
or catches up with old friends.

He has charm, he has good taste in music—
and the sight of him in running shorts is dangerously
distracting. But when he loves her old town and she
can't wait to check out, their new romance
is surely destined for the book drop . . .

"Jo? Joey Green?"

And that, in one frustrating nickname, was the reason why Joanna Green never came back to Halikarnassus. The fact that it was a nosy little town with one bar and few people worth drinking with, she could deal with. It was more the fact that everyone in town seemed obsessed with the Joanna she had been in high school—a screw up and a hellraiser and a general bad influence. She hadn't been home in years, and that one nickname made it abundantly clear that no one was going to try to get to know Joanna the Adult.

Not that Joanna the adult was any less of a screw up. Hell, that was why she was standing in the airport, waiting in baggage claim for the suitcase holding all of her worldly possessions (with the exception of her guitar, which she would never, in a million years, trust to baggage handlers).

Coming home as an abject failure with your tail between your legs was one thing, Joanna thought. Having to explain that failure to a bunch of people who didn't expect anything more from you was a new level of humiliation she wasn't sure she could deal with. Just keep an eye out for your suitcase, she told herself. You don't have to talk to anyone. You just need to grab the bag that is holding all of your worldly possessions, convince a cab to take you all the way to Halikarnassus, and hope that Granny is home to lend you cab fare.

Totally an adult.

"I thought it was you!"

Joanna could no longer ignore the persistent nostalgia at her elbow. A young woman in an enormous gray scarf was looking at her expectantly. Joanna tried to place her . . . she looked vaguely familiar . . .

"Oh my gosh, you don't remember me. Skyler Carrington?" Scarf Girl gave her a hopeful look.

"Holy crap, Skyler? I thought you were like . . ." The last time Joanna had seen Skyler, Joanna was getting in big trouble for making her cry because she wouldn't let her play with her very expensive guitar. Skyler had been what, five? Seven? She was ten years younger than Joanna, a fact that had caused Trina, Joanna's best friend and Skyler's big sister, a minor adolescent breakdown. Then, of course, Trina was ruthlessly protective of her sister who was, frankly, a brat.

Skyler had been three. Or five. Or whatever. That was a long time ago. She was probably much better now. And wasn't that why Joanna had avoided coming home? Because she knew people would only see her as she was back then? Pot and black kettle and all that.

Back then Joanna was a foul-mouthed, rebellious, broke teenager. Now she was . . . well she wasn't a teenager.

God, how depressing. She'd left town to shake off the image everybody had of her, only to find that the reason they had that image was because it was who she was.

Except that now she was old. And Skyler Carrington was as tall as she was.

And Skyler Carrington was leaning forward to give

Joanna a hug. "Trina's not going to believe this! What are you doing here?"

"Just, uh . . ." Skyler Carrington didn't need to know the whole sad, sordid story, and it made Joanna feel a little better that news of her epic failure had not reached Halikarnassus yet. At least, not the airport two hours from Halikarnassus. "Just visiting."

"Granny! How is Granny?"

"Good, fine." She hoped, anyway. Granny hadn't answered her early-morning call. But then, ever since Granny retired, she was always busy. Still, she usually returned calls.

Joanna waved her hand. "What are you doing here? Love the scarf."

"Oh my God, I just finished a semester in France. I'm, like, so not used to speaking English! And everyone here is so . . . American!"

"You'll get that, what with being in America," Joanna suggested.

"I'm just having, like, culture shock. Literally everything in France is, like, so much better. I can't even with this." Skyler waved her hand around.

Joanna couldn't even with the baggage claim, either. She also couldn't with this kid having adventures in France while Joanna had been working hard, making music, then throwing it all away in one stupid night. Skyler had probably done more in her teenage life than Joanna had in her . . . more than teenage life. They both talked big; this kid had actually done big things.

Fortunately, the baggage claim started to move and, as if the gods of Joanna's hometown shame were looking down upon her struggle to keep it together in a conversation with her old friend's formerly bratty toddler little sister, her suitcase came out first.

"Well, this is me. Nice to see you."

Skyler reached forward to help Joanna with her suitcase. "Are you going to be home for a while? Trina is going to die when I tell her I saw you."

Joanna pretended not to hear. She just waved and lost herself in the crowd, dragging all of her worldly possessions behind her.

Connect with Us

Visit us online at
KensingtonBooks.com
to read more from your favorite authors, see books
by series, view reading group guides, and more.

 Join us on social media

for sneak peeks, chances to win books and prize packs,
and to share your thoughts with other readers.

facebook.com/kensingtonpublishing
twitter.com/kensingtonbooks

Tell us what you think!

To share your thoughts, submit a review,
or sign up for our eNewsletters, please visit:
KensingtonBooks.com/TellUs.

Books by Bestselling Author
Fern Michaels

___The Jury	0-8217-7878-1	$6.99US/$9.99CAN
___Sweet Revenge	0-8217-7879-X	$6.99US/$9.99CAN
___Lethal Justice	0-8217-7880-3	$6.99US/$9.99CAN
___Free Fall	0-8217-7881-1	$6.99US/$9.99CAN
___Fool Me Once	0-8217-8071-9	$7.99US/$10.99CAN
___Vegas Rich	0-8217-8112-X	$7.99US/$10.99CAN
___Hide and Seek	1-4201-0184-6	$6.99US/$9.99CAN
___Hokus Pokus	1-4201-0185-4	$6.99US/$9.99CAN
___Fast Track	1-4201-0186-2	$6.99US/$9.99CAN
___Collateral Damage	1-4201-0187-0	$6.99US/$9.99CAN
___Final Justice	1-4201-0188-9	$6.99US/$9.99CAN
___Up Close and Personal	0-8217-7956-7	$7.99US/$9.99CAN
___Under the Radar	1-4201-0683-X	$6.99US/$9.99CAN
___Razor Sharp	1-4201-0684-8	$7.99US/$10.99CAN
___Yesterday	1-4201-1494-8	$5.99US/$6.99CAN
___Vanishing Act	1-4201-0685-6	$7.99US/$10.99CAN
___Sara's Song	1-4201-1493-X	$5.99US/$6.99CAN
___Deadly Deals	1-4201-0686-4	$7.99US/$10.99CAN
___Game Over	1-4201-0687-2	$7.99US/$10.99CAN
___Sins of Omission	1-4201-1153-1	$7.99US/$10.99CAN
___Sins of the Flesh	1-4201-1154-X	$7.99US/$10.99CAN
___Cross Roads	1-4201-1192-2	$7.99US/$10.99CAN

Available Wherever Books Are Sold!
Check out our website at **www.kensingtonbooks.com**